The vast fleet emerged with battle screens full out and all its projectors began as one to blaze; and Axolgan got the shock of his not-too-war-filled life. All space around the planet was full of warships; the Garshan fleet was larger than his own! He said something to Knuaire, but got no answer. The psiontist-fusion was busy. *Very* busy. They were doing the work that Rodnar and Starrlah would have been doing if they had not been so hard at work elsewhere.

It is impossible to teleport anything into any volume protected by a capable psiontist; and Rodnar had insisted that every warship of Grand Fleet, of whatever tonnage, should have a psiontist aboard. Thus Grand Fleet could have been larger than it was, but Axolgan did not object to that. He thought it already four to five times too big for the job.

While the Garshan fleet was, at the moment of engagement, larger than the Justiciate fleet by two hundred twenty one units, the Guards outnumbered the Garshan psiontists by three hundred sixteen. Wherefore, in the first thirty seconds of plus time, five hundred thirty seven Garshan ships were blown out of space. Ragingly incandescent, furiously expanding fire-balls appeared where each unprotected warship had been . . .

By the same author

The *Lensman* Series

Triplanetary
First Lensman
Second Stage Lensmen
Grey Lensman
Galactic Patrol
Children of the Lens
Masters of the Vortex

The *Skylark* Series

The Skylark of Space
Skylark Three
Skylark of Valeron
Skylark DuQuesne

The *Family d'Alembert* Series (with Stephen Goldin)

The Imperial Stars
Stranglers' Moon
The Clockwork Traitor
The Bloodstar Conspiracy
Getaway World
The Purity Plot
Planet of Treachery
Eclipsing Binaries

Other Novels

Spacehounds of IPC
The Galaxy Primes
Subspace Explorers

E. E. 'DOC' SMITH

Subspace Encounter

Edited and with an Introduction by Lloyd Arthur Eshbach

PANTHER
Granada Publishing

Panther Books
Granada Publishing Ltd
8 Grafton Street, London W1X 3LA

Published by Panther Books 1984

A Granada Paperback Original

Copyright © Verna Smith Trestrail 1983
Published by arrangement with the original publisher,
Berkley Publishing Group, New York

ISBN 0-586-06014-6

Printed and bound in Great Britain by
Collins, Glasgow

Set in Times

For
VERNA

Contents

Introduction

Subspace Encounter is the last science fiction written by Edward E. 'Doc' Smith. Other novels bearing his name and first published since his death in 1965 were either expanded short stories or new books based on his notes or concepts – but this is Doc's work, and except for an unpublished 'whodunit,' his last.

In the late 1960s rumors circulated among his fans who had known him well that there existed an unpublished sequel to *Subspace Explorers*, but since no manuscript had surfaced the rumors had died and the story was forgotten.

This was the situation when in the winter of 1978 I visited David and Ruth Kyle in Florida. Dave had begun writing additional Lensman stories at the suggestion of Frederik Pohl, then editor of a major paperback publisher; and Dave showed me a photocopy of a Smith manuscript which Fred had sent him with the suggestion that he might be able to use some of the ideas in his plotting.

I read the manuscript – and was startled to find notations in my own handwriting and signed 'LAE' – suggestions I had made to Doc early in 1965. The typescript was a copy of material I had sent to Fred shortly after Doc's death, thinking then that something might be done with it. But it was not a complete story.

Memory started working and pieces began falling into place. After returning home, taking a copy of the script with me, I consulted my correspondence files and was able to reconstruct the total picture.

In 1962 Doc had completed a novel called *Subspace*

Safari with John W. Campbell's *Astounding Science Fiction* in mind. It was a sequel to a novelette, *Subspace Survivors*, which Campbell had published. Campbell wanted extensive changes made – Doc had refused to rewrite the story, disagreeing with John – so he had a novel on his hands which he couldn't even submit to other magazines since he had used parts of the original novelette in the sequel.

He began reworking the manuscript and in the course of time decided the story could not be told in one book. He completed the first section of the story, which he called *Subspace Explorers*, and which appeared in book form in 1965. With the novel accepted he got to work on the second book, using me by correspondence as a sounding board – then one evening he phoned to tell me of an exciting new idea for the story that had just occurred to him. He began working on this development, sending me the pieces as he wrote them, asking for my suggestions and comments. He took time out to write *Skylark DuQuesne* for Fred Pohl – and then Doc died.

I felt the book should be published – but the story was incomplete. There were tantalizing directions written on the part I had, such as: 'See Page – of the one book version.' I finally phoned Doc's daughter, Verna Smith Trestrail, telling her I wanted to get the book ready for publication, giving her the background information, and asking her to search for the one book version and any other pertinent material that might be in her possession. It took a lot of searching, but finally the one book version turned up. And that was all she found. The copy of the later work that I had sent Fred Pohl was the only one to survive. If I had not sent and Fred had not kept that manuscript this story wouldn't exist.

I know what Doc had had in mind – and certainly I am the only one who knows – so from the pieces in my possession I have been able to reconstruct the present book, *Subspace Encounter*. I believe Doc would have approved what I have done.

Lloyd Arthur Eshbach

Prologue

To ascribe the occurrence of two or more events to coincidence is either to admit ignorance of, or to deny the existence of, some fundamental relationship. Nevertheless, all previous investigations into the Early Psionic Age 'explained' it, as can be shown by rigorous analysis, by employing coincidence to an extent that is scientifically preposterous. This one does not: as a matter of fact, it denies the existence of coincidence.

This work is the result of years-long study of that Age. It is not, however, strictly speaking, a history; since it does contain some material that is not incontrovertibly factual. On the other hand, it is far from being a mere historical novel. Therefore it should, perhaps – and using the term more or less loosely – be called a chronicle.

At the time in which this chronicle is laid, interstellar flight, while not the one-hundred-percent-safe matter it now is, was far and away the safest means of travel known. Insurance companies offered odds of tens of thousands of dollars to one dollar that any given star-traveler would return unharmed from any given startrip to any one of the ninety five colonized planets of explored space aboard any starship he chose.

There were a few accidents, of course. Worse, there were a few complete disappearances of starships; cases in which no calls of distress were sent out and of which no traces were ever found.

Aboard the starship *Procyon* there were four psychics.* Barbara Warner was a full-fledged psiontist. She knew it

* Recorded in *Subspace Explorers*.

and worked at the trade. Whenever her father, the owner of WarnOil (Warner Oil, to give the business entity its full name), wanted another million-barrel gusher she went out, looked around, and told him where to bore his well. In ten years, on ninety six planets, WarnOil had not drilled a dry hole. All were gushers of fantastic production.

The other three were latents. Carlyle Deston, First Officer of the *Procyon*, and Theodore Jones, its Second, had always had hunches, but neither had ever mentioned the fact. Bernice Burns, a post-deb of upper crust Society, was actually a clairvoyant psiontist, but she would not admit the fact even to herself. Deston and Barbara fell in love at first sight and were married a few minutes later, and Jones and Bernice were not far behind them.

Catastrophe struck – without warning, with split-second speed and with utter and incredible devastation, reducing the great starship to a fused hulk of destructively radio-active metal. Its cause? There was nothing whatever to indicate the source, no follow-up attack; and for almost all aboard the *Procyon* it was instant death. Like all starship disasters, there was no time for any report to be made.

The four – Carlyle Deston, Barbara Warner Deston, Theodore Jones and Bernice Burns Jones – being highly psychic, had enough warning of catastrophe so that each couple reached a lifeboat. The Destons found already in their lifeboat, studying subspace, one Doctor Andrew Adams, a Fellow of the Institute for Advanced Study. These five were the only survivors of the disaster to get back to Civilization.

Decontamination – thorough but most unpleasant – followed; as soon as it was safe to do so, they reboarded the hulk, finding all subspace gear inoperable. Most normal-space equipment, however, would work – after a fashion. It would take a year or more to reach the nearest solar system, but they had plenty of power, air, water, and food.

13

Shortly after the shipwreck both girls became pregnant; and long before the year was up, it became evident that both periods of gestation were going to be extraordinarily long. This gave super-mathematician Adams new data with which to work, and he proved that time was not an absolute constant, but could, under certain conditions, become a parameter. (Cf *The Adams Theory* and *The Adams Effect*.) He deduced: 1) That the *Procyon* had struck a field of subspatial force that he called the 'zeta' field; 2) That the entire mass of the ship and all its contents were charged to an extremely high potential with a force more or less analogous to that which produces lightning; 3) That the ships which had disappeared had been completely destroyed by the discharge of zeta force to a planet upon approach; and 4) That extreme precautions must be observed if they themselves were not to be destroyed in the same way.

In due time – or rather, about five months *after* due time – two babies were born: Theodore Warner Deston and Barbara Bernice Jones.

A barren planet was found and plans were made to rid the *Procyon* of zeta force. Extreme caution was observed. The force was discharged in successive decrements by means of twenty-five-mile lengths of ultra-high-tensile wire. With all potentials at the zero of normal space, the subspace communicators were again in working order and Deston reported in. It was of course a simple matter for the subspace-going machine shops to jury-rig enough subspace gear for the *Procyon* to get back to her home port under her own power.

Both Deston and Jones were promoted on the spot; but, since both were now married, neither could serve InStell (The Interstellar Corporation) in either subspace or space. Captain Theodore Jones went back to Earth – Bernice was not very rich – to work in the main office.

14

Captain Carlyle Deston resigned and went with Barbara to the palatial Warner home – her home now, since her parents had died in the wreck – on the planet Newmars. He was not going to live on his wife's money all the rest of his life.

Barbara knew that Deston had tremendous latent powers, and she helped him develop them. He became able to do with metals what she had done with oil. He found a mountain of uranium, which Deston and Deston, Incorporated, sold to Galactic Metals. He also found copper in quantities which made automation feasible, a discovery which played an important role in early psionic history.

The Destons and Joneses (psiontists now, too) and Adams went into space in search of other natural resources. They found everything they sought and eventually what Maynard of GalMet wanted most – rhenium, the rarest and costliest ingredient of an ultra-alloy, Leybyrdite. Deston met Doctor Cecily Byrd, Director of Project Rhenium; a woman whom Maynard described as 'a carrot-topped, freckle-faced, shanty-Irish mick – with the shape men drool about, with a megavac for a brain and an ice-cube for a heart.'

The source of this rarest of minerals they called Rhenia Four, a hellish planet indeed, one of its creatures, the 'kittyhawks,' having teeth and claws of the very alloy MetEnge had been developing. 'Curly' Byrd proved herself able to set up full automation even there. She was helped by, among others, an engineer named Percival Train, whom she married. Surprisingly, the Trains also developed psionic abilities, as did Dr Adams and his wife Stella, to bring to eight the unmatched psiontists who made up the brains of the new super starship *Explorer*.

The remainder of the first volume of this chronicle is devoted to the beginnings of the Psionic Age on Tellus;

the three-pronged conflict between Communism, corrupt labor and capital, and what became the Galactic Federation; and the unaccountably rapid growth of psionics through the ninety five colonized planets.

Volume two continues the chronicle – the record of two psionic civilizations.

CHAPTER 1

The Gamesmen

The Justiciate, composed at that moment of one hundred eighty three Tellus-type planets, lay in a part of the Cosmos the very existence of which no mind of the ninety six planets of Tellurian civilization had ever envisioned. Not even the farthest ranging subspacer of either civilization had ever discovered any hint of the presence of the other. Nevertheless the Justicians were human beings to the last letter of classification; human even to the extent of varying skin color from white through different shades of yellow and red and brown to almost black. Unlike racial distinctions as they occurred on Tellurian planets, with different races inhabiting single worlds, normally each world of the Justiciate was the home of a single race. There was little interracial marriage, joining lives as they put it – not because any race felt itself superior to any other – except for the insufferable red-brown Garshans – but because most ordinary people never left their home worlds.

All the Justician planets were linked together by hundreds of subspace freight or passenger lines and by hundreds of thousands of subspace communications channels. They were also linked together in that they were ruled by, and were more or less willingly obedient to, a harsh and dictatorial government known as the Council of Grand Justices; of which His Magnificence Supreme Grand Justice Sonrathendak Ranjak of Slaar was the unquestioned and unquestionable BOSS.

The planet Slaar was and is the Justiciate's most populous planet; and the city Meetyl-On-Slaar, the Justiciate's largest city – population ten and a quarter million – was and is the capital of both planet and the empire.

To Tellurian eyes Meetyl would have looked very little indeed like a city. It was built on and inside a rugged, steep – in many places sheerly precipitous – range of mountains; it extended upward from an ocean's rockily narrow beach to an altitude of well over ten thousand feet.

If structures built inside of and outside of a mountain can be called, respectively, internal and external buildings, some of Meetyl's external buildings were one story high, some were a thousand; but all were in harmony with each other and with the awesomely rugged terrain. There were no streets: all traffic, freight and passenger alike, moved via air or via tunnel.

In a pressurized section of the ten-thousand-foot level, in a large and sumptuous office on the glass door of which there was an ornately gold-leafed gladiatorial design and the words 'Sonfayand Faylor – Games,' a fat man reclined at an elaborately-inlaid piece of free-form furniture that was his desk. He was a big man, with a fish-belly-pale face and small, piercing, almost-black eyes. He was three-quarters bald and what hair he had left was a pepper-and-salt gray.

Three of the room's walls, its floor, and its ceiling, were works of sheerest art in fine-particled mosaic. Its front wall, one great sheet of water-clear plastic, afforded a magnificent view of turbulent ocean, of stupendous cliffs, and of cloud-flecked, sunny sky. The man was concerned, however, neither with art nor with nature; he was watching a young man and a young woman who, arrowing through the air from the north and from the south respectively, were climbing fast and would apparently hit his landing stage at the same time. He glanced at the timepiece on his desk and said aloud to himself, 'Good – they're both exactly on time.'

18

He pushed the button to open the outer valve of his airlock and turned on the 'Come in and shed and stow' sign: the two visitors let themselves in and, without a word, began to 'shed' their flying harnesses and to 'stow' them in a closet designed for the purpose.

The male visitor was of medium height and medium build, with the broad somewhat sloping shoulders, the narrow waist, and the long-fibered, smoothly-flowing muscles of the hard-trained athlete who specializes in speed and maneuverability rather than in brute strength. His eyes were a cold gray; his thick, bushy hair was a sun-faded brown. So was what little clothing he wore – singlet, shorts, and plastic-soled ground-gripper canvas shoes. His smooth-shaven face and bare legs and arms and shoulders were deeply tanned – and were marked and cross-marked with the hair-thin, almost invisible scars of the expertly-treated wounds of the top-bracket knife-fighter. Top bracket? Definitely. Only the very best of the best lived long enough in that game to acquire as many scars as this man bore.

The girl, rid of her flying helmet, shook her head vigorously, so that a mass of brilliant violet-colored hair, hitherto so tightly confined, swirled about her head. Then, reaching up with both hands, she fluffed her hair into shape with her fingers. She was almost as tall as her fellow visitor, was not too many pounds lighter than he in weight, and was super-superbly built. Her eyes were a gold-flecked hazel. Her clothing, while newer and more ornamental than the man's, was no more abundant nor cumbersome, and – femininity all solar systems over! – she wore, dangling from a fine platinum chain encircling her left ear, a two-inch octagonal diffraction grating.

Like the man's, her face and shoulders and arms and legs were deeply tanned; and, like his, they too were plenteously and finely scarred: if not quite as abundantly

19

as his, numerously enough to show unmistakably that the worn rawhide haft of the knife at her belt did not get that way from skinning orksts.

With no change of expression – or rather, with no expression at all on his face – the male visitor tuned his mind to the girl's and drove a thought. 'You're Daught . . .'

'Quiet!' she interrupted mentally. Not a muscle of her face moved. Her eyes showed, strictly unchanged, only the customary interest in a strange young man who was as much of a man as this man very evidently was. 'Are you *sure* this fat slob can't varn? Or anyone else within range, so you're sure you're not making eaglemeat out of both of us?'

'Positive,' he telepathed. 'He's no more psionic than the toad he looks like, and Knuaire of Spath's on guard. You know him?'

'Songladen Knuaire? The theoretician? I've met him once, is all. He's an operator.'

'You can carve *that* on the highest cliff in town.'

All this, of course, at the transfinite speed of thought, had taken the merest fraction of a second of time. The fat man was speaking. 'Sonrodnar Rodnar of Slaar – Daughtmarja Marrjyl of Orm – I greet,' he said formally, and the two replied in unison, 'Sonfayand Faylor of Slaar, I greet.'

'You two haven't met, I understand,' the gamesmaster said, and went on to introduce his two visitors to each other, using the informal mode. 'Rodnar, Status Thirty Eight . . .' – the person of higher status was always named first – '. . . and Marrjyl, Status Forty, meet each other.'

Both smiled and bowed. 'I'm very glad to, Marrjyl,' and 'I am, too, Rodnar – *so* glad!' they said; and as they clasped hands firmly, Rodnar went on, 'No, Faylor, we've never met before. And Marrjyl, when I said I was

20

mighty glad to meet you, I wasn't just being polite. I've heard a lot about you – all good.'

She smiled again. 'Thanks, Rodnar, but not half as much as I've heard about you, I'm sure.'

'Maybe you know, then, Rod,' the fat man said, 'that she isn't a real pro, either. Like you, she's a spare-time gamesman, in it partly for the junex, but mostly for augmentation of status. She's a Designer First – just in from Orm – this is her first stab at the big time and the big chance and the big money – but, as you can see, she's good. Okay, peel your jerseys and turn around.'

The word 'peel' was strictly appropriate, especially in the girl's case. Her upper garment was almost as tight as the skin of an orange.

Her jersey came off to reveal that her firm, boldly outstanding breasts were startlingly white, showing that she was not in the habit of exposing them to the public eye. Yet she neither showed nor felt any twinge of embarrassment at baring them here. Also, her breasts were not scarred, showing that she wore breast-shields in combat – which was logical enough. Female gladiators, if they lived long enough to become mothers, were such excellent breeding stock that their mammary glands were held inviolate.

Naked to their waists, the two turned their backs to the promoter, showing fourteen-digit numbers tattooed in black across their backs from shoulder to shoulder. The fat man aimed a mechano-optical instrument – that looked like a cross between a typewriter and a Questar 'scope – first at Rodnar's back, then at Marrjyl's; and the machine, after chattering busily for a few seconds, disgorged four eighteen-inch lengths of tape. Faylor thumb-printed all four of these slips, then handed two of them to the man and two to the girl; who each thumb-printed both and handed one back.

'That for that,' the fat man said. 'Thanks. And here are your checks – a thousand each – for signing the contracts.'

Marrjyl nodded. 'Thanks a lot,' she said, and Rodnar added, 'Thanks, Fay, this'll do me fine.' He then quirked an eyebrow at the girl. She nodded, and the two harnessed up and took off.

As they were jetting along through the air, side by side, Rodnar said in thought, 'When I said I was glad to meet you, Marrjyl – or why not make it Marr?'

'Yes, do, Rod. If this thing works out at all, we'll be working together too long and too closely for formality.'

'My thought exactly – so, to proceed, I wasn't just flapping my tongue. I didn't want to let on to Fatso Sonfayand, of course, but my personal treasury's lower than the proverbial snake's hip in a swamp. Everything we could raise on Slaar and Spath both. Knu has assets, of course, but they're mostly frozen. And anyway I couldn't let him carry the whole load. And buying your way through channels takes junex, lots of 'em. We got as far as His Magnificence's second secretary . . .'

'You did? Already? That's better than almost anyone expected.'

'Yeah. As you said, Knu is really an operator. And the purse I'll get tomorrow night should get us past her. *If* I kill the Masked Marvel, that is.'

'*If* you kill him? Of course you'll kill him: Why shouldn't you?'

'You know why not. He's got a mighty good record – too good altogether for a non-psi – in fact, I've checked him out and he is psionic. Evidently a renegade – a loner – out strictly for number one instead of for the good of all psiontists as a group.'

She nodded, assuming an expression that was startlingly ugly for such an attractive face to wear. 'Uh-huh, they're the ones that need killing the most of anybody . . . but you're more than somewhat nuts to think any such scum could have what it would take to kill *you*. The worst he'll do is nick you a little, maybe, instead of you letting him nick you to make it look like a contest.'

'We *hope*,' he said, with not too much conviction in his tone. 'Who are you fighting, and when?'

'I don't know who yet; I'm signed to fight the survivor of the eliminations now going on for female finalists at the next Most Magnificent Eagle-Feeding – a week from Saturday night, you know, in Games Hall One. On form, it'll be Daughtmargann Loygann of Gloane and she'll be a summer breeze.'

He nodded. 'On form, yes – but just remember to probe her hard and plenty, because any bladesman who has lasted very long has *got* to be more or less psionic. But to get back to money – I hope you brought along a bale.'

'I did. I fine-toothed both Orm and Skane. Over a hundred thousand junex.'

He whistled. A hundred thousand Justician Units of Exchange was a lot of cash; much more than he had expected from the underground psionic groups of those two comparatively young, comparatively underdeveloped planets. '*That's* the kind of talk I like to hear, girl. Just for that I'll cash this here check, take you up top to the Eyrie, and ply you with drink and with prime-orkst steak.'

'And *that*, man,' she laughed, 'is the kind of talk *I* like to hear.'

Games Hall One was a subterranean amphitheater, so designed that every seat in the whole vast cavern afforded a perfect view of what was going on in the small central arena; a view that could at will be reenforced by individual tri-di viewers at each of all seats except 'ringside'. The whole splendidly-decorated Hall was illuminated by an apparently sourceless light of just the right quality and intensity for maximum viewing pleasure. Its atmosphere was pure, briskly-circulating air, at a temperature of seventy two degrees Fahrenheit and a relative humidity of twenty nine percent.

Every seat of the Hall's many thousands was occupied. The spectators were fairly evenly divided as to sex, and were of all ages from babies in arms up to white haired oldsters. All the people except the infants were keyed up and tense: all were reveling vicariously in the mayhem, carnage, and sheer slaughter of the Games.

The eagles had been fed. That is, brutish executioners, after breaking convicts' arms and legs with their mauls, had thrown their helpless but still living bodies into great cages of steel bars; there they had been torn to grisly bits and devoured by deliberately-starved, forty-pound Mountain King eagles.

The five preliminary bouts, in ascending order of skill and of savagery, were over; two women and three men had died. Bloodily.

Now Gamesmaster Sonfayand Faylor stepped up onto the 'table' – the circular platform twenty five feet in diameter and twelve inches above the arena's floor – that was the site of action. Unlike the squared rings of Tellus, this site had no ropes or guards: any gamesman leaving the table during combat, for any reason whatever, became eaglemeat then and there.

'LADIES AND GENTLEMEN!' Faylor bellowed happily. Like so many sports announcers, he liked to bellow and always stood ten feet away from the nearest microphone so that he could bellow. 'On my right, the champion professional bladesman of Meetyl! The one and only – the world-renowned Masked Marvel . . .!'

Amidst a tremendous roar of applause a tall, trim, splendidly-muscled man leaped in one bound to the center of the table and bowed four ways, saluting the crowd gracefully with his knife at each bow. He wore fighting shoes, a tight breech-clout, and a light mask of yellow gold – a mask that did not conceal his Garshan beak of a nose, to say nothing of interfering with even his widest peripheral vision. The gamesmaster finally broké into the applause; still bellowing and still loving the sound of his own voice.

'All I'm allowed to tell you about the champ is that he's a Garshan, and . . .'

'*You're telling us?*' a stentorian voice came raucously from ringside – and that statement had been entirely unnecessary. The Masked Marvel's reddish-brown skin and his veritable beak of a nose could not possibly have belonged to anyone except a native of Garsh – the home of the proudest, the haughtiest, the purest of blood and the most intransigently warlike of all the Justiciate's races of men. '*Chop it off – get on with the fight!*' the heckler howled, and the crowd went wild – clapping, stamping, whistling, shrieking, cat-calling, booing.

'*QUIET! SILENCE! SHUT UP!!!*' the gamesmaster yelled; so loud now and so close to a microphone that even the Hall One's super-powered public address system squawked under the overload . . . and the crowd did quiet down enough so that his voice could again be heard. 'He's a Garshan, and he's always had high status and a number, and he's got an awful lot of kills on his belt. Forty six. Enough so he's now Status Ten point Nine Nine Four.

'And on my left the challenger – Sonrodnar Rodnar of Slaar – Status Thirty Eight – an amma-CHOOR . . .'

There was some applause – not very much – as Rodnar leaped lightly to the purple-and-gold triple-ringed star in the table's center and made his four-point bows. Most of the noise seemed to be the offering and taking of bets as to how long the challenger would last.

'Although he's an ammachoor,' the fat man bawled

happily on, 'he's got nineteen good tough kills chalked up and he's one of the very few men who is actually good enough to bet his life that he can take the Champ. Like all championships, this match is unlimited and to the death, not to any set number of bleeding wounds or to incapaci-ation. *Unlimited!* Anything goes! To the winnah the diamond-studded gold belt, the purse of twenty five thousand junex, and two full numbers in status. To the loo-zah one free cremation. Take stations, gentlemen!'

The Garshan sprang to the ring's center, as was the champion's right, with his back to the gamesmaster; Rodnar stationed himself half a radius out from the center, facing his opponent, with knees and elbows slightly sprung and with knife at the ready.

'*Go!*' Faylor yelled.

Simultaneously with the word a bell clanged and the gamesmaster, surprisingly agile for a man of his bulk and mass, leaped from the table and took the seat of Arbiter-In-Chief.

At the first sound-wave of the bell's clangor both gladiators sprang furiously into action. The Garshan leaped straight at the Slaaran; his eager knife in his right hand, point outthrust; the fingers of his left hand spread and flexed to grab anything grabable.

Each man had long since studied his opponent, of course, and also his opponent's seconds. The Masked Marvel's mental shield was as solid and as tight as was Rodnar's own; nothing whatever could be read through either. So also were those of the two strapping Garshan seconds seated to the right of the Arbiter-In-Chief; as were those of Knuaire of Spath and Marrjyl of Orm, sitting at that official's left. Although no non-psi even suspected it, the real business of those seconds was to protect their respective principals against such psionic shenanigans and low blows as telepathically confusing the opponent's thoughts or by imperceptibly – to the non-psionic judges, that is – teleporting that opponent's knife and hand an inch or so off-target at critical instants of the engagement. Or in the threat of sure death a Gamesman 'porting himself to safety. Those seconds, all four, were very good indeed at their business.

(There was of course no outward hint or sign whatever of any psionic activity. Since all officialdom was not only non-psi but also rabidly anti-psi, psionics did not officially exist, and at any display whatever of 'witchcraft' the offender became eaglemeat on the spot. So all fighting was strictly honest – no psionic fudging was or could be permitted.)

Rodnar leaped, too – or, rather, made a spectacular gymnast's dive – and faster even than the champion; but not directly toward him. Off-line slightly to his own right, and flipping his knife into his left hand while still in air: with the double purpose of flying unscathed *under* the Masked Marvel's blade and of slashing his left leg half off.

The smaller and faster man's normal strategy would be to take all possible advantage of his superiority in speed. Thus, whatever the crowd might think of his tactics and however it might yell and boo at him, he would ordinarily get onto his bicycle and stay on it out of the taller man's longer reach, and try to wear him down.

Wherefore Rodnar's instantaneous and slashing attack, a fractional instant ahead of the champion's, took all of the experts by surprise and almost succeeded. In fact, and in a very small way, it did succeed. In spite of everything the Garshan could do to change the trajectory of his leap, to get his leg out of the way, and/or to cut, kick, stamp or grab Rodnar's suddenly-wrong-sided knife hand, the very point of Rodnar's knife did nick the champion's leg and Garshan blood did begin to flow.

It was not at all a serious wound; it was the veriest nick.

Since such wounds bleed quite freely, however, when made by razorsharp cutting edges, it looked much worse than it really was and the crowd went even wilder than before. For, in spite of that crowd's innate and long-cultured savagery, practically everyone who did not have money down on the champion was in favor of the under dog; especially since that under dog, instead of running away from the champion, had actually taken the fight to him in the first fractional second of the match and had actually scored first blood!

Slamming the non-skid soles of both fighting shoes against the resined texture of the table's tightly-stretched plastic cover, Rodnar sprang erect and whirled around, hoping to find the Garshan off balance and unready. He wasn't – but he wasn't quite organized for attack yet, either, so Rodnar maintained the offensive. He feinted another dive at the champion's back-hand; then as the Garshan began to lower his guard and to whirl, he leaped high into the air and somewhat to his own left, swinging his right leg – with the fullest intention of driving the steel-lined toe of his fighting shoe into and through the champion's face.

But the Garshan had been feinting, too. Or, if not exactly feinting, he knew his trade well enough to be very skeptical indeed about this apparent exact repetition of technique. Wherefore he was prepared to straighten up instantly; and it took everything Rodnar had to arch his belly out of the way of the Garshan's ultra-fast and ultra-vicious riposte – a return slash intended to spread Rodnar's bowels all over the floor. In fact, he should have had just a little more, for he did not escape entirely unscathed. The frantically-wriggling twist that saved him from disembowelment brought his left hip into the knife's line of drive and he took a nick – about as serious a wound as he had inflicted on the champion a few seconds before.

28

Still in air, Rodnar grabbed the wrist of the Garshan's knife-hand and, with the anchorage thus afforded, spun and twisted like a cat and struck with foot and hand – to kick his foe in the solar plexus and at the same time to cut his throat. The Garshan, however, was familiar with that maneuver, too. He seized Rodnar's wrist and yanked it; simultaneously moving his solar plexus just enough so that the combination resultant of the motions made Rodnar miss both objectives. Then, both knife-hands being immobilized, the Garshan went viciously into close quarters. This, he thought exultantly, was his dish: he had broken a dozen men's backs from this exact situation.

To break a man's back, however, you have to hold him at least momentarily in some position or other; and Rodnar of Slaar was as hard to hold as a double armful of live eels and angleworms. Thrusting his head in close, he went for the champion's throat with his teeth. Foiled there by a hard and bristly chin, he went for his ear, but only got his mask – the first time that the Masked Marvel had been unmasked in combat. Then, wriggling and wrenching himself partially free, he shoved with all the strength of arms, torso, and legs; and as the two gladiators reeled apart the spectators saw the stream of blood running down the Slaaran's thigh – and the whole vast crowd exploded into pandemonium.

Then, for the first time, Rodnar mounted his velocipede. No athlete, however hard and however well trained, could maintain that pace of violence for long. He was fairly sure that it was taking more out of the champion – an older, heavier, slower man – than it was out of him; but there would be no cessation of combat until one of them was dead and he would have to save some of his strength. But not too much – he could not afford to let the Garshan get very much rest – he would have to wear him down to where he would make a mistake.

Wherefore very shortly he resumed his harrying, sniping, lightning-fast attacks; circling, reversing, feinting, thrusting, leaping . . . giving nicks and taking them . . . but as time wore on giving more than he took . . . until both men were literally plastered with slowly- congealing, sweat-streaked blood and foot-wide areas of the ring's floor were slippery with gore despite the resin . . . and the sadistic uproar of the crowd mounted higher and higher . . .

Until finally, after what seemed like hours and was actually twenty eight minutes, the champion did make a mistake. His knife was too high and he was a fraction of a second slow and a bit awkward and a couple of inches out of place in coping with a triple feint; and Rodnar, with chin and left shoulder protecting the vital areas of heart and throat, drove straight in for the kill.

He knew he'd have to take a savage counter-stroke, a slash or a stab; but there'd be only the one and in his position it wouldn't kill him – this was too good a chance altogether to miss. Wherefore he drove in, swinging. He deflected the champion's slashing stab to shoulder and arm and ribs, even while he was driving his own blade to the hilt into unresisting flesh and twisting it viciously, in a mangling spiral, as he withdrew it.

The ex-champion collapsed; and Rodnar, deafened by a roar of noise that seemed almost solid, stood there, holding his ghastly, gaping, blood-spurting wound together as best he could with his right hand, while his surgeon with his tool-kit and Knuaire and Marrjyl with a stretcher rushed up to him. Rodnar did lie on the stretcher while the doctor did his preliminary work. That done, however, he stood up and, refusing all help and acknowledging the bedlam-roar of the crowd with a couple of nods, he walked under his own power to and through the fighters' exit of Hall One of Games.

Outside that exit, however, he was very glad indeed to rest most of his weight on his friends' shoulders, and to let them half-carry him to the ambulance that was to take him to the hospital.

CHAPTER 2
The Grant

Nothing like the civilization and culture and government of the Justiciate and its tyranny had ever come to flower on Tellus or any other planet of Tellurian civilization. To approximate them there would have to be something possessing in combination the dictatorship of Communist Russia, a caste system but little less rigid than that of old India, the brutality and savagery of ancient Rome, and a technological advancement fully equal to that of the Western Hemisphere of Tellus.

Impossible? It might seem so. Nevertheless, it worked. Creakingly at times, it is true; and by dint of occasional blood-lettings and purges of horrible scope and type; but, after its fashion, it had been working for many thousands of Justician Standard years. It had been kept working, all these millennia, by the Tyrant's enforcement arm; the hated and feared planetary police, the Guard of the Person – disrespectfully called the 'Purps' from the gold- and silver-trimmed purple splendor of their full-dress uniform.

At the top of this sweet-smelling heap there was one and only one o'stat: (Overstat. Above status or zero status.) The Dictator – the Tyrant – the Supreme Grand Justice – His Magnificence Sonrathendak Ranjak of Slaar.

In Status One to Status Five, inclusive, with their status numbers carried out to three decimal places from 1.000 to 5.999, were the members of the Dictator's Board of Advisors, the members of the Council of Grand Justices, and a few *very* VIPs. In Status Six to Status Fifteen, equally finely graded, were all other major executives of the Justiciate. Any one of these persons could act as judge and jury and could impose the death penalty.

Status Sixteen to Status One Hundred, inclusive, none of which were fractionated, contained everyone else of any importance at all; and every person having status, and also the o'stat, had his or her fourteen digit Citizen Number tattooed across his or her back.

This status-and-number system of caste and regimentation did not include the millions of teeming millions of un-stats – people under status, beneath notice or consideration – people who, being non-citizens and possessing neither status nor numbers, had little or no recourse against exploitation. In the musty tomes of law they had some rights – rights which varied considerably from planet to planet – but in everyday life the extent of realization of those rights varied just about inversely as the status of the citizens concerned in the exploitation.

These un'stats were not exactly serfs; nor were very many of them slaves. On most of the planets of the Justiciate it was perfectly legal for any citizen to enslave any number of un'stats at will, but such enslavement was a very risky business indeed. Most un'stats preferred death to slavery; and, in dying, it was their custom to take as many numbered persons as possible with them into the hereafter.

And many un'stats, the ablest physically and mentally or both, won citizenship and numbers and status in many and various ways. Rodnar's great grandfather, for instance, had been born an un'stat. Having inherited psionic genes from both parents, however, he became an outstandingly successful bladesman and advanced himself and his line accordingly.

Perhaps it should be mentioned, though it hardly seems necessary – through the millennia the Justiciate had outlawed all languages except the dominant one, that of

Slaar; so a universal language was spoken on all the one hundred eighty three planets; with one notable exception, proud, recalcitrant Garsh.

A few days after winning the championship of Meetyl, Rodnar – now of Status Thirty Six and with his left arm in a sling – took an aircab to the edifice housing the outer offices of his Magnificence the Supreme Grand Justice. Armed this time with a letter of introduction to the First Secretary herself, he was ushered immediately into that Able's inner private office.

Her Ability First Secretary Daughtelna Starrlah of Slaar, Status Eleven point One Nine Zero, was a tall, brown-eyed, breasty muscular – swimmer type – young woman; with muscles and other attributes startlingly on display through a tightly-stretched jersey made of white nylon gauze. She wore the dangling, sparkling ear-pendants that were the mode of the moment; her shining, jet-black hair was piled high in what would be the mode of week after next. She was made up to the eyeballs.

She was sitting in a posture chair at an oversize desk littered with correspondence baskets, folders of all colors, business- and star-charts, hand-books, technical journals, tapes and viewers. In her left hand she held a green folder with Rodnar's name printed on it in black. As Rodnar entered the room she stared at him intently; she fairly riveted his eyes with hers with a look as old as woman and man.

While the usherette was showing Rodnar where he was to sit, the FirSec half-rose behind her desk and half-extended an exquisitely-worked crystal flask. 'A whiff?' she asked, but went on without a pause, 'But I don't suppose you inhale, though, at that,' and she withdrew the flask and sat down again.

'No, thanks, Your Ability, I'm in training; but please go ahead.'

'Uh-huh; I don't really like the stuff – my inhaling is strictly social.'

The office-girl having left the room and closed the door behind her, the FirSec flipped the switch that turned on the red 'IN CONFERENCE' sign across the outer side of that door. She then said 'No Calls' to her squawk-box and flipped its power-switch to 'OFF'; continuing the while to look at him with an intensity and a purpose that surprised him to the core.

It was not that a woman was taking the initiative – in their culture that was the woman's inalienable right and her exclusive privilege – it was that this particular woman would deign to make a pass at *him*. She was a high Eleven, an Able, and he was a mere Thirty Six; more than one-third down the status scale toward being nothing at all. Beyond making sure she was a non-psi he had not read her mind, not even the most superficial of her surface thoughts, and he did not read it now. Very few if any top-bracket psiontists were or are Peeping Toms.

'Subspace Technologist First Sonrodnar Rodnar of Slaar, I've been . . .' she began, formally, but broke off and went on in a strangely altered tone, 'Oh, down the cliff with *that* stuff!' Dropping the folder onto the desk, she got up, walked around to face him – he got up, too, of course – took his right hand in both of hers, and squeezed it hard. Her face paled, then flushed, and her nostrils began to flare as she went on, 'I watched you kill that utterly unspeakable louse of a Garshan the other night . . .'

A light flashed on in Rodnar's mind. He knew the connection, in strongly passionate women, between violent death and sex; and his own quick passion began to flame into being. But he wondered. That was days ago

. . . it wouldn't last this long . . . or could it? And how could a top-drawer FirSec – an Able – ever have had enough to do with even a high-stat Garshan to hate him that much?

But there was more to come, and worse. '. . . and I reveled in every second of it,' the girl went on. 'Death of Eagles, how I hated that slimy, nolligenous pfauld! So when your dossier, with your request for an interview, hit my desk I became completely unstuck. I owed you *so* much . . . I'd been wondering *so* much what – or how to . . .' She broke off and licked a lip with the tip of her tongue, for the man was moving.

He tossed his sling to the floor and, with left arm dangling carefully loose, he stepped up to her until his chest just touched her breasts. 'Yes?' he asked quietly.

She started to nod, then shook her head. 'Uh-uh,' she said, quite evidently very much against both will and desire. 'I shouldn't've – we mustn't – that ghastly wound; we'd tear it wide open.'

'Uh-uh,' he disagreed. 'It ought to be stuck together strong enough to hold by this time, I should think. Anyway, so what? Even if we do pull a few stitches Doc can stick 'em back in.' He put his good arm powerfully around her and the dam broke – their two bodies tried mightily to weld themselves full length into one . . . and, all unconsciously, his left arm came up and went to work in sync with his right.

'Um-m-m-nh?' he asked, after a little of that. His mouth was in no position to talk.

Neither was hers. 'Umnh – hmnh!' she agreed, enthusiastically, and managed to move her head enough, without interfering in the least with what they were doing, to indicate what was evidently the door to a room that was even more inner and more private than her inner private office. And, awkwardly – blissfully unwilling to give up any iota of contact – still straining together – the two turned toward the door . . . and Rodnar caught his breath, flinched uncontrollably, and stopped dead in his tracks, his face turning white.

'Oh? . . . Oh! . . . Oh, *no*!' she cried, in three entirely different tones, pulling away from him far enough to see that the whole left side of his shirt was soggy with blood – blood that was already plastering her thin nylon jersey to every fine contour of her right breast. 'Death of *Eagles*! I thought I felt something! All-Powers damn me for a fool! . . .'

'Think nothing of it, Starr!' he protested. 'Just a little leak, is all, and it's strictly my own fault – I should've known enough not to use that arm . . .'

'Lie down here!' she snapped, paying no attention to his protests and practically forcing him down onto her office couch. 'Lemme look . . . oh, good . . .' She sighed deeply in relief. 'It isn't spurting, so it'll be all right to get your doctor – he's mine, too, you know – or did you? – in here instead of rushing you to the hospital.'

'Doctor? Nuts to that. Maybe we'd better take a rain-check on these doings until that slash heals a little more, but it won't take long to transact our bit of official business. *Then* I'll go see Doc.'

'Nuts to that right back at you, Rod.' She flipped the switch to her com, punched a number, and waited until a handsome, forty-year-old face appeared upon her screen. 'I'm awfully sorry to have to bother you, Doctor,' she said then, 'but I wonder if you could dash over here to my office right away and sew Rod up again?'

'What? How in . . .?' The pictured eyes looked search-ingly at the patient, then glanced at the girl. 'Cancel. I see how. *What* a brain! Rod, if your brain was solid U-235 and it all fissioned at once it wouldn't crack your skull . . .' he paused, grinning at them both, and emitted a chuckle that turned into a belly laugh. 'But I can't say I blame you – either of you – at that; I might even do the same thing myself. Don't worry, Starr; he's perfectly all right and I'll be right over.'

The doctor punched off. Starrlah, without changing the adjustment of her set, said 'Lanjy' and a top-half view of the usherette, seated now, appeared on the screen.

'Yes, Your Ability?' the picture asked.

'I just had an accident, Lanjy – please skip down to Brazzoin's, will you, and get me a zero-gauge white See-Mor jersey, Sec-Style, size thirty eight?'

'Right away, Your Ability; thank you!' the girl caroled, and took off on the run.

Starrlah cut com, sat down on the edge of the couch, licked her lips, and gulped twice. 'I feel better, darling,' she said then. 'The way that hyena of a doctor howled, you can't be in any real danger . . . but I thought I'd *killed* you . . . and what *could* I have . . . it simply petrifies me, to think . . .'

'Nothing like that, sweetheart.' Their hands met and clung. 'In fact, I'm pretty sure we could . . .'

'But I'm *absolutely* sure we won't,' she declared. 'Not without permission in writing. Being scared to death *once* is enough.' She bent over and kissed him, gently but with plenty of meaning; and he returned the caress fully in kind. 'Besides, it'll keep – and without spoiling. So as you were saying? No, not that, either – say something else.'

'Okay, I've been wondering. I know that high-stats have as much grief as anybody; but I can't visualize you as being either close enough to a Garshan – even a high-stat Garshan – or near him long enough to develop that much hatred.'

'I wouldn't let him get close to me at all. Ever. That's what started all the trouble.'

He didn't say anything; just looked at her questioningly. She went on, 'I know. Practically every man from a planet barbarous enough so that men still make the approaches is decent enough to act civilized while he's on a civilized planet, but that egregious stinker wasn't. I also know that Garshans are absolutely pure of blood – no monkey business with any member of any other race. Any Garshan who fathers or mothers a cross-breed feeds the eagles. Together with the 'breed. But he, the putrescent monster, wasn't even a good Garshan – except in that the harder I smacked him down the more determined he became to make me.'

'Sure. That made it a point of Garshan honor. He'd get you if it was the last thing he ever did in this life.'

'That's right. Well, as long as I had status on him I could kick him in the teeth and I did, in spite of his terrific in with Grand Justice Laynch of Garsh, and his gutsy assumption that being a champion bladesman gave him the right to push an in with His Magnificence. What I didn't think of was that I was already at the very top of my status possibility and he wasn't. So when he got status on me he began really to close in on me, with every slimy, poisonous maneuver he could possibly execute. So I finally had to do one of three – and *only* three – things. First, start looking past that revolting, gloating puss. Second, kill him myself or hire it done – with every chance in the world that the Purps would pin it onto me and feed me to the eagles. Third, engineer it so that the insufferable monster would die legally and naturally. Actually, inevitably – of an occupational hazard.' She paused and gazed at him innocently, eye to eye.

He got it instantly. 'Eaglesdeath!' he exploded. 'So *that's* how I got onto the table with him so easily! But how? Even with your status, how could you work *that* trick?'

She laughed. 'It was so simple, really, that when I

39

finally thought of it I cursed myself all over the place for not thinking of it sooner. First, I picked you out – out of all the bladesmen of civilization. Then I started a lovely little rumor and kept it spreading that he was afraid of you; scared to death. That he'd run a mile rather than meet you in anything except a prelim to first scratch. So, being a proud and stiff-necked Garshan . . .?'

He whistled expressively. 'I see. That would work on practically anyone, let alone a Garsh . . .'

A tiny signal light flashed yellow, accompanied by a softly unobtrusive buzz. 'Okay, Lanjy, bring it in, please,' Starrlah said, and the usherette came in. Without looking at either the FirSec or the man she strode up to the desk, placed a small package on its top, about-faced smartly, and marched as unobservantly out.

Starrlah looked down at Rodnar's bloody shirt. There was no fresh blood; that already there was pretty well clotted. She bent over, kissed him – quite playfully, this time – said 'Stay put, you, I'll be back in a jiffy,' and picking up the package *en passant*, went into the back room.

Rodnar sat up carefully, experimentally. Good – there was no stab of pain; no gush of blood. He stood up, as carefully . . . walked half across the room toward the desk . . . sat down in the chair he had occupied before and buried himself in thought.

One phase of this operation he didn't care much for, being used without knowing anything about it . . . but Great Powers, what a woman! He'd never been in love, he didn't think, and there wasn't supposed to be any such thing as love at first sight, but if this wasn't love, what was it? And love aside, he'd never dreamed of having an in with any such powerful official as the Tyrant's First Secretary . . . so he'd have to have a horrible lot of guts to do any squawking about it even in thought . . .

Starrlah came back in, fresh and clean from her shower and wearing a new jersey and a short, slit skirt to match. Her hairdo and makeup had remained untouched. 'Oh!' she exclaimed, and rushed over to look. 'Darling! Are you *sure* it's stuck?'

'I'm sure, sweetheart. All dry and hard. See? No fresh blood at all.'

'Oh, wonderful!' She kissed him lingeringly; went around her desk; took her accustomed seat. 'But before we go into this grant business,' she touched the green folder with a freshly-glitter-nailed forefinger, 'there's just one more thing about this Masked Marvel business. Very few people know anything about it, or are ever going to.'

'I understand,' he said, a little uncomfortably in spite of himself. 'Those who can do you some good and those you're serving notice on to tiptoe around you because you've got more teeth and claws than a jungle tiger . . .' He paused, then went on with a markedly lightening mien, 'It was a kind of a shock at first, thinking of myself merely as one of your teeth, but the more I think it over the better I like it. It cuts both ways, you know.'

'Of course it does!' She laughed delightedly and reached out; their hands met and held. 'I was hoping you'd see it that way – there are lots of men who wouldn't. It won't do you a bit of harm, you know, to be the only person I've ever given a ninety-minute appointment to.' She picked up the green folder; began to flip its pages.

'*That* long?' He was amazed. 'I'll say it won't! You'll never know how much I appreciate this, Starr.' He slid a yellowish-green slip – the Games check for twenty five thousand junex . . . across the desk's top toward her. 'This'll be enough, won't it, to pay the costs of a quarter-hour audience with His Magnificence? The investigation, security checks, and so on?'

She glanced at the figure, whistled sharply, and pushed

41

the slip back toward him. 'No, my dear,' she said. 'We'll forget the polite fiction about "costs", please – I'm not down to where *you* have to bribe me. Or can. Put it back in your wallet.'

'Nix. No deal. Partners help each other, don't they? Didn't this job cost you? And plenty?'

'Of course it did. Two hundred fifteen thousand junex. But I gathered a lot more posies on my way up here than I put out.'

'But not that many.' He shook his head. 'You aren't old enough yet. Even though that desk is a flower-garden de luxe, you're still in hock up to your beautiful ears. Confess.'

'All right. I still owe the bank seventy-five thousand; but they aren't worried about it and neither am I. Not many bouquets are this big . . .' she tapped the check lightly, '. . . but they come often. I'll make out. And I won't take this check or any part of it. That's flat and final.'

'You just think it is, little chum,' he said firmly. 'This isn't bribery any more, it's a partnership deal; your authority and my money. Either I at least chip in or I pick up my marbles and go home and start all over on Spath – and *that's* flat and final. So call your shot, Starr.'

She studied his face for a long moment, then smiled radiantly – a smile that made her look to be about eighteen – and said, 'You really mean that, don't you? I'm amazed . . . I never knew a man before who . . . very well, I'll meet you half-way; we'll go halvers on it.' She put the check into his hand and this time he accepted it. 'So bring me one half that big sometime, you wonderful guy, and I'll accept it with glee. Maybe more than that, even – whoops! More than glee, I mean; not more than half. Not a *kinto* more than half! But to get back to this grant business:

42

'You're petitioning for the re-issuance of the research charter your father had, that lapsed when he died. Your proposed charter is identical with his, except for your name instead of his, and is the most masterly piece of legal befuddlement I ever scanned. What isn't sheer gobble-degook is equally sheer flapdoodle. Under that charter you don't *have* to do anything whatever and you *can* do anything you please. Including psionics!' She spat that word out as though it offended her every sense, then went on:

'I fine-toothed the records, and your father and his group apparently never did anything except meet a couple of times or so a week and turn in reel after reel of metaphysical blatherings and blah. And, if I'm any judge, if they found out anything it would have made eaglemeat out of every one of them right then. So before I sign, seal, and deliver this, and authorize headquarters and an operating fund, I'll have to . . .'

'Huh?' he broke in, staring. '*You* sign – and authorize? You mean I don't have to petition the Throne?'

'Just that.' She threw back her head and laughed. 'Exactly. A special bonus. I told you His Magnificence likes smooth work, and the way I got myself out of that jam – and him, too, for that matter – he hated the crumb, too, and had been wondering how to get rid of him without . . .'

'Wait a minute!' he broke in. 'The more you talk the more baffled I get. If the Tyrant didn't like him he'd feed him to the eagles, wouldn't he? And wouldn't he do it anyway, to back you up?'

'Uh-uh.' She shook her head. 'The answer is "No." To both questions. In theory perhaps he could, but in practice no ruler ever has been or ever will be the absolute despot most people think he is. That is, not for long. He has to play footsie with the biggies or die quick, even surrounded

by Purps by the dozen. So His Magnificence has to –
cooperate with the Grand Justice of Garsh – as the
Number One of the Council of Justices he swings altogether too much weight to be offended needlessly, and
the Masked Marvel had a kingsize in with the Grand
Justice of Garsh. See? As for taking *my* part; don't be
naive. Why should he? He was watching that fight with his
eyes out on stalks – all a-quiver to find out whether I had
the stuff or not. If a FirSec can't fight her own battles and
bury her own dead she gets fed to the eagles – or at least
gets kicked down-status to a job she *can* handle.'

Rodnar whistled. 'Wow and *wow*,' he said. 'When I said
high-stats had their griefs . . . well, *that's* one I certainly
never thought of.'

She shrugged. 'To each his own,' she said, then went
on, 'The reason that's so trite is because it's so true.
Anyway, he liked the operation so well that I'm in with
him so strong I can scarcely believe it myself. He got the
point instantly when I suggested my taking care of you and
your grant and tossed you right into my lap. So you see I
can't cross the old boy up, Rod; not even for you.'

'Of course you can't, my dear. I don't want you to. I'm
not out to cross *anybody* up.'

'No?' Her lovely face hardened. 'Then you are *not*
going in for any of this psionics squank?'

This was it; the place where he'd have to walk a
tightrope. 'The possibility is not excluded,' he said,
carefully.

He actually felt her withdrawal. 'A while ago I would
have said you were either a fool or a knave,' she declared,
'but before I staked my life on your quality I learned very
well that you're neither. So I'll listen. Especially since
there's no use pretending that our relationship is anything
ordinary any more. But Rod, I simply *can't* swallow such
abysmal nonsense as ectoplasm, talking to the spirits of

44

the dead, flying saucers, telepathic little blue men from the third moon of Skane, precognizing my own death from being shot in the flank with a spear-gun, kinestheticking a . . .'

'Hold it!' he broke in. 'Good for you! I can't, either, but I'll bet my half of that check that you have intuitions, and I *know* that I have hunches.'

'Of course I have – but what has that got to do with the price of orksts in un'statland?'

'Plenty. Neither intuitions nor hunches can be explained.'

'Of course not; they're . . .' Beginning to see where the man was heading, she broke off.

'Yeah,' he said. 'So-called "psionics" does contain a lot of squank. But after the squank is shucked off, there is a residuum of truth that has never been explained, either. What do you know about X-storms in comparison with magnetic storms?'

'Oh?' she asked, startled. 'Oh. Nothing at all, compared to your specialized knowledge. Just that the College has been studying them for ages and hasn't – oh-oh! I see. Since a strictly orthodox – what you'd call a hidebound – approach has failed completely, you think that even such a wildly *un*orthodox one as psionics should be tried?'

'You're a smart girl, sweetheart.' This was an understatement of the first magnitude, and Rodnar now knew it. 'But all I can say is a variant of what I said before: no possibility whatever is excluded.'

'And that's enough. I told you I'd studied you intensively, but some corollary data didn't click into place until just now . . . you, one of the top techs of all civilization, eating out of the same dish with Marrjyl of Orm and Knuaire of Spath . . . She being a Designer First – and that *doesn't* apply to clothes – and he a Theoretician First and probably the greatest mathematician now alive . . .

Well, I don't want to know any more, my dear; I may know a little too much already . . . so there's just one more question. Will you swear on your honor and by your status not to work against Sonrathendak Ranjak as Supreme Grand Justice?'

'I'll do better than that, Your Beauty.' He raised his right hand. 'I swear on my honor and by my status to *support* Sonrathendak Ranjak in office as Supreme Grand Justice of the Justiciate.'

'Oh, thanks, Rod – that's *wonderful*! I'll get your Institute for Advanced Study stuff going through the mill right away . . .' She paused; and, eyes holding eyes, they went carefully but very meaningfully into each other's arms . . .

'How would it be,' he asked finally, 'for me to come back after quitting time and take you up to the Eyrie for a prime-orkst-steak supper and take you home, after?'

'I'd *love* it! The Eyrie, anyway – about the taking home part, not unless we absolutely . . .' She broke off as the tiny light lit up again and the soft-voiced buzzer again sounded. 'Oh, drat! I'll bet that's that odious hyena of a doctor!'

And it was.

CHAPTER 3

The Institute for Advanced Study

The First Secretary had given Rodnar a really choice office. It was as high up as the Gamesmaster's and it, too, was pressurized and overlooked the ocean. Also, since it had to seat more people, it was larger. Being larger, its works of art were of greater size and of more magnificent scope. The entire back wall was an ages-old masterpiece of mosaic, of overpowering force and poignancy and beauty, portraying a frightful storm at sea. A great sailing vessel, heeled over until her lee rail was awash, tearing through the water with only tattered rags of canvas on her almost-bare poles and spars but with a tremendous bone in her teeth, was making what was very evidently a climactic last-ditch effort to survive – and it was just as evident that her fate hung dreadfully in the balance. To look at that masterpiece, especially for the first time, was a shattering experience; and all the other art in the room – on floor and ceiling and both side-walls – led the eye inescapably toward it.

When Starrlah had first taken Rodnar to look at that office, both had stood entranced for minutes, studying that mosaic and appreciating it and feeling its impact in the very marrow of their bones. The girl had finally said, with her eyes showing a trace of unshed tears, 'Rod, that is the most utterly *marvelous* thing I have ever seen in my life. It simply tears at me; it's one of the very few things I've ever seen that makes me go all weepy inside.'

Rodnar, staring in fascination, had nodded and had said, 'It's got a terrific wallop, no question . . . If I can have *this* office, Starr, I certainly don't want to look at any more or have one built. I'd never forgive myself if I let this go.'

He had worked in that office for some three weeks now; had become accustomed enough to it so that he *could* work in it. Marrjyl, however, who was now approaching at high speed through the air, had been in the new headquarters only a couple of times. Also, since she was just in from Orm, she had never previously seen a copy of the younger Naizlon's immortal *Ship In Distress*. She looked in, shed and stowed; and then, after flashing a thought of greeting at Rodnar and Knuaire, she put both hands on her hips and stared at the mosaic in frowning concentration.

Rodnar grinned at her. 'I know,' he directed a thought. 'It's got the wallop of a battering ram. But why all the scowls? Every time you come in here you scowl at it.'

'Was I scowling? I didn't realize that I was . . . not that I'm at all surprised. Wallop? *Huh*!' She emitted a more or less ladylike snort. 'It leaves me as cold as a basket of fish. I know that nobody now alive has ever sailed a vessel of that type or tonnage and I've never read up on the theory, but that thing sets my teeth on edge something fierce. It doesn't make sense in any partic . . .'

'Huh?' Rodnar demanded. 'Why, that's the greatest . . .'

'I don't care *how* great it is!' she broke in in turn. 'You simply can't assume that the captain of a sea-going vessel that big would be or could be an utter nitwit. That's ridiculous. And if he wasn't – if he had a living lick of brains – he'd've had his tail section there – ' She pointed, then swung the finger in a quarter-circle clockwise, ' – pointing straight back into the wind, so it couldn't possibly blow him over. And I'll bet you seven junex to two that if you put appropriate data into a computer you'll find that those waves are all askew too. Absolutely wrong in size,

48

shape, aspect, and deployment for the evident direction and apparent velocity of the wind.'

Rodnar was shocked. 'But *Marr*!' he protested. 'That's art! You *feel* it – 'way down deep in your guts and with everything you've got – you don't run it through a computer or analyze its components for stresses and strains.'

'The hell you don't,' Knuaire put in, speaking aloud. He was a tall, lithe young white-skinned man with gray eyes and curly brown hair, who had not been making any secret at all of the fact that he thought Marrjyl of Orm was really a something. 'It's a fact that many such vessels were destroyed in storms. That makes it all the more unjustifiable for Naizlon the Younger to have employed an indefensible figment of his own imagination when an actual happening, accurate in every detail, would have served him just as well artistically and emotionally, and infinitely better in every other way. Marr – ' he turned to the girl, ' – you're a sweetheart – a darling – a girl after my own heart. My profound congratulations! You're the first person I've ever met who didn't bow down and worship Slaaran art, cockeyed as it is. If permitted, I'd kiss you on both cheeks.'

'Thanks, Knu! Wonderful! The way Rod was looking at me, pinning my ears flat to my skull, I was about to begin to be ashamed of myself, but now I won't have to. And as for kissing, there's a lot nicer places for that than that,' and she proceeded to demonstrate.

'There is, at that,' the Spathian agreed, as he cooperated enthusiastically in the demonstration. Then, when the girl broke contact, he jerked his thumb to indicate a group of people flying toward their landing stage on a sharply downward slant from the north and said, 'Some of our gang coming in. If the rest of them are on time – and they probably will be – everybody will be here in less than fifteen minutes. So listen, Marr. If you don't want to get skinned alive, rubbed with salt, drawn, decapitated, and quartered *before* being fed to the eagles, don't ever again tell anyone except me the truth about Slaaran art. Not even Rod here, and I won't either. We'll keep it a secret between ourselves; just whisper it to each other once in a while,' and, with a conspiratorial grin, Knuaire of Spath, Vice President of the Institute and – unofficially – its Assistant Chief Psiontist, went to the lock to welcome the visitors.

There were twelve people in this group. While they were unharnessing, six more came in at short intervals; two couples and two singles. Eighteen people; the highest-powered psiontists of eighteen different worlds; white, yellow, red, brown, and black. There were other groups of psiontists on many worlds, but they were more isolated, less organized; and at this point it seemed prudent to exclude them from the Institute's plans. Few of the eighteen had previously met any of the others, but each knew at least one of the three hosts; and, while everything was peculiarly silent, the ether was full of greetings and of flying thoughts.

Most surprising, perhaps, was the meeting of two persons who had attended a seminar together right here on Meetyl, had met several times before, but without either having had any suspicion that the other was psionic. One was a tall, yellow-skinned, brown-haired girl, very attractive in an awkward, coltish way, who couldn't have been a day over fourteen, Tellus-equivalent. She glanced once at a short, brown-skinned – Malayan type – youth, a few years older than herself, and uttered a piercing shriek that was physical as well as mental;

'Dal! Of all the people I never expected to see here, you, Sonrogo Dallarr of Brith, are posi-*tutely* the last! What a *gorgeous* shield you've got!'

50

'Same to you, Kitten – or, for any of you others who haven't met this obstreperous young squirt yet, Daughtanja Arla of Crayme. I'm as happy to see you here, Kitten, as I am surprised.'

She had rushed up to him and had seized one of his hands, at the same time extending a two-ounce flask cut from one perfect crystal of sapphire. 'Whiff?' she asked. 'Or do you still use that corrosive squampf that eats holes through the top of your head and the soles of both feet all at once?'

He laughed. 'Rather corrosive than vapid, Arla; I like it to hit bottom.' He extended his flask, which was of simple rose quartz. 'Try it again, why don't you?'

She shook her head, grinning engagingly. 'What you'd better do with that noisome squampf is pitch it down the cliff where it belongs. Here's cheers!' She clicked flasks with him, inhaled deeply (from her own flask), and turned to the Spathian. 'You're Knuaire, the Theoretician First, aren't you? I've been studying your monograph on the application of Grizzon's Criterion to the use of the Chi function in the fifth determinant . . .'

After ten or fifteen minutes more of general mixing and of getting acquainted, Rodnar called the meeting, which was not really formal, to order and said:

'Since this is our first actual meeting, I propose to go into the situation quite thoroughly. Most of the material will be familiar to some of you, but much of it will be new to others of you, particularly to our younger members.

'Mysterious, persistent night lights – Unidentifiable Flying Objects – have been reported for many hundreds of years. Skipping the ancient ones, concerning which we have no reliable information, we know that during the last century there have been many sightings that no scientist has been able to explain. They can be explained

51

only by psionics; we psiontists are the only human beings able to perceive anything in the fourth dimension.

'About seventy years ago a psiontist found a very high probability of a connection between two particular sightings and two extremely severe disturbances then thought to be magnetic storms. Subspace communication had been perfected only a short time before. Before that, it was hard to tell whether any particular failure was or was not due to faulty apparatus or technique. As technology improved, however, and interference increased year by year, it was learned definitely that the increase was due to a certain type – we still call it Type X – of non-magnetic storm.

'During the next twenty years psiontists determined that everyone who sighted a genuine unidentifiable flying object was, to a greater or less degree, psionic; and three completely authenticated sightings occurred during three very severe X-type storms. Continued study confirmed the conclusion that Type X storms were caused by something occurring in the fourth dimension.

'Psiontists informed the authorities of their findings; but they were ignored. Non-psionicists believed, then as now, that all psionics was fakery, imagination, and crackpotism; that what actuality, if any, it had was witchcraft and black magic and must be stamped out wherever and whenever found. However, the terribly disruptive Type X storms continued to increase and the Council of Science could not even touch the real problem. So finally, in sheer desperation, our Grand Justice – Supreme Grand Justice Sonrathendak Ranjak of Slaar, you know; he was a young man then and able to think a little – gave my father a status rating of forty seven, a grudging go-ahead, and a small appropriation to found an "Institute for Advanced Study". When my father died I took over, and we kept on working. Surreptitiously, until now, when I'm adding you new members to our staff.'

Rodnar's face darkened, his thoughts turned bitter. 'And that's what we still are. No hint whatever, ever, of our real abilities or of what we can do and should be doing, or we feed the eagles. If the damned old fat-head glumpfs would only . . .'

'Damp it down, Rod!' Marrjyl broke in. 'If just one bit of *that* squampf ever gets out you'll certainly be eagle-meat.'

'Not a chance, Marr.' The man's sober mien lightened. 'I'm awake. They're too stupid – no, not stupid; impervious. And if, some day, one of the meat-heads does get a sudden rush of intelligence to the brain and sets their damned purps on us, I'll see to it that non-magnetic storms blow all their transistors out of all the rigs they can set up. Okay?'

'Okay.'

'To get on with it, our results to date have been ver*ee* ungood. We finally analyzed the stuff – it's a new type of energy, originating in the fourth dimension and completely unknown to any planet of explored space – and we've built counter-generators – generators of a force to neutralize it. However, to put it mildly, space is big; subspace is bigger; and we don't know much of anything about the fourth dimension. So, while we have managed to destroy a few of the generators of X-storms, we don't average one in two years and no wreckage has ever been found.

'Now. The Justices don't like us; the Grand Justices especially. They don't want to believe in psionics at all; and, to the extent that they're forced to, they're afraid of us. And jealous – of anything we *may* have that they haven't got. So:

'Admittedly we haven't done much; but nobody else has done anything at all. The Council of Science tried to write off our successes as due purely to chance, but their statisticians couldn't get anywhere with that. Hence, for that and certain other reasons, we're here – along with some not-too-subtle hints that if I don't produce I'll be considered an ex-citizen and eaglemeat.

'That hits the high spots to date. Now. I know that the energy originates in the fourth dimension. I think that it is not a natural phenomenon, but is a product of parascience – psionics – and of technology. I infer that it is produced by generators designed and built by a race of highly intelligent entities, at least some of whom are psiontists. Not ordinary psychics or mystics, but highly-skilled, highly-trained psiontists; experts of at least our own grade. I deduce that there exists, somewhere, hitherto completely unsuspected, such a race. I conclude nothing, as yet. I request full and frank opinions from all of you. Sonjormel Wayrec of Garsh, you seem anxious to be heard; over to you.'

Wayrec – a burly, black-haired, reddish-brown skinned, hawk-nosed man of thirty, the only Garshan in the Institute – came in without a moment's pause. 'You have of course considered the point as to whether or not these X-storms are deliberately inimical.'

'I have. They may be. They may, much more probably, be accidental. Incidental, rather; a by-product of the normal activities of this postulated race.'

'It is my considered opinion that X-storms are both deliberate and inimical. That there is such a race; a race that is studying us and harassing us. That, whenever they are ready to act, our communications will be blanketed continuously and they will attack us.'

'Nonsense!' snapped a big, massive, almost-black woman, Daughtlanarr Monarr of Tsalk. 'I believe firmly that X-storms are purely natural phenomena; just as natural as magnetic storms but we don't know yet what causes them. Your inference, Rodnar, is based largely

54

upon the fact that such storms are increasing in number. You are ignoring the over-riding fact that all Nature waxes and wanes, in one way or another. And Wayrec, your thinking is altogether too deeply colored by your heredity and environment of ceaseless warfare. You are extrapolating from an indefensible assumption to utterly indefensible conclusions. Knuaire, what is your . . .?'

'Hold up!' the Garshan snapped, his dark, proud face hard set. 'As a mysto-pacifist, Monarr, who does not wear a knife, you should not insult a whole man. An apology is in order.'

'You hold up, Wayrec,' Rodnar said crisply, before the black woman could say a word. 'I asked for full and frank opinions. Censored, pussy-footing opinions are valueless. Therefore the insult, if any, was mine. I wear a knife and I am at your service . . .'

'Hold up, both of you!' Knuaire drove the thought. 'Rod, are you conducting a forum or a games? Wayrec, did you come here to learn something or to pick a fight?'

'You've got a point there, Knu, at that.' Rodnar grinned sheepishly at the Spathian; then went on. 'I apologize, Wayrec, especially since I'm a semi-pro bladesman; and I apologize to all of you for conduct unbecoming a presiding officer. Wayrec, you still have the floor.'

'The error was mine,' the Garshan admitted stiffly, carefully concealing the fury that raged within. 'I gave my opinion. I will add only that my mind is open to facts and to sound reasonings, but not to sentimental vaporings and mystic denials of reality. Over to you, Theoretician First Songladen Knuaire of Spath.'

'While I am not convinced that such a race does in fact exist,' Knuaire said, 'I am willing to postulate, as a first-approximation working hypothesis, that it does. We have explored only a minute fraction of one galaxy, and it is probable that all the planets of all the galaxies are mutually accessible through the fourth dimension. Thus, without introducing any additional unknowns, almost anything is possible; but idle speculation is not productive. We should, I think, concentrate on X-storms and how to abate them – "how" is much more important at the moment than "who".'

'Check,' Marrjyl agreed, 'if we want to keep on living.' The meeting settled down to solid study.

They had built twelve counter-generators. They were kept out in subspace, powered and ready, but the few successes that had been achieved in aborting X-storms had been due largely to luck. The trouble was that the storms moved altogether too fast; they did their damage and disappeared before the defending installations could get within range.

'You said "moved too fast," Knu,' Rodnar said. 'Is there an implication that the cause may be the mere passing of a postulated vehicle? That perhaps something in its operation may inadvertently create our problem?'

'Unlikely as it may sound, it's a possibility that must be considered. The fact that our own operation does not interfere with communications does not preclude the possibility of others doing so. That line of thought should be followed up.'

Rodnar nodded. 'It should. Marrjyl and I will follow it. Since Orm and Slaar have had more X-storms of late than other planets, we're in the best position to do the job.'

Work went on for hours; until, long after supper-time, the first courses of action had been roughed out. They all had supper *en masse*, harnessed up (no one ever teleported if any non-psi could possibly catch him at it), and sped through the air to a nearby spaceport, where they slotted the claim tokens for their subspeedsters.

Eighteen of them lined out for their home planets. Rodnar went to a point in space about one-third of the way from Slaar to the planet Orm, to cover one of the locations where X-storms had seemed most frequently to originate. Marrjyl, who as a top-flight designer had been involved with Knuaire in the production of the counter-generators, went with him; and shortly thereafter Knu 'ported aboard.

With Knuaire's entry, Marrjyl exclaimed fervently, 'I can't *stand* that Wayrec! I don't trust him one kinto's worth. He may be – no, he is – a strong psiontist, but he has only one interest – Garsh.'

'Let's not be influenced by his bad manners,' Knuaire commented. 'He can't help being a Garshan.'

Days passed, during which the three spent a lot of money. Other psiontists came, in other subspace speedsters. Huge space-going machine-shops came, carrying hundreds of mechanics. Weirdly-wired, terrifically-powered devices were planted, in a carefully-computed four-dimensional pattern, throughout all 'nearby' subspace – some of them, of course, being many parsecs away in normal space.

'But suppose it *is* intelligent beings who are making these X-storms without even knowing it?' Marrjyl deman-ded one day. 'Beings who don't know anything about us any more than we do about them? Don't even know we're here? We shouldn't kill intelligent creatures, no matter how monstrous they are, just because they're using this sector of the fourth dimension. We don't own all sub-space, Rod; you know we don't.'

'Of course we don't; but listen, Marr. First, I don't believe that X-storms are or can be caused by subspacers. Not only Knu, but a dozen others of the best mathemati-cians alive, with our biggest computers, have been work-ing on it; and every answer comes out N hyphen O dash in capital letters. They can't find any theoretical basis what-ever for a drive that can possibly make the stuff. Second, if you stretch your imagination enough to imagine intelligent life completely unknown to us . . .'

'That's not much of a stretch, and you know it.'

'Of itself, no; but there's a terrific snapper. No matter where they live – with so many of them flitting around for so long a time, *some* of them – certainly the ones we wrecked – would have normalized close enough to us to have been detected. Nothing ever has; not even a bit of wreckage. Play *that* on your piccolo, Marr.'

The girl caught her lower lip between her teeth. 'Maybe some things *have* been seen . . . some of those non-psi sightings, you know . . . no, too vague, nothing tangible – typical crackpot stuff.' She pondered, then cried triumphantly, 'But there could be a type that *lives* in subspace!'

'Oh, poppycock!' he snorted. 'How far out into the wild blue can you go? If so, they'd be incomprehensible by definition. Anyway, our generators are not designed to kill anything. They don't generate death-rays. You know what the stuff is as well as I do.'

'I know; but there's still the possibility of it making their drives backfire and kill everybody aboard.'

'Oh, for the love of . . . cut it, Marr. Get conscious and get with it.'

'I am with it!' she insisted. 'Making that assumption, the very least it would do would be to . . .' She broke off and scowled in concentration, then went on, 'Uh-uh. Assumption untenable. Matter remains in subspace only under impressed force, so it would emerge . . . and nothing ever has . . . but listen, Rod!' She stopped short; her eyes widened. 'If not in our space and not in subspace – what *other* space can there be?'

Marrjyl of Orm was the first entity to have any inkling of the truth, but she was neither willing nor able to support her theorizing against even mild opposition – and Rodnar's opposition was anything but mild:

'Oh, stop blowing your nozzles and land somewhere,' he exclaimed. 'And think of this. The most we'll be doing to them isn't a patch to the least those X-storms are doing to us. Disruption of communications, – business, – time, – money, – tens of thousands of very expensive com units and instruments. Don't be a weeper, Marr; especially since I am and you ought to be pulling full weight with the Law on this project. Not only to keep from being eagle-meat, either; this is the first chance we've ever had and the best one we ever will have to ram psionics down the damned old glumpfs' fat throats.'

'On *that* you're clicking,' she agreed. 'Put that way, this kind of theorizing goes down the cliff: we're certainly more important to us than any purely hypothetical entities can be,' and nothing more was said about alien entities, intelligent or otherwise.

Space is unimaginably vast. Also, by the very nature of things, subspace is incomprehensibly larger than is mere space. And one of the peculiarities of subspace is that no two subspacers leaving the same place for the same destination ever do or ever can take the same 'course' unless they immerge at exactly the same time – at *exactly* the same time, to within an immeasurably infinitesimal fraction of a nanosecond. Thus Rodnar and Marrjyl did not find any subspace traffic lanes: there were none to find. And thus their generators did not abort any X-storms – then.

And it was just as well for the peace of mind of all humanity of the ninety six planets of Tellurian civilization that it was the mighty *Explorer*, and not one or a succession of InStell's passenger liners, that eventually put those highly capable defenses of Slaar and Orm to the test.

CHAPTER 4

The Adams Fusion

Alone in his office aboard the super Starship *Explorer*, the leybyrdite monster which MetEnge and DesDes had built in partnership, Dr Andrew Adams paced restlessly, a frown of complete concentration on his long, lean face. He seemed to glide across the heavy pile of the floor, oblivious to the comfortable furnishings, the necessary electronic equipment, his tall, lithe, gray-clad form avoiding them by instinct. His wife, Stella, had left the room quite a while ago, sensing his need to be alone.

Adams was annoyed – annoyed with himself. He ran one hand through his thick gray hair. Time and again he had considered his problem and always without result, always concluding that the solution was beyond him. And inevitably he had returned to the question that *had* to have an answer.

What – no, *who* – was behind the psionic explosion that in an incredibly short time had opened vistas of knowledge, produced powers of accomplishment that normally should have taken decades? He thought of his own development – his and Stella's, rather, since what they had done had been accomplished through their mutual efforts. Of course he had a good mind to start with – but of psionic ability there wasn't a trace. The same must be said of Stella. The Destons had given them their first real insight into telepathy, and, through it, their first inkling of the universe of psionics. That had been less than a year ago – and through their studies of metaphysics, paraphysics, occultism and every other kind of esoterica; through telepathic consultation with sages in India and China,

Tibet and Central America and everywhere else where a germ of truth might be gleaned, they had made of themselves psiontists of extraordinary ability.

Was it logical? It was *not*! It was entirely too much of a lifting by one's bootstraps.

He thought again of the list he had once compiled: eighteen coincidences. Impossible! There had to be an Operator – with a capital 'O'.

At first thought it would seem to be Barbara Deston, for she had been an oil-witch with extraordinary powers before any of the rest of them had manifested any psionic abilities beyond the simple matter of hunches that worked. But he didn't believe it was Barbara. No – and again he was back to the idea which in earlier go-arounds had brought him up against a stone wall. It must be some power completely outside their knowledge and association. A puppeteer pulling strings!

Assuming this were so, *why*? Altruism? The bettering of the human race? Certainly this was being accomplished through the opening of the universe in a manner never dreamed of before. But that was a most unsatisfactory motive. Something, someone playing God.

Adams scowled. If this *were* so, how could he – or it – possibly be detected? Why try? Because he had to know! But how? Where to begin? He'd gone over all this before. Well, it didn't promise any tremendous revelation, but there was one thing he hadn't done before – a study of the six top psiontists, all of whom were aboard the *Explorer*. Perhaps a hint, the mark of the Operator.

He sent a thought to Stella, in the great lounge in conversation with Bernice Jones and Cecily Train. Quietly she excused herself and joined Adams in their quarters, where in flashing thoughts he appraised her of his thinking and what he planned.

Stella's response was slow in coming. 'But, Andy, I

61

don't like the idea of secretly examining – probing – the minds of our friends. But if we ask them we'll be – '

'Putting them on their guard? All the better, my dear. An area guarded might be just what we're seeking.' Her objection vanished, and he sent a thought to the six psiontists.

'Pardon this intrusion, please. I've been thinking – ' He ignored Deston's barely suppressed, 'Andy, what a surprise!' 'I've been thinking again about some of the problems of psionics; and I've arrived at a need to study your minds individually and in the aggregate. Stella and I in fusion will do the investigating. May we have your permission?'

Though they were surprised, all six gave immediate consent, Deston speaking for the group: 'Of course, Doc, if you think there's something to be gained we'll be glad to cooperate. Any suggestions?'

'Just that you be yourselves. Go about whatever you're doing. I should not have to tell you that we won't be prying. Our study will be confined to the functioning of the mind, the upper levels of cerebration, Campbell's Fourth Nume, if you will. You should not be aware of any intrusion.' He added apologetically, 'Believe me, we don't like this any more than you do and if I didn't consider it necessary I wouldn't be suggesting it.' Unanimous reassurances came, and Adams withdrew.

Stella and Andrew Adams faced each other, holding hands tightly across a small table, eyes meeting unwinkingly. Their minds merged in an indescribable fusion, functioning as one.

Barbara Deston. In perfect visualization they sensed the trim, five-foot-three yellow-haired oil 'dowser' who as Barbara Warner had found oil wells for WarnOil throughout the ninety six planets. The Barbara whose nickname had progressed from Barbry through Barby to the dynamo they affectionately called Bobby. The physical Barbara vanished in the personality – a woman who on the one hand was warm, empathetic, loving; and on the other a coldly driving, rigidly direct force that moved unswervingly toward any predetermined objective. A blending of opposites that in Barbara did not seem contradictory. But all of this was surface inspection, a foundation for the probing that followed.

Concerning the Adamses' study of Barbara's and the others' minds little can be said. What they actually did cannot be told in ordinary words or any symbology except that of the psiontist. The sifting, the penetrating, the delving into one mind by another lies beyond description. Yet when their study of Barbara ended, the Adams fusion realized that though they had greatly widened the scope of their own thinking, they had made no advance toward their primary aim – the Operator. Certainly she had the ability to help in the psionic development of other minds – had done so – had developed for herself abilities in every phase of psionics – but there was no indication of the super-psiontist they were seeking.

Even as they withdrew, certain that their invasion had not been detected, they were aware of one very strong impression. There were depths in the intellect they had studied which defied their most penetrating probe – not the impression of a strongly held mind block, but limitations in their own powers.

Carlyle Deston, Carl or Babe to the others. Short for a spaceman, stocky, whose only psionic manifestations before he met Barbara Warner were hunches that never failed. Bobby, sensing his latent psionic abilities, helped him develop the power to detect metals, communicate telepathically, as well as precognition and telekinetics. They probed. A highly intelligent, well-balanced mind with additional psi powers still latent, still in need of greater development. Again they learned more about mental functioning, but that was all.

Theodore 'Hercules' Jones, Captain of the *Explorer*. Like Deston, given to hunches. A big, powerful man, the source of his nickname – Herc to the others – highly efficient in his field, a strong member of the psionic team, but certainly not the Operator. His wife, formerly Bernice 'Bun' Burns, a tall, svelte platinum blonde, the most sensitive psychic of the group with a range of perception that was truly incredible. Other psionic abilities that now had to be considered normal; nothing more.

Equally disappointing were Cecily and Percival Train. Red-headed, freckled Cecily who had been a top level engineer, a power house. Perce Train almost as big as Herc Jones, and a power on his own. The Adams coupling found the usual psionic abilities, with the para-kinetic strength intensified to an unbelievable degree. They were power personified. They were the movers – they the pair who alone could 'port the great mass of the *Explorer* with precision and ease that was near-miraculous. In addition they possessed an affinity for each other that enabled them to achieve a fusion unmatched even by that of Andrew and Stella Adams. But the Operator? Negative. Marks of manipulation? None that they could discern.

Beside the negative findings concerning the Operator, the Adams fusion had learned – rather confirmed – two facts. All six psiontists had in varying degrees all the psi powers – telepathy, precognition, teleportation, telekinetics, levitation, clairvoyance, clairaudience – in some of them more highly developed than in others. And he and Stella of course were adepts in all. Only the Destons, strangely, were 'dowsers.' In addition, no mind alone had the power, the completeness, the unity that the couples in combination possessed. In the full meaning of the term each was the complement of his or her mate, especially in things psionic.

Adams thought of the two children – Theodore Warner Deston and Barbara Bernice Jones, Teddy and Babbsy – and the fusion sensed them vividly – two romping toddlers among a dozen others in the fairyland playroom designed by Bobby and Bun. Adams had observed them in a technical fashion from conception in the zeta field in subspace; it was he who had brought them to light after a fourteen month gestation period; his medical skill that had examined them in every possible way during their growth to this moment. A lovely and delightful boy and girl, normal and healthy, mentally precocious, bright and alert, but not uniquely so.

The fusion touched their minds – and shockingly they were blocked! Startled, with all the strength and skill they had developed through endless hours of concentrated study they drove with fused power – and bounced! No penetration whatever.

Then in a time so immeasurably brief that afterward neither Andrew nor Stella Adams could be certain that they had really sensed what they thought had touched their minds – a flash of intellect with breadth and power and scope beyond anything they had ever encountered. It was the mere hint of a glimpse – gone instantly – and it was followed by something so unexpected, so inexplicable and alien that it left them momentarily numbed.

They seemed to be looking into a large office, garish and brilliantly colorful in its opulence. The walls were an exquisitely wrought pictorial mosaic, a continuous scene that completely encircled the windowless chamber, even the single door continuing the design. Colors were harshly vivid, the subject gory and violent, what appeared to be a great arena, the banked seats filled with red-brown men and women with cruel mouths and great hooked noses, their scant apparel brightly colorful. In the arena was a melange of semi-naked, knife-wielding duelists, of great taloned birds of prey tearing light-skinned human victims to bits with great, rending beaks.

There were two men in the room, standing facing a great contour desk, its top also a garish gemmed mosaic. Both were of the same race as the spectators in the wall scene, with enough gold chains and bars and jewels on what were evidently uniforms to indicate high rank indeed. And both were manifestly obsequious, almost cringing. At that instant the fusion realized that they were viewing the scene through the eyes of a third personality behind the desk – and that being was intoning in a voice of venomous, savage power:

'Make your plans with only one thought – one purpose – and never lose sight of it. There is no room anywhere – not in this System, not in this galaxy, not in the total universe, for any race of power except ours! Except for the necessary slaves, none can be permitted to live. This is our destiny – and Great Day is rapidly approaching. Plan well – make no mistakes – but take no action until I give the command.'

There followed the barest touch of a mind of savage arrogance, of fierce pride, of ruthless drive – alien, inhuman. Then nothing!

Stella and Andrew Adams found themselves staring into each other's eyes like suddenly awakened sleep-walkers, their hands limp. It was one of those very rare moments when the thoughts of the imperturbable Dr Adams were disordered and confused. In moments, almost by instinct, he touched the minds of the two children – and found them as they had always been – unusually intelligent, showing tremendous latent psychic powers – but only a little boy and girl.

Frowning, Adams stared intently at his wife, then spoke aloud:

'Stella – what did we see?'

'I – don't – know! It would seem we caught a glimpse of a mind beyond any we ever touched – at the moment we were trying to probe Teddy and Babbsy – but that can't be. Then for a moment we saw what they – or the entity whatever its nature – observed – but I just *can't* believe it!'

Adams' eyes narrowed and his head sank forward, his chin resting on one tight fist. 'Or we sensed what something or someone wanted us to see.'

Complete silence followed as Stella and Andrew Adams, with utmost concentration, considered what had happened. Minutes passed unheeded while every nuance of thought, every detail of what they had sensed from the beginning of their experiment was subjected to closest scrutiny by the keenest, most penetrant mind of that age, reenforced by an intelligence that was complementary and in its own individual way little less able than Adams' own.

How long they were immersed in their appraisal they had no way of knowing. During part of those minutes of thought Adams found himself reverting to concept after concept that had occupied his mind for days on end. They crystallized. Space having four dimensions. Psiontists working through that fourth dimension. Subspace itself – why not many spaces existing in subspace? Perhaps an infinite number of spaces with subspace a separating yet a containing medium? He groped for an analogy – found none. But the staggering thought seemed strangely logical.

Finally Adams spoke. 'Of that supermind little can be said. Certainly we haven't enough data to arrive at any conclusion – though I believe more firmly than ever that there must be an Operator. Identity? Impossible to say. We were blocked out of the minds of the children – but there is no proof that theirs was the screen. That scene we saw seemed to be revealed through the eyes of an entity behind that desk – but if that were so why did we see the setting in such great detail? Illogical to think that the individual who spoke would have been looking about the room. So I lean toward the view that we saw what we were supposed to see. Why? No data. But I'm certain we did not stumble upon something that was supposed to remain unknown. There was a reason for our seeing what we saw. What reason? Again, no data.'

His expression grew somber, and an intense, distant look came into his eyes. 'There is one more thing we should try. We have a thought-pattern of that being behind the desk. I know there's little hope of success – it actually is absurd – but let's try to find that entity.'

At Stella's instant assent they joined hands, locked eyes, and their coupled minds roamed cosmic space, open for a particular thought matrix. They had never attempted anything like this before, and it was a staggering experience. Alone in vacuity. As world followed world a flood of thought, a cosmic hubbub, smote their senses – like the prayers of humanity rising to the ears of God. On and on endlessly – but never that specific mind, nor any akin to it.

Finally they desisted, slowly coming out of a black emptiness that was yet filled with thought, again aware of the solidity of four walls. Ruefully Adams smiled at his wife, then drew a deep breath. 'Quite an experience though obviously doomed to failure. I actually knew better.' A pause, then he said, 'I see you agree that for the present we should say nothing about all this. But we'd better call the others.'

Six minds found themselves in full telepathic communication with Andrew and Stella Adams; and Adams said,

'I thank you, friends, for your coöperation. By studying your minds and with your help I have been able to open my own mind and Stella's to a larger segment of reality; finding that reality is much simpler, and yet at the same time far more complex, than I had supposed.

'I theorize that there may be an infinite number of spaces in subspace, but at the moment this is not subject to mathematical or any other kind of proof. It is probable that what we do, when we traverse what we call subspace, is move through the actual fourth physical dimension of space. A rigorous analysis of the zeta field shows' – here he poured into the linked minds a long succession of equations so abstruse as to be meaningless to all – 'that there must in fact be at least one other three-dimensional space coexistent with ours; imperceptible to us because no one of their three dimensions coincides with one of ours. The fourth dimension is common to both and is of course perpendicular to all three of both . . .'

'But, listen, Doc!' Deston protested. 'In that case – '

'They must be coincident, or at least parallel? By no means. That aspect of reality is a little difficult to grasp, but the equations explain the phenomenon perfectly. With a common fourth dimension, their time rate is of course the same as ours. Their time vectors and parameters may be different from ours, as may also be some of the physical properties of their space itself.

'The composition of the zeta field indicates that it is not a natural phenomenon, but the product of science and technology, whether intentional or inadvertent. It is therefore clear that Second Space contains science and technology of at least the same order of magnitude of advancement as our own.'

'There must be Tellus-type planets, then,' Jones said.

Adams shook his head. 'Not necessarily. That much extrapolation at this point is unwarranted.'

'Are you suggesting,' Bernice asked, 'that the subspace disappearances of starships have been zeta field explosions – if that's the term – caused by the close approaches in subspace of First and Second Space Vehicles?'

'I am postulating this as a strong possibility, the most logical assumption in the light of our present knowledge, nothing more. There are other possibilities. Perhaps instead of near-collision of vehicles from both spaces our losses occur when starships inadvertently attempt to enter Second Space – though as I think about it, it seems highly unlikely. In short, we're guessing . . . A related thought. What influence might such near approaches to Second Space by our vehicles bring to bear on their worlds? Perhaps be briefly visible. Mere speculation, of course.'

'Is it possible,' Cecily inquired, 'that other space vehicles might perhaps unwittingly touch the – edge, if that is the proper reference – of our three-dimensional space, and perhaps be momentarily visible?'

'It is conceivable,' Adams agreed, half smiling; 'visible to one with psionic ability.'

'Then that would explain UFOs,' Deston said.

'That is implicit,' Adams agreed, 'in our assumption that psionic ability is the ability to perceive, and to work in, the fourth physical dimension of space. This, however, is not to suggest that UFOs are necessarily involved in starship accidents.'

'You mean – ?'

'It is conceivable, given our woeful lack of data, that any number of other explanations might apply; even that such impinging might originate in spaces other than Second Space – assuming that there are such. I am simply suggesting that the *sightings* of UFOs might occur when such interspatial contacts occur. That, if this is the explanation, sightings indicate psionic powers, active or latent.'

'Oh, wonderful!' Barbara exclaimed. 'Then anyone

70

who has ever really seen a UFO would have to have been psychic.'

'That follows, and that is my opinion. But of course they did not see them with their physical, optical eyes.'

'How else could they . . .' Jones began, then broke off and went on, 'I see. Transference. Since they didn't know any other way of seeing, they had either to see them with their eyes or go nuts.'

Deston nodded. 'That makes sense. This whole thing is a horribly big bolus to swallow, but . . . what do you think, Bobby?'

'It *is* big,' Barbara agreed. 'Tremendous. But in a crazy way it carries internal evidence of being the truth. The big question is – do we or don't we?' She was referring, of course, to the matter of exploring – or invading? – Second Space.

'We do,' Deston said, flatly, 'if for no other reason, to determine if our theorizing about subspace accidents is correct. And *if* correct, to find a way to prevent recurrences. That is, if we can figure out any possible way of crossing into Second Space. After all, this is not mere teleportation.'

'Why, that's easy,' Cecily contributed. 'Look – it'll take both Perce and me to do it, but all we have to do is rotate the ship in the common fourth dimension until its three normal axes coincide with those of the other space.'

'You *say* it's easy,' Jones said, 'but just what are you going to do it with? The by-your-bootstraps-lifter they used in the old sub-light drive? Run that out into the fourth dimension, Babe, and what would you have?'

'I wouldn't know,' Deston replied. 'Curly, can you design a Byrd-Train machine to swing as much mass as the *Explorer* has got? And can you teach anyone else to run a Byrd-Train after you've built it?'

Cecily shook her head. 'No mechanism at all.

71

Psychokinetic energy only. Something like teleportation, except it's 'way up in the Fourth Nume.'

'Fourth Level of Organization, yes.' Barbara nodded. 'Sex and meaning. Determination and power. Both male and female elements necessary.'

'And sufficient,' Cecily declared.

'Perhaps.' Barbara was not yet convinced. 'But all of us . . . no, we couldn't all synchronize closely enough; not possibly. Can you and Perce, even? And would just the two of you have enough of it?'

'Yes,' Cecily said, positively. 'We're one. In sync to the skillionth of a whillionth of a nanosecond. And we've got it. More of it than the Pacific Ocean has water. Besides, you others will have jobs of your own, won't you?'

'You're not just . . . chomping . . . your choppers . . . Doll,' Deston said slowly, and Barbara put in, 'But can we do it at all? Would we live through it? Uncle Andy, what will the effect be on human bodies? Especially on those who aren't psychic?'

'I don't know.' Adams frowned in thought. 'My analysis does not cover the point and can not be made to cover it . . . there is no present applicable theory . . . and very, very little pertinent data.'

Wherefore all eight of those heavy-duty psiontists bent their every energy to the task of acquiring additional pertinent data. The problems were many. The zeta field was bad, but it could be neutralized by mechanical generators. But what *was* it? If it was a subspace phenomenon, generated in subspace and therefore consistent with it – that was one thing. If it was merely a leakage from something built in and native to Second Space, that would be something else entirely. What would such a construction be and how could it be handled? Second Space was different from First Space; its properties and non-temporal constants could be different. How different? In what way? By how much?

Adams did the theoretical work and the analyzing and the synthesizing; the seven others, straining their psionic powers to the utmost, observed everything they could reach and reported and recorded their findings and their conclusions.

The work was not done in a day – nor in a week. There were fumblings and stumblings and setbacks galore. New psionic techniques had to be developed, practically from scratch. Hitherto undreamed-of machines had to be designed and built and tested – machines that burned out; machines that blew up; machines that mis-functioned; machines that did not function at all. And much of the project depended – had to depend – upon machinery. The zeta field was only one of many things that could not be handled by psionic ability alone.

The job was finally done. That is, all they could do, had been done. No one was completely satisfied with it, but no one could point out anything more that could or should be done. No one suggested staying in their home space. All eight psiontists sat in the Destons' office, in a silence that could have been carved with a knife. Deston finally broke that silence.

'Us eight,' he said, tensely ungrammatical. 'All of us or none. I wish . . . but you all do too, of course . . . so skip it. Let's get at it; the sooner we try it the quicker we'll know.'

'Not tonight,' Adams said, definitely, shaking his head. 'We must be fresh – rested. Shall we meet here again, say at eight?'

At eight as arranged a quiet group met in the office. Now that they actually faced the venture into the completely unknown, none had much to say.

'Any last minute ideas?' Adams asked.

Jones spoke somewhat hesitantly. 'What about the possibility of our making the first crossing in Lifecraft Number One before going in the *Explorer*? I don't think we should involve the others aboard until we know what we face.'

'My idea, precisely,' Adams agreed. 'I was about to suggest it. Though we won't have the benefit of all we've worked on so long, we should be able to make the round trip – over, back, almost instantly – without it.' Quick assent came from the others, followed by silence. Then Train put his arm around Cecily.

'Shall we go?'

'Not quite yet,' Deston said, and turned to Jones. 'You're the skipper, Herc. Get on the com.'

'Not the com, Babe.' Jones called in his First Officer, Lieutenant Meng Chi, and told him, 'We are going through subspace in Lifecraft One. Not into subspace, but through it, to see what's on the other side. We don't expect to be gone long, but give us a week. If you haven't heard from me in seven standard days from now' – both men glanced at their chronoms – 'flit for the Galaxian Science Institute and turn everything over to Doctor Adams' first assistant.'

'Very well, sir.' The officer saluted smartly, his broad face expressionless, turned and strode away.

'Now we can go,' Deston said; and in Lifecraft One, 'Not too long, you two, remember,' he cautioned, looking at the Trains' faces. Train's jaw-muscles were lumped and Cecily's freckles were more apparent than usual; otherwise they showed no emotion.

'This is it!' the Trains said as one, and the torture began. It was just that – indescribable torture, as though every cell in their bodies tried to repel, or absorb, every other cell – violently, achingly in a twisting, rending, vertiginous nervous nightmare. Only a fraction of a second in duration, it seemed eternal.

All six, however, came through the ordeal not only alive, but not permanently damaged. They found that Second Space, itself, felt normal. It was passing from one space to the other that was so bad. The second experience was no easier than the first. Back in the *Explorer*, they gathered by common consent in the lounge.

Deston said feelingly, 'A little of that goes a long way. I for one am not ready for another trip without a bit of mental adjusting.' There was silent acquiescence from the rest; all were pale and drawn.

'Was it worth it?' Barbara finally asked. 'Did we learn anything?'

Dr Adams answered quickly. 'Indeed we did! That trip wasn't – pleasant – but there was no reason for my ceasing observing or thinking because of discomfort. Actually we learned much.

'Second Space, whose coordinates – ' he gave them ' – are implicit in my analysis of the zeta field and which I now fully believe is only one of an infinite number of such spaces possible, does in fact exist. Most important, psionics is in fact the all-embracing science. Out of our total thinking experience we are able to formulate four hypotheses which may be among the basic laws of the science. Before we take the *Explorer* across, however . . .'

'Wait up, Uncle Andy!' Barbara exclaimed. 'What are those laws of psionics? I'm very much interested.'

'Hypotheses merely, please. I make no claim . . .'

'Hypotheses, then. Go ahead with 'em.'

'If you insist. First: The map is the territory. Second: The clarity of perception of any future event varies directly as its inevitability. Third: Subjective time is measured by the number of learning events experienced. Fourth: Communications concerning reality are neither accurate nor complete.'

A brief but animated discussion followed as the import of these tremendous – albeit confusing – generalizations made their impact; following which Deston cut in all speakers of the ship. He explained briefly what they had done, then went on.

'We are going to take the *Explorer* across. I can give you no assurance of safety. The worst part of it, the crossover, is worse torment than anything I ever felt before. Imagine yourselves with the worst toothaches you ever had and the sickest you ever were. Boil it down, heap it up, and double it, and you'll have a faint – a very faint – idea of what it'll be like. The fact that eight of us came through alive doesn't mean that all of you can or that any of you want to chance it. So it'll be an all-volunteer project and all volunteers will be screened hard and fine.'

The screening was done. A third of the great starship's population went back to civilization. The *Explorer* made the BIG JUMP and after a very short time indeed in Second Space – jumped right back.

Nobody died. Many were sure they were going to; several almost did; but no one actually died. Men yelled and swore; women shrieked and fainted; children screamed and howled and went into hysterics.

But they made it!

CHAPTER 5

Lives Are Joined

After the first meeting of the Institute for Advanced Study, days passed, and a couple of weeks, and still nothing happened; but there was of course a great deal to do. Knuaire and Marrjyl worked together on the all-but-impossible theory of the fourth dimension; Rodnar and Marrjyl – she with her unsurpassed talent for design and he with his unsurpassed knowledge of and ability at subspace technology – worked together with everything they had at reducing that theory to practice. And, as time went on, Marrjyl found more and more occasion to work with Knuaire and less and less with Rodnar. Theory, she said, was a lot tougher than technology and was getting farther and farther behind – but neither man believed that that was the reason for the switch.

As soon as it became certain that there would be no more real shortage of money, Rodnar retired from games-manship as the undefeated champion bladesman of Meetyl. He did not surrender the title immediately. It would have smelled to high heaven. Four matches were arranged by Sonfayand Faylor, only two of them unlimited, ending in the death of Rodnar's opponents. He suffered no serious injury in any of these bouts. He was *good*. With the four victories on his belt, and with no logical contender in sight at the moment, he announced his retirement. He turned in the diamond-studded gold belt of championship to Gamesmaster Faylor, who thereupon happily announced a whole new series of games for its possession.

Very shortly thereafter Rodnar dug out, from the very

bottom of his bureau's bottom drawer, the heavily-jeweled two-ounce platinum flask that he had not carried for so long. He filled it with the hard-hitting aromatic compound he had never stopped craving, and whiffed a deep inhalation – which of course brought tears to his eyes and made him cough. Nevertheless, it felt and smelled and tasted so wonderful that he could not help but emulate the storied fillamalloo bird in crying 'ka-pooh-pooh, ka-pooh-pooh!' which translated from the vernacular means 'Great Guns, how good!' (Illustrated Lectures, Series F, Slide 92, somewhat condensed and more than somewhat cleaned up.)

Marrjyl, however, would not stop fighting; nor would she tell either man why she kept on with it . . . and of course neither man would try to probe her mind . . . especially since both knew her mental shields were as impenetrable as their own. She kept on fighting until she met a woman who came within a fraction of a split red hair of being her match. Marrjyl won, after almost forty minutes of desperate effort; but at fight's end she wasn't in much better shape than was her opponent – who was dead. Realizing foggily that she *had* at long last won, Marrjyl dropped her knife, slumped down, and sprawled out flat on her back, bleeding from a score of wounds; the goriest and last-received of which was a savage slash that went from her left hip down almost to the knee.

Rodnar and Knuaire, her seconds, rushed to her aid; as did her surgeon and his team of top-bracket nurses.

'Grab some of those pads – hold them there and there and there – we've *got* to stop this bleeding!' the doctor snapped at Rodnar and Knuaire, while he himself was going to work on the big one and while the nurses, working with the smooth, fast precision of their highly-skilled craft, set up and tubed in gravity-feed bottles of everything from Type O whole blood to normal saline solution.

There never had been any question whatever of moving the patient until a great deal of preliminary work had been done. They could not possibly have got her off the fighting-table alive. And, by some freak chance, the crowd did not bellow and scream for her blood too; and howl for action and riot at the delay. Instead, enthusiastic gamblers all over the place made noisy book as to whether or not the desperately-wounded gladiator would live – and if so, how long!

She lived, however, to reach the ambulance; and she was still alive – just barely – when they got her into an intensive-care room in Meetyl's finest hospital; and she stayed in that room for four days before she began really to mend. Once over the hump, however – with her physical condition and the care she was getting – she gained strength rapidly. Wherefore, a few days later, the doctors yielded to her demands to let Knuaire of Spath come in to see her.

He came in and for a few minutes nothing was said; scarcely anything was thought. He sat beside her bed and they held hands. Gently. And for the moment that was enough. Her blocks were up, full strength; but for a time that didn't matter, either . . . but finally he spoke aloud:

'Don't you think it's a little on the silly side, my dear, blocking me out *now*?'

She flushed, and softened her guard a little, but not very much – not enough to permit exchange of thought. 'I suppose it is, at that,' she agreed, aloud. 'I suppose I was broadcasting everything all over the place . . . and I know I owe you my life. Without you to hang on to, when I was low, and you holding on to me so, I couldn't possibly have come through . . . but listen, Knu!' Her grip tightened in his. 'I *can't* ask you to join me until I win six more status points – I *won't* have those noisome knangs gabbling

79

behind my back that all I joined you for was to make your status!'

As has been said, it was the woman's right – her inalienable right, her sole and exclusive privilege and prerogative – to take the lead in all matters sexual; however serious or however trivial. For a man even to try to do so branded him as inurbane, uncouth, and a loutish oaf. But Marrjyl – deliberately or not, and it had been deliberate, Knuaire thought, that was why she was blocking so hard – had left the door wide open for even a most meticulous gentleman to walk right in. So Knuaire did.

'The trouble with you is, Marr, you aren't thinking straight. As long as you and I both know better, what difference does that make? Besides, I can't see you making six more points on the table. You're now the challenger – but even if you can take the champion, that'll give you only two – and it'll be a hell of a long time before you're back into good enough shape for a championship fight. Also . . .' he paused, then went on, '. . . I hate to say this, Marr, but whether you know it or not, you left something behind you on that table.'

'I know I did,' she said somberly. 'You can't come that close to the big one without losing some of your fine edge . . . and a bladesman with her mind full of question marks as to whether she's going to make it or not isn't worth a damn . . . can't cut her way out of a paper bag . . . I've seen too many of 'em get it . . . but Knu . . .'

'But nothing, Marr,' he broke in, pressing his point. 'And there's another thing. Even if you were a high-stat, so that I'd be the one getting elevated, don't you think those same stinking gossipy bitches would be carving you up the back for joining lives with me for my money?'

'Money!' She snorted. 'Who cares about *money*? I can make my own mon . . .' She broke off in the middle of the word; her face took on a thoughtful expression. 'I knew you were well padded, of course – they don't give yachts like yours – that spacegoing palace – away as premiums or door prizes – but *that* much? Honestly?'

His answering grin was more than a little wry. 'More than that. Enough more so you'll never realize how glad I am that you were never interested enough in that angle to look me up in the Green Book. You're the only woman I know who hasn't. The question is, does that make the situation better, or worse? Better, I think . . . definitely, much better.'

'Huh?' she demanded. 'How do you figure *that*?'

'Because status is out.' He ticked off the point on one of her fingers. 'You know most women think vastly more of money than of status, or think they go together; therefore you now realize that those women are not going to accuse you of tying me up for my status, but for my money. Therefore you will retire from gamesmanship and keep on living; and you'll have to admit that a dead Daughtmarja Marrjyl wouldn't be in any position to do either one of us a bit of good.'

She grinned in spite of herself. 'You've got a point there, Knu, I concede.'

'Thank you, hon. Now. You have such a thoroughgoing contempt for any woman who *would* join lives for money that any remarks about you on that score, unlike those concerning status, wouldn't bother you at all. They'd simply bounce off like . . .'

'Heavens!' she broke in. 'If a girl wants to keep any secrets at all she shouldn't team up with a theoretician, should she? But you know something?' She sobered quickly. 'I simply don't care a lick if I *never* have a secret from you – Knu sweetheart, *will* you join lives with me?'

'*Will* I? Cut your shields and come in and see!'

She did so; and the kiss that followed – in which his lips barely touched hers, with scarcely any pressure at all, since they both knew exactly the shape she was in and what she could do and what she must *not* do – was as meaningful as it was gentle.

After an interval of bliss she said, 'Oh, that's wonderful, sweetheart – I love you so *incredibly* much!' She picked up the pendant-switch of her bedside com, pushed its red button, and went on, 'Will you have a public recorder come in as soon as he can, please?'

He looked at her in surprise, but didn't say anything, and she laughed. 'Uh-huh,' she said, gleefully. 'The sooner the quicker, ain't it?' and they held hands and exchanged thoughts (that need not be detailed here) until the head nurse of the floor, frowning her disapproval of the whole procedure, ushered the official into the sickroom.

'Cheer up, chum,' Marrjyl grinned unabashedly at the nurse. 'It isn't going to be nearly as bad as you think. Nothing at all strenuous. No rough stuff, I promise – I'm just nailing him down before he changes his mind or some other harpy gets her hooks into him.'

'I understand.' The nurse smiled a little in spite of herself. 'With Songladen Knuaire of Spath up for grabs that might be top technique at that. But I should have put him out five minutes ago, so as soon as this is over out he goes . . . here, I'll help you roll over and get your number into sight.'

The visitor – a public servant something like an assistant county clerk and something like a notary public and something like a justice of the peace, but not very much like any one of the three – was a small, bird-quick, fussy type. Taking his 'gun' out of his case, he aimed it at Knuaire's broad bare back, thus putting his number on imperishable film. Then, while the nurse supported her patient in position for her number to be plainly visible, he did the same for Marrjyl. Then, after gabbling a burst of gibberish that sounded very much like the oratory of a

Tellurian tobacco auctioneer, he said distinctly and almost slowly:

'Repeat in unison after me – "We, Songladen Knuaire of Spath and Daughtmarja Marrjyl of Orm" . . .' and they repeated after him, phrase by phrase, '. . . declare that there is no reason . . . known to either of us . . . why we should not join lives . . . and we go on record that . . . we are now joining lives.'

The official put his instrument back into its case and Knuaire reached for his wallet.

'I thank . . .' the little man began. Then, as he saw the size of the bill the bridegroom was handing him – it was a hundred instead of the customary three or five junex to cover the legal registry fee – he stopped talking for a moment and goggled. Then he went on, in a markedly different tone, 'Oh, *thank* you, sir, very much indeed!'

'Okay, Gladen's son,' the nurse said then. 'You can kiss her *once* – an easy one – then out you go until tomorrow. This gal's just about to fall completely apart.'

CHAPTER 6

Catastrophe

Lifecraft Number One was small. Its energies were small. Moreover, it had emerged into Second Space so far away from any inhabited planet that it was not detected. Thus nothing happened that was not due to the intrinsic differences between the two incongruent spaces. And because of the vastness of Second Space, like any other space, the first brief cross-over of the *Explorer*, not too surprisingly, also went undetected.

The case of the *Explorer*'s second visit to Second Space, however, was an entirely different matter. Fortunately, because of the extreme discomfort of the first crossing, and because they expected to do some exploring, the crew had been cut to a minimum, only very essential staff and the top-psiontists remaining aboard for the trip. The *Explorer* was the biggest, heaviest, most powerful, most heavily armed and armored superdreadnought of her time. And this time, on the way to emergence into Second Space, she went through the Slaar-Orm mine field. Mines designed, built, powered, triggered, and placed by Rodnar of Slaar, Marrjyl of Orm, and Knuaire of Spath, three of the universe's best.

When the *Explorer* immerged, Deston sat tense at his board. His eyes were tightly shut; his ears were closed to any sound. He was deliberately blind and deaf; for in that job his banked and tiered instruments were completely useless. Electricity was far, *far* too slow. Its pace was a veritable crawl.

Crawl? Just that, yes. In subspace the term 'speed' is meaningless, and the velocity of thought has never been determined. While it may not be infinite, or even trans-finite, it is a quantity with which no instrumentation has as yet been able to cope.

And anything that happened in the zeta sector of activity would be Deston's dish. His alone. No one could help him; there would not be time enough. There would be almost exactly no time at all. And besides, the others had their own jobs to do. Barbara sat behind Deston, mentally backing up her Carl with all the power that was uniquely hers. Herc and Bernice in complete synchronization were scanning subspace, tensely alert for the first indication of Second Space, seeking with all they had for anything inimical before it materialized. The Adams fusion, of course, was observing and mentally recording all that took place. The Trains, needless to say, as one were waiting, if need be, to *move*!

Carlyle Deston had been just as tense and just as watchful in the earlier venture, and nothing had happened, but he did not relax. He knew subspace as few other men knew it.

And Carlyle Deston, as has been intimated, was a full-fledged precog, and the Second Law of Psionics is: THE CLARITY OF PERCEPTION OF ANY FUTURE EVENT VARIES DIRECTLY AS ITS INEVITABILITY. Thus any event only a few seconds ahead was sharp and clear; but one a few milliseconds in the future, under conditions such as these, was not.

For it must be remembered that the Third Law of Psionics is: SUBJECTIVE TIME IS MEASURED BY THE NUMBER OF LEARNING EVENTS EXPERIENCED. Thus, in a state of such terrifically high tension as Deston's mind then was, he could and did experience a large number of learning events, and perform a very large number of acts of thought, in a very short space of time; and his subjective time rate adjusted itself accordingly.

Thus Deston perceived, a millisecond or so before it happened, the triggering of the counter-generators, and thus he energized, in the merest flick of objective time, mighty *Explorer*'s every defense against those ravening fields. His engines and generators – Chaytors and Wesleys and Grahams and Q-converters – had been designed and built to carry frightful loads, and they carried enough of that super-frightful initial load so that those fiercely-driven probes, bolts, beams, and floods of energy touched the huge subspacer's leybyrdite armor only lightly and only here and there.

Then, almost simultaneously with the energization of his defense, Deston yelled his mental warning and launched his counter-attack. His Z-guns, designed specifically for this sort of emergency, were operated by thought and hurled bolts of energy so devastatingly disruptive as to convert any matter they struck into sub-atomic debris at thermonuclear temperatures.

Thought is super-fast. The passage through subspace of a bolt from Z-gun to inimical generator took, as nearly as makes no difference, no time at all. Thus fifty nine Slaar-Orm generators were blown into superheated subatomic pseudo-vapor in a space of subjective time so short as to be scarcely measurable.

Deston, however, furiously and obliviously concentrated upon destruction, had not considered one supremely vital fact. The *source* of the power of the Chaytors – the total kinetic energy of the entire macrocosmic universe – was practically infinite; but the ability of the Chaytors to deliver power was very strictly limited. No Chaytor had ever before burned out; but no bank of engines had ever before been called upon to deliver the starkly incredible myriakilowattage of energy Deston used. Fortunately, he did not have control of all the Chaytors aboard, for all of his blew out at once. Thus, when he triggered a bolt at the sixtieth generator, nothing happened.

He came back to his surroundings, opened his eyes and ears, and gasped. Half of the bells, buzzers, and whistles on his board were yelling their warnings of disaster most dire; more than half of the lights were glaring red. He braced himself and scanned – he didn't know what he could do, but he'd do *something* – but the fullest stretch of his sense of precognition could perceive nothing of danger. The *Explorer* was through subspace and into Second Space; and the crossover back into First Space was uneventful.

The Trains had seen to that. They both knew that something extraordinary was going on, but they had no idea what it was. Nor did they scan. They couldn't. Every iota of their fused minds was supremely busy at their own job of handling the huge subspacer in its inter-spatial jump; an operation that had passed the point of no return in the instant of its beginning.

They knew without consultation that the *Explorer*'s stay in Second Space was to be cut short. Wherefore they held her in Second Space only long enough to make a lightning-fast mental computation, then hurled her back into First Space along a path very widely different from the path of entry.

The five other Prime Psiontists also knew that something very serious was going on, but no one of them knew anything more about it than did the Trains. Like each of the Trains, each of the others had his own fish to fry; and the fact that this particular fish did not appear – that time – did not set him free.

Captain Jones' board was noisier and redder than Deston's; and he was of course the first to scan the ship. He and his vessel were one, in a real, true sense; and what had happened to her almost broke his tough and burly heart. She was an out-and-out mess.

Half of the engine-rooms were junk. Copper and silver had run like water. What had been beautifully-fabricated steel was now pools and blobs and partially-melted lumps. The air was still a translucent fog of vaporized metal and smoke from smoldering and sputtering and flaming insulation. Chaytors, Wesleys, and Q-converters were starkly unrecognizable – if Jones had not known exactly where each machine had been, he could not have identified any one of them. What had been Grahams could be recognized; but only because nine-tenths of their mass was made up of ultra-high-tensile-alloy wire. And all that wire was now an obscenely tangled and interwoven engineer's nightmare. That horrible snarl's bottom was still quivering in a pool of molten metal on the floor; its top was jammed solidly against the ceiling.

Nor was the ship herself unharmed. No zeta stuff had penetrated into her interior, which was why no lives had been lost and why she had not gone the way of the *Procyon*; but wherever those viciously destructive fields had touched, frenzied damage had been done.

The *Explorer*'s armor was three inches of leybyrdite. Nevertheless, in many places that armor was split and rent and chewed and weirdly torn. Nor was any area of damage like any other. Strips of armor were curled up like shavings from a carpenter's plane, spiraled like turnings from a Gargantuan lathe, twisted and power-formed grotesquely into shapes defying geometry or description. And in dozens of places cleanly-, sharply-bitten-out chunks of various shapes and sizes had simply disappeared.

She still held air, of course. If she had lost all of her armor she would still have been an air-tight and completely navigable subspacer.

Deston and Jones stared at each other somberly. Barbara and Bernice stood together, arms around each other, silvery-white hair close to hair of brilliant yellow. The Adamses and Trains were elsewhere, inspecting damage.

Deston spoke aloud. 'We sent a boy to do a man's job, Herc. More accurately, a baby to do a giant's job. But who in all hell would have thought . . .' His voice died away.

Jones' hard, craggy face could not get any gloomier than it was, but it tried. 'You can play *that* clear across the board . . . so it's back to the salt mines . . .' He paused, then uttered a blistering deep-space oath that was actually more prayer than profanity. 'And I'd give my right leg to the hip and my immortal soul to keep on going.'

Bernice sat down and reached for his hand. 'Well, none of us got hurt, and that's all that really matters,' she said, as cheerfully as she could.

''Smatter, you two!' Deston snapped. 'You don't think we're *licked*, do you?'

The big captain's expression did not lighten. 'I don't *think* it, no. I know it. So will you, as soon as you start using that half-pint of blue mush you call a brain.'

'The hell I will. We'll rebuild – or rather, build a . . .'

'How?' Jones growled. 'Don't kid yourself, Babe.'

'I'm not. How? Easy. She didn't have enough oof, is all. Next time we'll have enough. What we *know* will be enough. Standby on everything. Reserves. Over-load cut-ins. The works.'

'I didn't mean that, meat-head. You know how much this ship cost and now every dime of it is down the drain. This thing you're dreaming up will be a new *class* of vessel; brand new from the drawing boards up. MetEnge is run for profit by money-men who think more of a buck than they do of their right eyes. They don't pour money down rat-holes, especially the megabucks your dream-ship would cost. After *this* shellacking the first jump across and with nothing to show for it? Get conscious,

chum. What Phelps says, money-wise, goes; and he'll simply have a litter of lizards.'

'I don't give a cockeyed tinker's damn if she costs billbucks. D'you think we're going to quit *now*? If you do you're crazy in the head. I think Maynard will still go along – pretty sure of it. But if Phelps can talk him out of it, Deston and Deston . . .' He broke off sharply and looked at Barbara.

'Of *course* we will!' She nodded vigorously. 'After all, that is exactly what we've been heaping it up for, isn't it?'

'Huh?' Jones' jaw dropped an inch. 'I know you two were rolling in it, but . . . but have you actually *that* kind of money to pour down the drain?'

'And then some. We're going on with it, Herc,' Deston said flatly. 'You can paste *that* right in the crown of your iron hat.'

As has been made clear, Captain Theodore Jones was not the excitable type, but at that emphatic statement of fact his face lit up like a sunburst. He leaped to his feet, whirled around, and began to bellow orders before he got half-way to his board.

'But what can we *do*, Babe?' Barbara wailed. 'You know what just *one* of those frightful things will do to any other subspacer ever built and we won't be ready again for positively *months*! And they won't stop all shipping – they can't – what will we *do*?'

'I don't know.' Deston frowned in thought. 'I can think of only one thing – Doc. Probably he can locate the things and hang OFF LIMITS signs around where they are, so our ships can give 'em a far miss.'

'Oh wonderful! I'm sure he can!' Then, on a tight beam of thought, 'Uncle Andy, where are you?'

Some six weeks after Knu and Marr had joined lives, Rodnar, wounds completely healed and back to normal in fitness and condition, was working in his laboratory when every piece of apparatus went dead all at once. At the same instant all the lights went out – an event that had never happened before – plunging the entire laboratory into the absolute darkness of a sealed subterranean vault. Even the red trouble-lamps failed to light up.

And in the same instant a silent shriek resounded throughout every chamber of his mind. 'Rod! Rod! I'm *scared*! ROD!'

'Hold everything, Starr sweetheart, I'm coming!' he snapped the thought; then, pausing only to snatch three flashlights from a hardware store half a mile away, he teleported himself into the FirSec's office and grabbed her in his arms.

To say that she grabbed him back is an understatement indeed. She tried with everything she had to pressure-fuse her body into one with his. 'Oh Rod darling!' she telepathed intensely, apparently unaware that she was not speaking aloud, even though her mouth was in no position to do any talking. 'Nothing works – not even the lights or the air – what *was* it? It even hurt my *head*! What happened?'

He did not answer her questions. Instead: 'Why didn't you *tell* me you were psychic, you fat-head?' he snarled the thought. 'And good enough to fake a perfect blank when I probed you!'

'But I'm no such . . .' she began to protest; then realizing what she was actually doing, her thoughts for a second or two were a really mixed-up mess: a potpourri of everything from seeing herself smashed into eaglemeat and thrown into a cage, up to ruling with her Rodnar the entire Justiciate. She forced herself to steady down, then went on, using telepathy consciously and perfectly, 'I never was psionic before, I mean. Honestly, I never had a psychic bone in my head!'

'I see you weren't. I'm sorry I popped off, Starr – I never even heard of such a terrifically sudden development in my life. You were a very strong latent – tremendously strong – and the shock blasted you wide open. So you're one of us now, whether you want to be or not. So I've *got* to take a second – give you enough stuff so you can protect yourself until I can really induct you – ready?'

'I'm eager!'

'Here it comes,' and it came. Such a mind as his could send, and such a mind as hers could assimilate, an incredible amount of information in an incredibly short time. Hence, in a very few seconds, she had learned what the true situation was, had accepted it, and had aligned herself solidly with her lover and what she thought of as being 'his' psiontists.

He released her mind and said, 'There. That'll hold you until I can finish the job. In the meantime, keep a tendril of thought hooked onto me wherever either of us may be and don't let your guard down for a fraction of a nanosecond without checking with me first.'

'Oh?' The thought was almost a schoolgirl's squeal of delight. 'It works at a distance, then? How far?'

'Nobody knows. Interstellar certainly – all over the Justiciate – probably all over the galaxy. But chop it; we've got . . .'

'Wait up, Rod. What *happened*? What was it? One of those X-storms of yours?'

'I don't know. If it was, it was the damnedest one that ever happened – nobody ever heard of anything like it before . . . but an X-storm couldn't do *that* to you. Not possibly. That was a psychic shock you got, not a physical one . . .' He paused in thought.

She thought, too, for an instant; then caught her breath. 'Then how about His Magnificence?' she whispered, even in thought. 'Suppose *he* got a psychic shock, too.'

'Uh-uh. Not a chance in the world that he was a strong enough latent, if a latent at all – it could hardly happen once, let alone twice. I'll show you. Come along; you do it like this,' and he insinuated their linked minds into the mind of His Magnificence Supreme Grand Justice Sonrathendak Ranjak of Slaar.

'Good Heavens! You mean he can't even *feel* us?' she demanded incredulously, flicking an exploratory feeler of her newly-acquired sixth sense over the hyper-surface of the Supreme Grand Justice's mind, which was now, to all intents and purposes, a monocellular layer; each individual element of which was wide open for her inspection.

'No, he can't feel us at all,' Rodnar assured her. 'Non-psionic minds are strictly three-dimensional; we're working through the fourth. This is a slimy trick and we do it only when we absolutely have to, but there's a reason, so go ahead.'

'Oh, the poor old guy,' she crooned, after a moment. 'Rod, he's simply scared to death – scared witless – he's sure it's a plot to assassinate him and he can't get hold of even *me* – he can't even find the door – Rod, I've *got* to . . .'

'Of course you have!' Rodnar snapped. 'That was what I wanted you to see. For yourself, not by my telling you. The solider an *in* you can get with him the better, and this is the chance of our lifetimes. Have you got a flashlight?'

'Of course not. Who ever needed a flashlight *here*?'

'You do now, little chum, so here's a couple of 'em. Tell His Nibs you've had 'em all the time in case of emergency. Blaster, of course?'

'Two, and I can take the left eye right out of a gnat either-handed.'

'Fine! It's possible you'll have a chance to use 'em. So dash in there – tell him you've sent a messenger – that's me but don't of course tell him so – to tell the engineers to get the lead out and to bring up three electric lanterns – I'll send 'em – and he'll have air and lights very shortly and the rest of the stuff as soon as possible. Then tell him you'll protect him until the purps show up and *do* it – guard him like a mother hen with one chick, with all your scanners out – you'll find you've got plenty of 'em – stiff spine, sweetheart! 'Bye!' He squeezed her tight, kissed her hard, and vanished from the inward-pressing circle of her arms.

Starrlah buckled on her blasters, dashed across the room to the door of the sanctum sanctorum, opened it a crack, and sent the powerful beam of one flashlight sidewise into the room. No one, not even his First Secretary and not even in such circumstances as these, ever intruded uninvited upon The Presence.

Even in such circumstances? Especially in such, the girl thought, as she looked on mentally while the badly frightened ruler, taking advantage of the diffused light of the FirSec's torch, dashed back into the chair behind his desk and fought for self-control. Then, as though there had been no delay at all – and, to give Ranjak credit, there hadn't been much – the girl said quietly:

'Your Magnificence, it is I, Starrlah. Have I your permission, sir, to bring you a light?'

She heard his uncontrollable gasp of relief. 'Indeed you may, Starrlah,' he said, quite uncharacteristically. 'Come in at once.'

She went in, closed and locked the door behind her, and clanged its triple bars of tool steel down into their hold-fast slots. She handed Ranjak one of the flashlights; then began to brace the other one upright on his desk so that its beam would bounce off of a cluster of jewels on the ceiling.

'Lights and blasters both, my dear?' Ranjak asked, quietly. His first flash of thought, naturally, had been that *she* was the assassin, but that hadn't lasted long. He was steadying down fast; this FirSec of his was becoming more and more of a revelation every minute. 'Thank you.'

'Yes, sir. Two of each in my desk, always,' she said crisply, piling one more book against the torch and testing the structure thus finished with a strong push of a fore-finger. 'There; that will give us light enough to shoot by.' The flared light formed a nimbus around the bushy white hair of His Magnificence. She pulled both blasters and handed one of them to him butt first. He accepted the weapon with an uncharacteristic, 'Thank you, Starrlah,' unrestrained relief in his voice, then added, 'Have you any idea what happened?'

'No, sir, I've no idea whatever. I sent a messenger to the engineers and your Guards of the Person . . .' and she went on with a machine-gun-fast report of what she and Rodnar had decided she should say; watching his mind the while to be sure that she was making the best possible impression – which she was – concluding, '. . . if they are our people they'll pound on that door in code, and I'll know it's safe to open. If they aren't . . . well . . .' she swung the barrel of her blaster so that it clicked lightly against the barrel of his, '. . . well, we've enough power here, Your Magnificence, to melt a million tons of rock down onto us before they burn us down.'

And that statement didn't hurt her standing a bit with His Nibs, either.

CHAPTER 7

The Great X-Storm

No previous single X-storm had ever affected more than one planet of the Justiciate, but this one struck four worlds – Slaar, Orm, Spath, and Skane; four of the most populous and most highly industrialized worlds of that civilization – at precisely the same time.

Marrjyl and Knuaire were the first persons to learn that such an incredible event had actually occurred. She, practically completely recovered from her wounds, was working with him in the Institute's library in Meetyl when all the lights went out. Their first thought, of course, was of a simple power failure, however unprecedented such a thing was; but it took only seconds for them to find out how vastly deeper than that the real trouble was. Nor did they exclaim about or discuss the fact that nothing like it had ever happened before. What to do about it was the important thing.

Quick as a flash – literally – Marrjyl's mind leaped out to Rodnar's, but stopped instantaneously at its very outermost fringe, before making any actual contact at all. 'Oh-oh!' she drove a thought at Knuaire. 'He's – they're – busy.'

'Oh?' he asked, carefully, not looking.

'No, not that. How *could* they be, after *that*? Don't be a dumbster! It's ... she's psionic ... a full-powered *psiontist*!'

'What?' he demanded, and peeked cautiously for himself. 'I see. Brand new. An extremely strong latent, initiated by psychic shock. It scared the living hell out of her – so much so that she reached out and grabbed him subconsciously – and hung onto him while her supermind opened up like a fissioning bomb.'

'Or rather,' she corrected him, 'he opened her up.'

'Of course; but if she hadn't had an ungodly lot of stuff she couldn't possibly have bridged that primary gap. Also of course he'd drive her; and keep on driving her to the fullest possible development: at *that* desk she'll be worth a couple of dozen good psiontists and a million junex in cold cash.'

Pitch dark as it was, he could not see her grin, but he could feel it. 'You think that's the only reason, I don't think?'

'I don't think, my sweet. The other ones didn't need mentioning. He was sunk anyway, probably, but now he's sunk without a trace . . . she's a tremendous lot of woman.'

Marrjyl nodded; and even in the dark, Knuaire 'saw'. 'You can carve that on the highest cliff you can find,' Marrjyl agreed. 'And I like her a lot – tremendously much – more than any other woman I know . . . It's funny, Knu, but I'm not the least bit jealous of her, even now, knowing that she's going to be as good a psiontist as I am.'

'That's natural enough,' he said. 'You're so completely different from each other that there are no points of conflict. If there were, hair would fly.'

'Could be – but that's a great plenty of this fuzz-witting around.' She gave herself a mental shake. 'He'll be busy a while yet, so I think I'd better start working on this thing without him. Let's jump to Orm – my lab – and find out what goes on. Agreed?'

'Agreed,' and the two stood, hand in hand, in a laboratory that was just as dark and just as dead, instrumentwise, as was Rodnar's own on Slaar.

'Well, ain't this something!' Marrjyl snapped, and Knuaire agreed in silence. Without wasting time in idle speculation and discussion of the extent of the disaster, he said, 'Let's try Spath. My boat – in her berth at the spaceport – in our seats at the board. Jump!'

They jumped; and, much to their relief, found that the yacht's lighting system worked perfectly. It was the only system aboard, however, that did. None of the more delicate, more sensitive apparatus – either aboardship or anywhere else on the planet – worked at all; and the entire subethereal level of thought seethed and boiled with the varitoned, varicolored, furious, baffled, and bitterly profane thoughts of the men and women who were trying so hard to restore a dozen different inoperative services.

'Hm-m-m-mnh.' Knuaire the Theoretician rubbed thumb and forefinger against the short bristles on his jaw. 'An X-storm, undoubtedly. Far and away the worst ever. A picture is beginning to form; we'll see how or if it hit Skane.'

'Skane? You'll have to carry me, then; I know hardly any landing-spots there at all.'

'No need to go in person; I'll ask.' He concentrated in thought for a second or so, then went on, 'Yeah. I thought so. That gives us enough data to do some guessing on.' He pressed the 'CLEAR' switch of a small visitank and set three tiny lights in it, saying, 'Call this the Spath-Orm-Slaar triangle . . .'

'I'll be glad to call it anything you say,' Rodnar's thought broke in at that point. 'Hi, people! Is this instruction private, Knu, or is the public invited?'

'Not the public, Rod, just you,' the girl said mentally patting the vacant seat beside her. 'We've been waiting for you to get done with that perhaps somewhat pleasanter job.'

'*Somewhat* pleasanter?' Rodnar demanded, unabashed, suddenly appearing in the flesh. 'You kidding? If I had my way I wouldn't come out here at all, but you know how it is, "Work is the part of life that makes it work," curse it. So, going around your triangle counter-clockwise, it's roughly nine lightyears from Slaar to Orm, twelve from Orm to Spath, and ten from Spath back to Slaar. Where do we go from there?'

'We construct the Skane–Slaar–Orm–Spath tetrahedron by setting this light up here to represent Skane.' The light appeared in the tank. 'Seventeen lightyears from Spath, nineteen from Slaar, and eighteen from Orm. Now. Those four planets were hit; no others. Slaar and Orm were hit terrifically hard, and about equally. Spath suffered much less, and Skane was scarcely affected at all – just a little of the most delicate stuff on the planet. While these data are not quantitatively exact, analysis shows that if a big enough X-storm originated at this point *here*,' a red light sprang into being well outside the Slaar–Orm–Skane face of the tetrahedron; 'seven, seven, ten, and fourteen lightyears respectively from Slaar, Orm, Spath, and Skane, its subspace reactions would do just about what was actually done.'

Rodnar stared at the red light and whistled through his teeth. 'Clear to hellangone out beyond nowhere,' he said, thoughtfully. 'However, I think that's still inside our mine field – we went 'way, 'way out. What do you think, Marr?'

'My guess would be yes, but we'd better get out there with our instruments and find out. With such a frightful storm as this, and the equipment we have out there, there certainly should be *something* left for us to find.'

'*Now* you're chirping, birdie,' Rodnar approved. 'Knu, can you spare the fifty-one percent for a few shifts?'

Knuaire, smiling, held out his arms and Marrjyl went into them, snuggling luxuriously. 'It'll be tough,' he said, 'but in such a good cause I'll try to get along. It'll take quite a while to repair the damage here, and she can't help much on that . . . I hope there's something out there to find, and if there is, you two are the two to find it.'

'Thanks, fella, and 'bye. Fuse minds, Marr, and I'll carry you – from here to my flitter's a tricky jump.'

She responded by relaxing completely, fitting her mind to his with the practised ease of skilled experience. 'Go.'

They went. Or rather, with no sense of motion and with no lapse whatever of time, they were standing in the tiny control room of Rodnar's subspeedster in its underground stall at Meetyl Spaceport.

The spaceport's controls and attendant robots were all inoperable, of course, so that no normal take-off was possible. The little subber's instruments were dead, too – but that fact wouldn't necessarily keep them on Slaar. He *could* 'port his speedster out, but *should* he? No psiontist ever had done anything like it, as far as he knew . . . and in one way he certainly shouldn't . . .

'How about it, Marr?' he asked then. 'The faster we get out there the more we'll learn, and if we wait for repairs I'm afraid we'll be too late to learn anything at all.'

'So am I.' She gnawed her lip. 'We've got to get out there *fast*, Rod, so I say go ahead.'

'Shall do,' he said, and went ahead; and, such was the turmoil and confusion, no one noticed that a certain subspeedster was in a certain stall one instant but was not in it the next. Even the thunder-clap (junior grade) of noise, of air smashing in to fill a vacuum, went unnoticed.

Since Rodnar's detectors, scanners, and surveying instruments generally had not been in operation during the storm, and since they were of necessity shielded to the limit against all known types of interference, it did not take long to replace the few super-sensitive relays and other extra-delicate components that had been burned out. Then the two psiontists gave their 'mine-field' a quick once-over . . . and when it was done Marrjyl put her head down on her arms on the table and cried . . . and Rodnar felt very much like doing the same thing.

For of their sixty protective generators, only one was in operation and it was limping. Where each of the fifty nine other great machines had been there was either sheer nothingness or, at most, a few shapeless blobs of once-fused metal.

After a minute or so Marrjyl sat up, gulped, wiped her eyes, and said, 'I think that was deliberate, Rod; don't you? I don't believe that anything natural could *possibly* have done that much of that kind of destruction.'

'I simply don't know what to think, Marr.' Rodnar's voice and mien were somber. 'But you said it – "that much of that kind". I can't imagine any natural phenomenon that would or could do it; it's all wrong in every aspect of scope, magnitude, and type. But on the other hand I can't conceive of any mobile structure ever built by man carrying that much power.'

'Who said anything about "man"?' she asked, quietly.

Rodnar scowled. 'You may have a point there,' he admitted, 'but let's not go clear off the deep end until we see what the cameras and recorders aboard that one installation got. If anything.'

It must be emphasized at this point that a subspace 'camera' is not an optical instrument, and that in subspace the term 'distance' is, in the ordinary sense, meaningless. Thus, subspace cameras operate practically instantaneously throughout starkly unimaginable volumes of three-dimensional space.

Ultra-powerful and ultra-long-range though they were, however, those instruments had obtained very little data; and that little was baffling, frustrating, and tantalizing in the extreme. For one thing, the action had been at such fantastically long range that the signal was almost com-

101

pletely drowned out by noise, and the pictures were almost completely obliterated by snow. And second, the forces there unleashed had been of such hellish intensity and magnitude that, even at that incomprehensible distance, the shielding had failed lamentably to protect vital elements of the instrumentation from damage.

Rodnar and Marrjyl did, however, get *something*; and, after doing everything possible to the science of their age in the way of cleaning up, de-lousing, re-enforcement, and intensification, they stared alternately at the product of their labors and at each other. It was a ship – but *what* a ship!

It was neither a sphere nor a cube, but appeared to be long and quite slender, with a ratio of about five or six to one. The thing's exact size could not be determined, of course, but every applicable criterion indicated a structure so huge that it could not possibly have been built on any planet of the Justiciate. It was not clear whether it had been attacked first or . . .

'It must have attacked, Marr,' Rodnar declared. 'Those generators of ours weren't weapons, they were simply neutralizers. They couldn't do any damage to anything.'

'To anything of ours, no. To anything we can think of as being possible of construction, no. But look there, and all along there.' She swept a pictured area with her hand. 'If that gigantic thing's armor isn't getting all chewed to bits I'll eat the first piece of it we find; and you don't think it's trying to destroy itself, do you?'

'I think you're stretching your imagination all out of shape,' he said. 'I think that those funny-looking markings are simply defects in the transmission and flaws caused by our own manhandling; it was right next door to being nothing at all, you know . . .' He paused in thought, then went on, '. . . but you could be right, of course. If so, they *could* have thought they were being attacked and fought back . . . but how could they *possibly* have destroyed fifty nine such installations as those in little over one second?'

'I've no more idea than you have, but it's one somewhat cheerful thought that they didn't destroy this sixtieth one, too, so their power at least isn't infinite. The worst thing is that they'll now think that we're savages; that we attacked on detection. Blindly, stupidly.'

'That doesn't necessarily follow. They must be highly intelligent . . .'

'That for sure. I wonder what they look like. Monsters, s'pose?'

'I'm not a damn bit sure I care ever to find out . . . but if they are actually as smart as they must be it's quite possible – maybe even probable – that they got enough data out of the meeting to deduce the whole truth. But to get back to our knitting, where in all the hells of space did it go to when it disappeared?'

Marrjyl gnawed her lip. 'I wouldn't know . . . it couldn't have stayed in subspace, and if it had emerged anyplace our lock-ons would have held it . . .' Her eyes narrowed suddenly. 'Remember what I said about "other space", Rod? I didn't really believe it then and it doesn't make any kind of sense now, but what else is left?'

'Oh, chop it off!' he snorted. 'There's no theory to cover even the possibility of any other space.'

'So? Answer my question, then. What's left?'

'The truth is left. The only thing possible. It emerged somewhere completely out of range.'

'So far away that *those* clamps couldn't hold it?'

'Since that's the only alternative I can see, that's the only one I'll buy; and it's certainly a lot easier to believe than yours is . . . and even if your cockeyed theory is right and that ship did originate in another space, any loose pieces of it would normalize in this, our normal space here. The only space. Matter in subspace emerges into normal space except when constrained by impressed force to remain in subspace. Right?'

'Well-l-l, up to now it always has.'

'Yeah, and the sun has risen every morning! You give up hard, don't you? If you're *that* sold on the idea, why don't you put Knu onto it?'

'Do you think I haven't already? As soon as I thought of it. He hasn't got anywhere with it yet, but he says it's a fascinating subject.'

'Maybe it is, for him . . . so, Marr, I give up. But what you and I had better do is beef up our detectors to the limit and go out and find either that alien ship or whatever pieces of it our generators did in fact chew off of it. If any. Agreed?'

'Agreed,' she said, and that was what they did; for day after day after fruitless day. Until, finally, they found a one-hundred-pound chunk of something that was neither ordinary space-flotsam nor meteoric stone or nickel-iron. In fact, it was something completely unknown to Justician science: a metallic alloy that approached the hardness of diamond, yet was ductile enough so that its surfaces of separation from its source were surfaces of shear, not of fracture.

'I pass,' Rodnar said, after he had applied all the resources of his little vessel to the stubborn stuff without coming even close to identifying it as any known metal or alloy. 'I think probably you'd better take it along with you when you go home tonight, so Knu can take it to a metallurgical laboratory and get it really worked on. It may even need an atom-separator.'

'Uh-uh.' Her fine eyes clouded. 'And I think I'd better stay at home and work with him, don't you? If this piece of metal turns out to be what I'm sure it is . . . well, about all you'll be doing for a while will be automatic, won't it? Combing a larger and ever larger sphere of space for that monstrous alien construct that I'm sure is nowhere in our normal space.'

'Frankly, I'm beginning to wonder, myself; but we've got to be sure . . . so you *would* be a lot more use at home than out here . . . computing, for instance, just how big my search-pattern will have to be to make the probability approach unity that said alien construct is nowhere in our normal space.'

She nodded. 'That certainly should be done and I'll do it . . . and you be *awfully* careful, Rod; especially going to visit Starr – and leaving. But I suppose she's keeping you posted on this horrible psychic mess?'

'Yes.' Rodnar's face hardened; his eyes became gray ice. 'She thinks there's something more going on than just the usual rounding up of pacifists, psychics and such and feeding them to the eagles, but she can't get an inkling as to what it is. When she does, I won't be here any more. Knu and I both are going to take steps.'

'Uh-huh, so I hear; but you want to remember *this* job is extremely important too, because if there can possibly be another space, and it's where X-storms come from, we've *got* to know about it. So – on with the search- pattern, my pal, my pal, huh?'

And on with the search-pattern it was. Rodnar searched the rest of the day, and Marrjyl went home to her Knuaire and stayed there, the chunk of alien metal going with her, of course. Rodnar searched, and went to visit Starrlah, and searched, and she came to visit him, and very good times were had by both – the only drawback being that all these meetings had to be the very subbest possible of sub-rosa meetings.

And as the days piled up into weeks the already tremendous sphere of space that did *not* contain the invading subspace |– if it *was* a subspacer – grew larger . . . and larger . . .

And ever larger . . .

* * *

When the weirdly-torn, fantastically-cut-up *Explorer* reached base on Galmetia she created a sensation. Maynard, after one good look at his tri-di, alerted his pilot and dashed for the roof. In one minute flat his 'copter was tearing a hole in the air for the spaceport with its sirens ululating and its big red lights flashing. He landed. He exchanged brief – *very* brief – greetings with the leaders of the expedition. He inspected the engine-rooms. He crawled through, over, and around those frightful rents and queerly-twisted, grotesquely-coiled strips of ultra-stubborn metal. For the first time in his life he was completely at a loss.

And the engineers – knowing so much better than Maynard could the actual power of those melted-down engines and the actual physical strength of leybyrdite, the ultimate alloy – were even more at a loss than Maynard was.

Without saying another word Maynard jerked a thumb at Deston and led him into the 'copter, which thereupon took off for the office. Maynard's face was gray and drawn; he looked as though he hadn't slept for a week.

'It isn't that bad, chief,' Deston said, quietly. 'A lot of money down the drain – but we have lots more. And nobody was hurt. And we learned a lot.'

'Maybe you're right. But what are we bucking? Tell me.'

'Okay, but while you're listening bear one fact in mind. We're going back there if it costs DesDes a billbuck and whether or not, after you've all heard the story, MetEnge has had it.'

'Don't be a nit-wit. As long as you stay in we will, no matter what kind of new ship you want. Fifty-fifty. Go ahead.'

'Okay,' and Deston began his story. He was about half-way through it when they reached Maynard's private office.

'Hi, Doris.' Deston smiled as he held out his hand.

'Hi, Babe.' She shook his hand warmly. 'I'm awfully glad you all got back safely.' Then to her boss, 'Full record, Mr Maynard, of course. Typed precis. And of course you're out.'

'Yes. To anything except the absolute end of the world I'm out, yes. But you may use your own judgement.' When they were seated in his inner office Maynard went on, 'Start over, Deston, for the record. I want to hear it over again, anyway.'

Deston repeated and then continued. He spoke without interruption until he came to the battle with the generators. He had to go over that repeatedly, from every angle Maynard could think of. He had also to go over and over the rotation from subspace into another space – Second Space – and the return to *First* Space.

At the end, Maynard sat silent for minutes; his eyes glazed and the fingers of his right hand drumming soundlessly on the soft plastic of his chair's arm. Finally he spoke. 'What you actually did, then, was *teleport* the whole tremendous mass of that ship out of space and *through* subspace . . . into – what? Dammit, man, how can there *possibly* be two *different* spaces?'

'It can't be explained. It just is; that's all. Dr Adams has an explanation, but only he understands it.'

'You said you were going after the unknown . . . you certainly found it . . . and you wonder if we want half of *that*? You must have developed tremendously since I last saw you. All of you.'

'That's the prize understatement of the year. It's reasonable enough, though, when you think about it. We'd all been hiding it, you know; but when we began pooling it – dragging out of each other everything everybody had – well, what *would* happen, chief?'

'Could be, at that . . . and that relieves me no end . . . we need you, believe me.' Maynard had shed ten falsely-added years in as many minutes. 'When do you want to get to work on the new ship – as though I didn't know!'

CHAPTER 8

Blow-Up

The message that broke up Rodnar's long search for the alien starship, however, did not come from Starrlah, but from Knuaire. 'Rod!' came the hard-drived, sharply-tuned thought. 'Give me your co-ords – we're coming out in the yacht.'

Rodnar gave them. 'But what's up, Knu?'

'*Ps-ss-ss-sst*! No more. The klant's in the fan! I don't know whether anybody can tap this thought or not and I don't want to find out. Be seeing you.'

The big luxury ship appeared; the little speedster was 'ported aboard. Then the yacht went somewhere else – fast. Only then did the Spathian relax.

'Hi, Marr,' Rodnar said then, to supplement the mental greetings that had gone before. 'Okay, Knu; spill it.'

'What started the whole blow-up was your speedster; when you 'ported out of the spaceport, you know. You didn't slot your token.'

'Of course I didn't. How could I?'

'There wasn't any way to, I guess, at that; but did you ever see a completely frustrated robot? For the first time in a long and errorless career not being able to account for a subspeedster left in its care?'

The other two laughed, then Rodnar whistled express-ively. 'No, I never did . . . I'm not sure I can even imagine it. Robots simply don't make mistakes. They can't.'

'That's right. Or lie. So when they got that robot back into working order again it proved, by every recorder in the place, that your subber was still in its stall, and to keep from blowing all its banks, I guess, it stuck to that story regardless. *That*, as you can imagine, blew the fan and the klant both clear into orbit. It not only brought psionics out into the open, it jammed it down everybody's throats. Then, when all the stuffed shirts of Slaar, Orm and Spath were denying it in public and in private wondering what in hell they could do about it – they hadn't yet decided to make eaglemeat out of all psis everywhere – I took that metal to Sonslehn Sleht for analysis and physical test. When he found out how much *rhenium* was in it, he . . .'

'Rhenium? That's just a chemical curiosity, isn't it?'

'It's more than a curiosity wherever *that* stuff came from, believe me. There's more rhenium in that hundred pounds of alloy than has ever been found before in all known space.'

'But what's it good for? No, cancel that – if it's obtainable in quantity, and it must be, somewhere, the question would be, what isn't it good for?'

'That's better. Its physical properties are so utterly fantastic that the Purps' snoopers wouldn't believe their own spy-instruments. They were sure that Sleht was faking the whole test for a gag; so he 'ported aboard here a couple of milliseconds ahead of a blaster beam. Re-runs confirmed his results, of course, and right then *everything* went to hell in a handbasket. They *knew*, then, that it was something we psiontists had developed strictly on the QT, and the Council of Grand Justices began to froth at the mouth. All psychics were declared eaglemeat, with an added feature. You and I and Marr, Sleht, Wayrec, and a few others – the top psiontists of the Institute – are worth ten thousand junex alive or two thousand dead.'

'But how . . .?' Marrjyl began, without thinking, then went on, 'Oh, of course.'

'Of course,' Rodnar agreed. 'With the methods of suasion they use, it wouldn't take the Purps long to find out who the prime operators of the Institute are . . . thank the Powers that nobody outside us three has any inkling whatever that Starr has any connection whatever with psionics.'

'I say amen to that, my love,' came Starrlah's thought into their threesome, and after a moment of mental snuggling with Rodnar she went on, 'I'm done working for today and I'm home and I've set full-ply psionic guards so can I join you now in person?'

'Come ahead, sweetheart,' Rodnar said, and she did, and for half a minute or so the snuggling was satisfyingly physical. (Marrlah and Knuaire both knew that Rodnar and Starrlah had joined lives; and, of course, why they had not yet registered that fact.) Then: 'I suppose it was you two who organized the exodus? I haven't been paying much attention, you know.'

'I know. We helped, yes . . .'

Starrlah snickered. 'They a lot more than helped, Rod. And you ought to've been there – in moving stuff out of apartments they actually 'ported things right out of Purps' hands. Talk about frustrated *robots*!'

Rodnar grinned and cocked an eyebrow at Knuaire, who said, 'Yeah. With everything blown wide open anyway, we figured that the bigger and more obviously impossible we made it, the better. But the whole thing is rolling under its own power now.'

'Where to? Not Psi, surely – that Garshan sucker-trap?'

'And become a steady source of eaglemeat? Hardly – not by several hundred clusters of suns! A new planet. Top secret. "Hope" we call it. It's to be developed as a completely independent, completely self-sufficient planet of psiontists.'

'Just like that, eh?' Rodnar objected. 'How many generations d'you think *that'll* take?'

'Not as many as you think,' Knuaire replied, unperturbed. 'You see, there'll be no ordinary psychics . . .'

'And no mystics,' Marrjyl broke in, 'and especially no mysto-pacifists, of any kind, age, race, or color.'

'They'd all rather go to Psi, anyway,' Starrlah explained. 'Those of them, that is, who'll go anywhere. Most of them, like that obnoxious Daughtlanarr Monarr of Tsalk, are going to revel in becoming martyrs in as spectacular a way as possible.'

Rodnar scowled. 'Could be . . . they seem to figure that if they sit on their hands long enough everything they don't like will all go away – and how they figure that torching themselves to death will help matters any has got me completely baffled. But how many real, genuine, indubitable psiontists do you think there are?'

Knuaire grinned and both girls laughed aloud. 'You'll be surprised, Rod,' Starrlah said. 'Everybody was. Astounded, in fact. When everything broke loose all over space all the thought-channels were absolutely jammed with psiontists who'd been hiding everything they had. There'll be at least a quarter of a million just from Slaar alone, in almost a thousand ships. With everything they'll need.'

Rodnar's scowl scarcely lightened. 'I'm glad your thought was "They'll" and not "We'll",' he thought darkly. 'All three of you know – especially you, Knu, as a top-bracket theoretician – what will happen if we desert Civilization and devote all our efforts to developing a purely psionic civilization of our own. It'll be either an outright collapse into savagery or, very much more probably, an infinitely worse tyranny – that of the strongest group to emerge from the catastrophe, which would be the Garshans. And I'll bet five to two in hundreds that not only there aren't any Garshan psiontists on our side, but you've got full psionic blocks set against any pattern whatever of Garshan thought.'

Knuaire held up a circle made of thumb and forefinger

and said, 'Check to here. Go ahead,' and Starrlah added, 'I'm glad, Rod. I was hoping you'd think that way. I'm almost sure what you're going to say next.'

'You probably are. In spite of its glaring defects, the tyranny has worked, after a fashion, for a long time; and it is getting better. Civilization has advanced tremendously and is still advancing. Ability is recognized; advancement in status is not only possible, but common; and there is no official racial discrimination at all, not even on the Council. And the present Tyrant, His Magnificence Ranjak, isn't too bad an egg; as tyrants go and in his own poisonous way.'

'He isn't either poisonous,' Starrlah the FirSec came strongly to the defense of her boss. 'He's nice, and I ought to know. He's the best Supreme Grand Justice the tyranny's ever had.'

'I think he is too,' Rodnar agreed. 'Not that that's saying too much in his favor, at that, as far as the good of the whole human race is concerned. But – now let's imagine that every Grand Justice in the Council is a Garshan, with Laynch sitting on the throne as Supreme-Grand-Justice-Tyrant. What kind of a book would you make as to how many years it would be before everybody with a number – everybody with any status at all, clear down to and including Status One Hundred – would have to be a Garshan?'

No one of the three answered the question; no one seemed surprised that he had asked it; no one disagreed with his thought. Instead, Knuaire said, 'We're pretty much in agreement on the basic situation, I think. The question is, what should we do about it?'

'I won't say I haven't got any ideas,' Rodnar said, 'but since you're the theoretician they probably aren't nearly as good or as complete as the ones you've already developed. So over to you.'

'Thanks. It's too soon, of course, to specify any details, but the first broad division into three main lines of effort should be as follows. One group, headed possibly by Marrjyl and myself and certain administrators and others, should continue, systematize, and intensify the work we have been doing haphazardly; the work of supporting actively the present Tyrant and his Council of Grand Justices.

'Second, the much larger but much more routine task of settling, developing, and guarding our new planet Hope. Marr and I both feel that this segment of the total task is already in thoroughly competent hands.

'Third, most difficult of all and least susceptible to either analysis or suggestion, and yet probably most important of the three, it is the considered opinion of the theoreticians that you two, Rodnar and Starrlah, are best qualified of us all to head up a group of your own choosing whose task it will be to develop whatever techniques and/or procedures may prove necessary to effect changes you may think desirable in the government of the Justiciate – with whatever that may imply.'

'Great Powers, Knu, have a heart!' Rodnar exclaimed, even as a shielded thought flashed through his mind. Knuaire alone – not a group – had come up with this idea, for none of the other theoreticians knew of Starrlah's entry into the psionic group. But it was logical, so when the Spathian paid no attention to his protest, he turned to Starrlah and said aloud, 'And he calls himself our friend!'

That night in bed, after attending to certain matters of urgency, Rodnar and Starrlah lay in each other's arms with their minds tightly fused and thought and thought and thought. They considered the Justiciate and its tyranny – element by element, planet by planet, government by government and faction by faction. Rodnar didn't know much about these latter, but Sarrlah did – what she didn't know about them simply was not worth knowing. Rodnar learned what she knew; she learned what he knew; and together they analyzed and classified and differentiated and tabulated their total information.

And next morning, before they got up, they went over all their data again; this time synthesizing, re-classifying, integrating, re-tabulating, and computing. And in four or more night-and-morning sessions of intensive study, they worked out a tentative, first-approximation plan of action.

They wanted to be together all the time, but of course that simply was not in the wood. The price on Rodnar's head was now twenty thousand junex, so he had to be very careful indeed. And she *had* to stay with His Magnificence, for three excellent reasons:

First: Since Sonrathendak Ranjak himself was in all probability essential to the success of their overall plan, his life would have to be guarded as only a top-bracket psiontist could guard it.

Second: As the Tyrant's First Secretary she was in the best possible position to know everything that was going on throughout the Justiciate.

And third: 'But *could* you quit the old boy, even if you wanted to?' Rodnar asked.

'I don't know . . .' Starrlah grimaced. 'The point never came up. No high-up ever wants to quit . . . not ever . . . but if anybody ever did I'm afraid he wouldn't like it and it'd be a case of eaglemeat.'

'That figures . . .' Rodnar paused in thought, then went on, 'But you can take a vacation, can't you?'

'I'm supposed to have three weeks a year, but I'm 'way overdue and he hasn't said anything about it; and neither have I, of course. That's the bad part of having such a solid in with him . . . he'd give me one, I think, but he might not like it and we simply can't afford to lose one bit

114

of the ground I've gained . . . no, the smart thing is for me to be so overworked that he'll take pity on me and insist on my taking a long rest. Three weeks of starvation dieting, with a couple of hours every evening of hard swimming and of course a gradual change in cosmetics toward the corpselike, and I'll be the haggiest-looking hag you ever saw.'

Shaking his head in wonderingly admiring amazement, Rodnar held her out at arms' length and examined her for a long half minute. He whistled softly and said, 'Starr sweetheart, all I can say is, you'll simply never know how glad I am that you're on my side and not the other.'

She chuckled happily, then laughed aloud. 'And all I can say is, look out Garsh! Here we come – the Rod–Starr simulation of an irresistible force!'

On Galmetia work had begun immediately on the new subspace and trans-spatial giant – for it actually was entirely new, so small a portion of the original *Explorer* being usable as to barely warrant mention.

A conference of the eight psiontists had preceded the actual beginning of detailed planning. Upton Maynard's inner sanctum was the scene of the gathering, with President Maynard himself, representing MetEnge, in attendance; but with Dr Andrew Adams in charge.

Although the destruction of the subspace liner was practically instantaneous, the super-psiontists had observed and recorded an incredible amount of detail. All of it was placed in a pool of common knowledge.

FirSec Champion was there – now Mrs Eldon Smith, wife of the second-in-command to the big boss – but still Doris Champion for business purposes. She was seated unobtrusively to one side behind the most advanced steno-recorder ever built. Hers was the task of recording every thought, every suggestion poured into that psionic reservoir.

An uninformed, non-psionic observer would have considered the entire proceedings madness. Not an audible word was spoken. The nine people were seated or sprawled in luxurious contour chairs in whatever position they found most comfortable; some from time to time rose and paced the length of the big room. There was no sound save the barely discernible stutter and click of Champion's electronic wizard.

Dr Adams rather formally opened the meeting, but from that point on formality vanished. Fortunately for the record they usually avoided simultaneous input; but with the speed inherent in thought transference, an amazing inter-change of ideas took place in a very short time. Despite this, hours passed before they broke for refreshments.

The details of the session would make interesting reading for students of the era; but since FirSec Champion's very complete minutes are available to researchers, it is enough to say that the plans which emerged from that conference laid the groundwork for a greatly improved interspatial ship. It was the first of several such meetings; but when the skilled staff at MetEnge, spurred by an outlay of funds which for all practical purposes was limitless, began to give their thinking concrete form, construction moved ahead with fantastic speed.

CHAPTER 9

Orkstmen

It did not take Starrlah three weeks to arrange for a vacation. It did not even take two. Supreme Grand Justice Sonrathendak was, as Rodnar had said, a good egg; particularly in his personal as opposed to his political relationships. And Starrlah liked her boss; both as a person and for the way he treated her and others near him – even though, like those others, she was afraid of him and was very careful indeed never to antagonize him in even the smallest way.

In these personal relationships Ranjak was considerate and, in his own mind at least, perfectly fair; and he liked his present FirSec immensely. Not sexually – for that business he preferred blondes and/or red-heads, which was why his FirSecs were always brunettes – but for her ruthless but velvety smooth efficiency, her poise, and her all-but-eidetic memory . . . and the way she had handled the matter of the Masked Marvel. Her actions during the X-storm crisis had put her in with him – but *solid*.

Ranjak was also smart, able, and observant: if he had not been he would not have lived to half his age.

Wherefore in just eleven days Starrlah was on vacation and was eating everything she could reach. Then, after announcing that she was going to Gafia, so far that it would take twenty six junex worth of postage stamps to mail her a postcard, she and Rodnar 'ported themselves aboard Knuaire's yacht and proceeded to make themselves look enough like Garshans to pass a casual inspection.

Starrlah needed only a false nose and a skin-dye job;

Rodnar had also to have his hair dyed black and get a pair of almost-black contact lenses. These lenses bothered him for a long time; but he finally got used to them so that he could endure wearing them during normal waking hours.

The adventurers did not do anything about their numbers except cover them with cosmetic paste. Not so much because the removal or alteration of a Citizen Number was a capital offense: principally because Starrlah would have to have her number, precisely as it now was, the minute her vacation was over. She could not go back to her job or to any other place of status without it. Also, numbers would not matter if they did not show: the same argument applied to them as to the disguises as Garshans, which did not have to be too good. The Slaarans were going to a Garshan un'statland; in which, since none except Garshan un'stats were to be expected, none else were looked for. And of course they could not possibly pass any kind of a psionic inspection anyway. All they could do should this emergency arise was to 'port away from any such inspector, instantly and far.

In due course then Rodnar and Starrlah, taking with them a young couple of psiontist-trainees, 'ported Rodnar's subspacer into a cavern on the far side of Garsh's first moon and put out all the screens the little vessel had. Then, ultra-cautiously, they began their survey, which took quite a while because their requirements were several and strict.

They needed a couple of Garshan un-stat complements, at least semi-permanently established in some ordinary, routine job, who lived and worked within point-blank range of Garshion, the capital city of Garsh. Within a hundred miles, since that was about as far as they could read accurately the faint side-bands and even fainter leakages of thought that they would *have* to have. This pair must be young, and the nearer they were to the Slaarans in size the better. They could afford to use some psionic compulsion, but not too much. And finally, the girl had to be in her first pregnancy, but not too far enough along in it so the condition showed. This was the toughest requirement of all; for at age twenty three Tellus-equivalent a female Garshan un'stat – as the Slaarans learned much later – was supposed to be having her third or fourth child.

They finally found a couple, each of whom was close enough to specifications; a couple of orkstmen living in a stone-walled, sheet-iron-roofed cabin in the middle of a mile-square field of rich, live-stock-covered pastureland only seventy five miles from Garshion and its Edifice of Garsh.

They 'ported their naked selves, then, into this cabin; and 'ported the previous occupants – without their soft leather breech-clouts and moccasin-type shoes – out into the speedster on the moon, where the trainees took charge of them. Killing this couple was not in order; when Rodnar and Starrlah got ready to leave the planet the two natives would be returned unharmed to their cabin. Not only unharmed, but also with exact memories of having done almost everything that the two Slaarans had in fact done in their places.

Except for a deluxe bed, the inside of the cabin was crude and bare. There was a shower-bath and a sink, each with hot and cold running water and a steel bucket half full of detergent. There was a flush toilet of sorts. There was a rough table of planks, upon which were two pottery bowls and a two-gallon jug. There were two three-legged stools. There were a couple of shelves of tools of various kinds – knives of a dozen different shapes and sizes, grinders and whetstones and hones, axes, hatchets, killing blasters, and so on.

119

Driven into the walls between the stones there were wooden pegs, from which hung other, larger implements of the orkst-raising business. Centered at the end of the room opposite the door there was a gas-burning stone fireplace with a big iron kettle. To the left of the fireplace was the king-size bed already referred to; a splendid affair made of resilient foam and steel springs and covered with soft-tanned orkst-skins with the hair-fur left on. To the right of the fireplace was the heavily-insulated door of a gas-fired walk-in deep freeze.

The two interlopers, after checking the empty garments for life and finding none – the whole place was scrupulously clean – put them on. Then Starrlah ran lightly across the room to the fireplace and sniffed appreciatively at the pot, in which a thick stew simmered.

'Well, Brosk, we eat, anyways,' she said aloud, in Low Garshan. They had both been studying that language for weeks; they were both good enough at it so that, with a little help from psionics now and then, they could get by. 'This here glop smells mighty good. The boss may be a grock, but he ain't no belly-robber. I'm hungrier'na bitch whanker with nine cubs, so let's get ta scoffin', huh?'

'Yah. Me, too. I c'd scoff tha tail-pipe right off'na ten-year-old skink. Dig in, Wilny.'

Taking the bowls off the table, they ladled them almost full of the richly aromatic stew. Then, after a short cooling period, they dragged the heavy stools up to the table, sat down opposite each other, and began to eat. Raising the heavy, clumsy bowls to their mouths, they drank off as much as possible of the liquid; then dug in with their fingers and their razor-sharp, needle-pointed knives; swigging by turns the while the mildly-fermented beverage from the jug.

After eating they washed their hands, faces, and utensils; picked up the tools of their new trade; and went out to get to work at their new job.

Orksts were highly-bred domestic animals larger than sheep but smaller than cattle, and similar to neither. Their flesh, in prime condition, was very fine eating. Their hair-fur – long, thick, extremely fine stuff somewhat resembling nylon – in prime condition was very useful and very valuable, especially so in the full pelt.

The trouble was that the peak of prime for each animal occurred only once in its life, was unpredictable, and lasted for only a little over one day. Thus orkstmen were well toward the top of all un'stat workers. They had to have intelligence enough and manual dexterity enough to be expert skinners and good butchers. Also, they had to be able to learn how to tell just when each orkst was 'priming up'. The better the orkstman the less sub-prime meat and pelt he put out: too much sub-prime stuff and he fed the eagles.

That afternoon Rodnar and Starrlah killed, skinned, and dressed twenty three prime orksts. That evening they began to probe, as delicately and as carefully as they possibly could, into the lowest-status minds in the Edifice of Garsh.

Next day they worked; next evening they probed; and so on.

At noon on the fourth day Rodnar punched the 'pickup' button and the owner came out, driving a twenty-five-ton reefer truck. He was about five feet eleven, was unusually fat for a Garshan, and had small, piercing eyes. He was of Status Ninety Nine – next to the very bottom – and completely non-psionic, so it was easy to make him see with his own eyes that he was dealing with the two people who belonged there. He went first to the pile of skins and riffled through them; his big, fat hands proving surprisingly deft and sure.

'Hunnert 'n' fourteen. Pretty fair stuff, Brosk.'

'Pretty fair, hell,' Rodnar-Brosk said, conversationally. 'Hunnert 'n' fourteen top primes.'

'Tell when I spread 'em. Lotta pelt; didn' know's ya c'd make out on all that extry stock, but I see ya took the chains offa yer wildy. Got 'er knocked up 'n' workin', uh?'

'Yeah,' Starrlah-Wilny said. 'Missed a bleedin' er two 'n' tha croaker says I'm stuck with it so I better stick around, fer a while anyways.'

'Aw ri', load tha pelt 'n' start shovin' tha meat in.'

They did so; while the boss, of course, looked on. After a time, while the hard-frozen carcasses were being trundled along the monorail into the frigid body of the truck, the owner – very highly pleased with the size and quality of this load – spoke again:

'Some say the wildies're better'n tha civ'lized feems sometimes. Mabbe so 'nless ye hafta cut their dam throats to keep 'em f'm knifin' ya. Wildies're bad thataway. Lotta men get gizzarded, tryin' ta tame 'em. 'Speshly that old. Smart 'nuf 'n' good 'nuf ta keep tha whankers f'm sniff'n'em out that long, they slice y'up into whanker-meat 'n' scram tha hell out. Me, I druther pay more 'n' keep my guts inside me where they belong.'

'Naw.' Rodnar-Brosk disagreed. 'If ya beat 'em up, shore. Why tha hell not? All ya hafta do is show 'em ya like 'em 'n' like ta have 'em around. She broke in good 'n' I never licked 'er once. B'sides, lookut whatcha get. Jever see a city feem with them lines er that quality? She's got breedin', boss. Thass why I wanted 'er, not 'cause she was cheap.'

'She don't look too bad now, fer a fact. Primin' up, ya might say.' The big man looked at the supposed Wilmy's firmly jutting breasts and at her superb figure in exactly the same way as he would have examined a prize-winning orkst in a stock-show. Having status and a number, he was infinitely above any un'stat. 'Looks like mabbe she c'n work good 'n'd have good get. How long was y'up in the hills, Wildy Wilny?'

'Ever since I was belly-high to a norkst,' she bragged. She was working smoothly, easily, without missing a hook. 'But ya can't dodge 'em f'rever once they start reely whank'rin' ya, so they fin'ly drug me in. But ya know sumpin? It's gettin' so I kinda *like* tha grock.' She jerked a thumb at Rodnar. 'I like ta eat reg'lar, too, 'n' sleep safe 'n' dry 'n' soft 'n' warm.'

'Noticed he gotcha a high-stat bed 'n' throwed tha bunk out. Yer cost'n'm, Wildy. Mebbe yer wuth it, though.'

'Depen's on where yer lookin' from, who's gettin' tha blade. I figgered first-off I was gettin' purely jobbed, but in some ways it's nice, knowin' where yer at. Mebbe I'll get all civ'lized 'n' even like brats, I dunno.'

'Thassaway ta talk, Wildy,' the fat man said. Then, the loading done, he climbed up into his cab, thought for half a minute, and added, 'This ain't a bad load for two orksters, tha time ya took; it ain't bad a tall.' That was a compliment indeed.

With the Garshan gone, Starrlah looked at Rodnar with an impish glint in her eyes and beamed a tight thought. 'So I "broke in good" and you "like them lines". I got breedin' too. Thanks so much, my dear.' Laughter came bubbling to the surface. 'Oh, Rod – wasn't it fun?'

As had been said, the two Slaarans could not stand psionic inspection; but that was to be feared only if they had given Wayrec or some other top-bracket Garshan psiontist some cause for suspicion – and they were pretty sure that they hadn't yet. They had been careful enough at every point to be virtually certain of that; even though they had no real evidence whatever that Laynch actually was plotting against the Tyranny of Sonrathendak Ranjak.

If any Garshans were so plotting, however, they would have been checking right along for spies; both inside their organization and outside it and using their very ability to varn (a word covering the full range of extra-sensory perception and capability). This checking would cover everyone down to and including Status Fifteen, certainly. To Twenty, probably; and to Twenty Five possibly. Below Thirty the possibility would be vanishingly small – there were so many people in those grades that any systematic psionic coverage of them would take vastly more time and effort than it could possibly be worth.

And as for the possibility of checking the billions of Garshan un'stats – that didn't warrant consideration.

No – the Slaarans' only risk of detection lay in the quality of their own varning. They would be safe unless and until they tripped some psionic trap hard enough to trigger a lock-on – and *that* they hadn't better do!

The real Brosk had requisitioned enough stock from the owner to keep him and his half-wild mate at work twelve or fourteen hours out of every twenty four. Neither Rodnar nor Starrlah, however, had to feel of or even look closely at an orkst to know when it was priming up. They could do many other 'impossible' things. Wherefore they spent much of their time lying flat on their backs on the big bed; varning.

Hour after hour their mental fusion scanned non-psionic minds – sifting indetectably the total knowledge of governmental, managerial, executive, and regulatory personnel up to and including Status Ten. That was as high as they wanted to go at first – people who, beside being non-psionic, were neither as smart nor as able as they themselves were. (They both were actually high Fives in ability; but there wasn't a thing they could do about it – yet.)

They did not learn very much from any one person; but the total knowledge of things Garshan obtained from the thousands of medium-to-high executives studied was impressive indeed. And when each item had been stored in Starrlah's near-eidetic memory; had been indexed and cross-indexed therein; had been analyzed and synthesized by both operators working in fusion; and finally, when a hundred or so different assumptions and hypotheses had been extrapolated and/or projected into the future: then and then only then was the Starr–Rod team ready to go to work on the really powerful psionic minds of Garsh.

This was fantastically tricky business; especially since one of the first discoveries they made rocked them right on their heels. *The highest high-stats of Garsh, up to and including the Grand Justices himself, were psiontists!*

Wow! With the Council of Grand Justice unanimously and continuously opposed to psionics in every form, what did *that* mean? The Slaarans did not exactly know; but their educated guess was that it confirmed their belief that Garsh was and had been planning on taking over the entire Justiciate. And the Garshan Wayrec, so outspoken at the Institute meeting, was obviously a spy. These new data did not, however, change either their objective or their method of operation. They would have to be even more careful than ever, was all. To be caught in their spying by *those* minds would be ver*ee* ungood indeed: they would never get another chance even fractionally as good.

Wherefore they did not actually touch any high-stat psionic mind at all. They attended, invisibly and indetectably, high-level meetings and conferences; listening to and recording all business transacted. They listened to high executives dictating via voice or thought to machines or secretaries. They held detector webs, for fifteen minutes at a time, to entrap leakages of thought from minds immersed in high-level planning. They hovered over tables in exclusive restaurants; especially over those tables at which strong drink was copiously imbibed, hence at which grievances against superiors were sometimes being aired. These data were very informative indeed.

Above all, they followed VIPs after important meetings, varning for leakages and unguarded, unconscious radiations of thought. There were reasoned or careless afterthoughts of differences of opinion concerning matters of high policy and decision and action. There were angry condemnations of and bitter recriminations against – too intense to be contained – the stupidities and the incompetence of persons mentioned profanely and luridly by name.

All these and thousands of smaller – and quite possibly meaningless – items were seized, studied, and stored . . . and to such good purpose did they work that by the end of Starrlah's vacation period they had everything pretty well wrapped up. Not in detail, of course; but in broad they had a fairly coherent and meaningful picture and they had figured out the first moves in the game they would have to play.

Wherefore they vanished from the orkstmen's cabin, leaving their borrowed garments behind; and, while those garments were still warm, the real Brosk and the real Wilny reappeared in them, with no knowledge whatever that they had been out of them except to sleep, or that they had been away from the orkst-ranch for any time at all. They knew as a matter of course that they had been on the ranch all along; they remembered distinctly every detail of the work they had done and every word of their various conversations with the ranch's owner. And both took it for granted that they had learned by doing to be better orkstmen than they had ever been before.

Both Slaarans reappeared in Rodnar's subspacer in the cavern on the moon of Garsh where, after thanking the psiontist-trainees for a job well done, they dismissed them; and with haste, though not without some difficulty, they removed every trace of their Garshan disguises. There followed a brief but fervent time of parting. Then Starrlah vanished by 'porting herself back into her one-room, one-girl apartment in Meetyl on Slaar; and next morning, it was a thoroughly refreshed, lovely, and buoyant FirSec Starrlah who went enthusiastically back to work at her regular job.

Rodnar, on the other hand, 'ported his subber to join Maarjyl and Knuaire, awaiting aboard Knu's yacht. With the little vessel stowed, they went into mind-to-mind discussion of what had been learned. Although some pertinent details were still lacking, it was completely safe for them to assume that Grand Justice Laynch of Garsh planned to overthrow the Justiciate and make himself the Supreme Grand Justice. And by everything that was logical and by indications picked up during their spying, he would be acting without delay. The flight of tens of thousands of psiontists, many of them undetected high-stats holding important positions, with the general chaos attending their disappearance, gave the Garshan a made-to-order opportunity.

Having reached this conclusion they acted.

CHAPTER 10

The Eagle-Feeding

Rodnar, Marrjyl and Knuaire, working together to avoid duplication, alerted two hundred-odd other Psiontist Firsts of six planets and they all went to Slaar. Five of those six planets did not require attention, since none of them had a Grand Justice on the Justiciate; but Slaar was all-important. As a matter of fact, it worked out that whoever held the City of Meetyl and its Edifice of Justice and its top-echelon Guards of the Person held the entire Justiciate.

The two-hundred-plus psiontists 'ported into Meetyl without any trouble. Most of them were unknown to the Guards, all of them had excellent covers, and a few hundred visitors make no impression at all upon a city of ten million. The three ringleaders – four, counting the metallurgist Sleht – who were well known to and wanted badly by the secret police, had no trouble, either. Meetyl had so many first-class hotels that, except for the tourist and convention seasons, there were many hundreds of rooms vacant every night. Food, of course, was no problem; and the fact that they could not pay for either lodging or food did not bother them at all.

They had no worries about anything three-dimensional, but subspace was something else. Something entirely else. They were watching subspace – all subspace through or by any part of which any approach whatever could be made to the Edifice of Justice and the person of the Supreme Justice of the Justiciate. Since time would be extremely important in the instant of attack – to be measured in milliseconds – they had set up an instantaneously-reactive webwork of warning; and the psiontist handling that webwork worked a shift only one minute long. That was as long as even those minds could stay at the peak of tension and awareness.

They were virtually certain that Laynch would make his move in daylight and in public. They were fairly sure that it would be at a big public affair, very probably the well-publicized eagle-feeding extraordinary to be held five days from then in the Room of the Throne itself, and which His Power the Supreme Justice himself was going to grace with his presence. Nevertheless, they took no chances. The Supreme Justice, although he had no suspicion of the fact, was being guarded as no entity in all history had ever been guarded before: guarded through every millisecond of every hour of every day.

Marrjyl, whose long one-minute shift followed Rodnar's, was just as tense and alert and keen as he had been. She, too, held a plasma-jet blaster in one hand and a razor-sharp bladesman's knife in the other.

The Edifice of Justice is not an edifice. Nor is it a cave. It is a thing of a thousand rooms built in the depths of a mountain. It is protected in every direction by more than two thousand yards of solid rock; as well as by all the weaponry known to a warlike race of men. Built of high-tensile alloy, it is much stronger as a unit than the volume of rock it replaced. It is air-conditioned throughout; its lighting is an apparently sourceless glow of daylight quality and intensity. The greatest, finest artists of all Second Space worked for more than two centuries on its decorating.

For those who lived there at the time in question – the elite, the *crème de la crème* of the entire Justiciate – it was the ultimate in luxury and of status. Anything that any one of those personages wanted, he or she in full measure had.

The Room of the Throne was immense; so tremendous that, while its shape was actually long and narrow, it was so wide that it seemed impossible for such a vast un-pillared cavity to exist so far underground. It was of a splendor and a magnificence not seen on Tellus since the glories of Babylon and of Rome. It was both barbarous and super-modern; it was utterly fantastic. The wall-to-wall carpet was of synthetic fiber, with a deep, rich pile, flaming out all the colors of the spectrum in bizarre designs. Walls and ceiling, in mosaics of exquisite artistry of tile and gold and jade and jet, portrayed in story after pictured story the triumphant history of the Justiciate.

But there were also cages of steel bars, within which huge mountain eagles beat their clipped wings fruitlessly and screamed in hungry rage. There were brutish men, naked except for leather belts, who carried heavy bludgeons and long, sharp-edged knives. There were guards in full space-armor carrying plasma-jet blasters in their hands. There were agile, hard-trained men and women in knife-fighters' nylons, wearing the beautifully-made tools of their trade.

Nine-tenths of the Room's great length of floor sloped sharply upward, to afford all standees – no one sat, ever, in The Presence – a clear view of what was happening on its level one-tenth. That immense ramp now held fifteen thousand people; all of whom had paid for their tickets by being of service to the Guards of the Person. Not in cash: *those* ducats were not for sale at any price in cash.

The Throne, on its dais of jet and gold and purple, was built against the end wall opposite the ramp. It was made of vari-colored transparent plastic; which, self-luminous, ra-diated bands and beams and ever-changing patterns of many-colored light. It was inlaid and laced and latticed with polished gold; it was studded with blazing, sparkling gems.

And the man who sat on that magnificent throne looked

every inch the power that he was. Seventy or so years old, he was tall, straight, and carried very little fat. His hair was white, but he still had it all, and his teeth – he was grinning savagely – were even, white, and natural.

Before the Throne, flat on their faces on the floor, were three rows of people. Three rows of naked men and women, each row a hundred and twenty feet long. Packed close, side by side. Psychics all; mentalists who had the inner strength – or the sheer stupidity? – neither to fight nor to teleport themselves out of harm's way.

The Supreme Justice, without rising, held up his ornately carved and jeweled scepter and spoke:

'Any trial of such vermin as these would be superfluous. They are not human beings; they have no right to live in human guise. I declare them eaglemeat. Keeper of the First Cage, to work.'

One of the brutish men leaped to the end of the first row of victims, seized a man by the hair, and dragged him over the carpet to the first cage of the long line. There, on a rubber mat – while the eagles screamed and flapped in ever-mounting frenzy – he slashed his victim's tendons, bludgeoned the limbs to break the bones, then flung the crippled body into the cage.

Everyone stood spellbound at this, the opening event of the long-awaited spectacle. Everyone, that is, except the two-hundred-plus uninvited psiontists. They were all watching subspace now. This was – or very shortly would be – the moment.

Since Rodnar and Marrjyl, while watching, were not wound up nearly as tightly as the psiontist whose shift it was, they were a flick of time behind that psiontist in materializing in the Room of the Throne. They appeared, however, close beside the Supreme Justice and in time. Laynch himself was there in full flesh, driving a knife at Ranjak's heart.

Rodnar swung his blaster, but he had made a very poor choice of weapons. Blasters were heavy, whereas knives are light. Thus Marrjyl's knife flashed three-quarters through that brawny wrist before the gun was in line. Instantly, almost instantaneously, Rodnar did what he should have done in the first place – locked mentally onto the knife and hand, stopping them cold a bare four inches from target – finding that he acted just in time. Laynch's mind was there, too, with all its power. For an instant those two tremendously powerful minds warred; then Rodnar found himself in possession of the knife, four almost-whole fingers, and a part of a thumb. The rest of the hand had vanished with Laynch.

Rodnar tried to follow the Garshan. He was sure it would be useless, but he had to try.

His departure and return were almost simultaneous. He got back in time to see the abandoned knife and five severed digits fall into Ranjak's lap. The knife, dropping point down, was so sharp that it cut effortlessly through jeweled robe of state and through ornate brocade shorts and made a wound in the royal leg that began quite freely to bleed.

'He won't be back in person,' Rodnar snapped the thought at Marrjyl. 'He'll have to have that hand attended to or bleed to death and by that time it'll be over. So watch here while I . . .'

'Why me, you noisome jerk?' she stormed. 'Watch him yourself!'

'Because I want somebody here who's got both brains and guts – and that down there's a job for professionals, not amateurs!' and he leaped into the melee.

All this had happened so rapidly that the Supreme Justice was just beginning to realize what was going on. He had no doubt at all, though, that he was still the supreme despot of all the planets of all space, and he reacted accordingly.

'*Shut up*, you egregiously slankerous kfard!' Marrjyl drove the thought so viciously that every cell of the non-psionic brain screamed in agony. 'You're not Lord of Space any more. You're a mass of meat worth exactly as much as that much eaglemeat. You started something. Nobody knows who'll end it or how. In the meantime you had better give thanks to whatever Force you recognize that we decided to save your life – at least for now.'

Rodnar was already deep in the action. A small army of Garshans – he never did find out how many – had 'ported into the Room of the Throne to kill a few thousand of the Justiciate's officialdom, and they were going about it in a thoroughly workmanlike fashion. Rodnar and his fellows were not defending the Justiciate to save the lives of any tyrant's minions. They did not care if all those vicious onlookers died. They were after the Garshan operators. It was now war to the death between them and the psiontists of Garsh, and both sides knew it.

All the guards, spacemen and savages alike, were already dead, of course. Neither side wanted interference, so the guards had died first, by mental force alone.

Unseeing, careless of footing, Rodnar materialized with both feet squarely upon the naked back of a slender yellow-skinned woman still lying prone on the carpet. She uttered one prodigious involuntary grunt, screamed once, and vanished; and Rodnar noticed, almost unconsciously, that the other pacifists were disappearing, too. Being sacrificed gloriously was one thing; to be trampled to death ignominiously, under the feet of a coarsely brawling mob, was something else.

The sudden drop through the space where the yellow woman's slim body had been, although only a few inches, disturbed Rodnar's aim so much that the needle beam of his blaster, instead of drilling a neat hole through the

Garshan's head at the bridge of his nose, cut him completely in two diagonally, from his right shoulder down and across through his left hip.

The Garshan's body did not impede the ferocity of Rodnar's beam at all. It went resistlessly on, slicing through the bodies of a score or more of spectators on the ramp, through the splendid rug and through the even more splendid mosaic of the floor, and deep into the rock of the subfloor before its frightful force was spent.

Rodnar gasped and scanned; but no ally-psionist had been in the way of that wide, wild slash. Fair enough – but this was no place for blaster work. He 'ported the gun away and went in with his knife.

As has been said, Rodnar wasn't big. He stood only five nine and tipped the beam at an unimpressive one sixty. He was, however, strong and tough and fast. He was in hard training and he had studied and practised bladesmanship ever since he was six years old.

In ordinary knife-fighting one combatant always knows where the other is. He doesn't disappear. This engagement, however, was knife-fighting *plus*. Either could disappear at will; to reappear in the same instant behind the other and stab him in the back.

Many tricks were tried on Rodnar during the seventy five seconds that the battle lasted, but none of them worked. Once he found himself facing Sonjormal Wayrec of Garsh – the disruptive psionist spy – who attacked viciously and whom Rodnar promptly disemboweled. Rod was covering the whole hemisphere of perception and he was very, *very* fast. Thus, before the battle ended, he was covered with blood – not his own – from one end to the other.

Suddenly all fighting stopped. All surviving enemies had vanished. Rodnar scanned. Two hundred thirteen dead Garshans. Almost all of his men had taken a slash or two, but only four of them were dead – and Knuaire and Sleht weren't wounded. Fair enough.

There is no need to detail here what happened and was still happening on the ramp. Everyone knows what occurs when a jam-packed mob goes panic mad. Almost a thousand people died in the Room of the Throne that day.

Rodnar 'ported to Marrjyl's side, getting there at the same moment as Knuaire. He took over the tasks she had been doing, including that of holding together the edges of Ranjak's wound, which was already beginning to clot. 'Thanks for the help,' he said aloud.

'Oh? You did know it, then?' she answered. 'Between Knu and you I was really busy. Knu needed help more than you; he's not a pro.' Her eyes were still stormy, but a slight smile was trying to make headway at the corners of her mouth.

Knuaire answered. 'Of course we knew. We're not that stupid. Otherwise I certainly would have taken a couple of nicks or worse – I'm not that good with a blade and some of those Garshans were experts.'

'But what are you sore about?' Rodnar demanded. 'You aren't notching your knife, are you?'

'No.' Marrjyl's half-smile disappeared. 'I wanted in! Besides, the girls will all think I glumpfed out.'

'Is *that* all?' Rodnar smiled broadly. 'You know better than that. So do they if they're listening – and they probably are. You were picked for this job, girl. I told you.'

'Don't *I* get any credit?' The question formed in the three minds. It was Starrlah who as FirSec had been holding the fort for Ranjak. 'I watched, of course, and though I may not be an expert at psionics or in bladesmanship, I know I kept a few of those knives out of your back, Rod.'

Rodnar's mental reply was contrite and warmly grate-

135

ful. 'I should have known, sweetheart – and thanks so much. I'll thank you in person after we take care of His Nibs.'

'You're not going to – ?'

'No – we'll 'port him out to the yacht. We'll see if we can't drive some sense through his thick, hard skull. If we can't I'll feed him to the eagles, just like he thought he was going to do to us.' He paused. 'We'll have to get behind a good tight screen somewhere with him before we can relax.'

He looked at Knuaire. 'We both need a bath, and . . .'

'I'll inform the attentive world you do.' Marrjyl wrinkled her nose in pretended distaste. 'Over all the loudspeakers of Slaar.'

Two men, the woman, and the ex-dictator vanished.

CHAPTER 11

His Magnificence Takes Instruction

Out in deep space, aboard Knuaire's yacht, Sonrathendak Ranjak of Slaar – he was not being called 'Your Magnificence' now – was having a bad time. It was not that he was being hurt physically. He wasn't, very much. Only when he tried to assert himself. Every time he tried that he was smacked down by a bolt of mental force that made all his senses reel.

They had dressed his gashed leg which, after all, was only a rather superficial wound; otherwise he was ignored. His quarters were purely utilitarian. He had no extra clothing. He had to get his own food out of storage and prepare it himself; and the fact that practically no preparation was necessary did not ameliorate the indignity. He had no service at table. Worst of all, he had to put his own used dishes, utensils, and so on into the converter himself . . . he refused to do that once; but once was enough. He finally tried a hunger strike, but when it became clear that they would be glad to have him starve to death, he resumed eating.

As day followed day, be became more and more appalled. What *were* these people? Or *were* they people? They never talked, or communicated with each other in any way he could perceive. They paid no attention whatever to each other, yet they all seemed to be working at *something*. No one paid any attention to the instruments or to the ship itself, yet everything functioned normally. They never went after anything or picked anything up or set anything down; whenever any one of them wanted anything it appeared at hand, and, having been used, it disappeared. Every once in a while one of them – standing, sitting, or lying – would go into what looked like a trance; but none of the others paid any attention to that, either.

One week of this reduced Ranjak to the human equivalent of a quivering pulp. Wherefore he felt only a great relief when Rodnar appeared in his room, sat down beside him, proffered his rose-quartz flask, and said, 'Hi, Ranjak. Whiff?'

Ranjak felt so low that he did not resent even such unbelievable familiarity as this. In fact, he was almost pathetically glad to hear a voice. He accepted the flask and inhaled – gingerly and not at all deeply.

As Rodnar had remarked several times, he liked it strong. Ranjak didn't. Tears came to his eyes and he coughed in spite of himself. As soon as he could talk he said quietly:

'Thank you, Sonrodnar Rodnar of Slaar. Just why did you people save me from the Garshan?'

Rodnar glanced at his chronom. 'That's a long story. Before I go into it, a couple of questions. First – apparently you recognized me. True?'

'Yes. I watched your duel with the Masked Marvel, and saw your bladesmanship in the Room of the Throne. Of course I recognized you – as I recognized Daughtmarja Marrjyl of Orm who helped prevent my assassination.'

'Question two. Have you learned yet that you are neither the Almighty Power nor an irresistible force?'

'I have. Thoroughly. It was very hard to discard sixty five years of belief, training, and experience, but I now know that psionics is a very real thing. A tremendous thing.'

'We hoped you'd be man enough to admit it. Since you are, I'll answer your question. The situation is just now becoming clarified enough for us to begin making plans.

Everything was brought out into the open by that parking-robot making all that noise about my subber disappearing impossibly from its stall. But it started long ago; Laynch has undoubtedly been planning that coup for years.'

'Are you sure that the Garshan who attacked me was Laynch? Sonednil Laynch, Grand Justice of Garsh?'

'Definitely positive. Both Marrjyl and I know him well – we've observed him psionically – and we both read his number. Besides, we kept all four fingers and the thumb of his right hand and the prints checked, so there's no question of identity. His plan was to kill all the justices at once. He, personally, was to kill you, take over the Edifice, declare himself Supreme Justice, and appoint his own Grand Justices. You can take it from there yourself.'

The ex-potentate did so, and his ruddy face paled. 'I had no idea that . . . but how could anything that large have been brewing so long? My Intelligence . . .'

'Don't blame your Guards. Ordinary spies are absolutely useless against psionics. And every high-stat Garshan is a psiontist, including Laynch himself. But we were ready for them, so they killed only ten Grand Justices . . .'

'That many? But there are still eighty one alive?'

'Not exactly. Forty one are still alive. Some died in the riot; we killed thirty two; just as I would have killed you five minutes ago if you still had been harboring delusions of grandeur after a seven-day exposure to the truth. The thirty two we executed were either thoroughly corrupt or unalterably opposed to psiontists, or both. In most cases they were guilty of gross atrocities against us. We're not fooling, Ranjak.'

'I see you're not.' The ex-monarch licked his lips. 'I'm beginning to . . . Laynch would have slaughtered billions of people. Literally, many billions . . . whereas you . . . ?' He paused, delicately.

'That is correct. Whereas we will have to slaughter only

one race, the Garshans.' Rodnar held up his hand to silence the old man's protest and went on, 'I know. Genocide is supposed to be reprehensible. But when a race has proved over and over, during a thousand years, that it is dedicated *as a race* to warfare and conquest, that race should be exterminated. Of course, if you gag too much at complete genocide, you might try saving some of them – all babies under one year old, say, in hope that you can train the lust out of them. Whether heredity governs or environment I wouldn't know – that might be a good way to settle that point.'

'*I* might try?' Ranjak's eyes widened. 'But you've . . .'

'But we haven't,' Rodnar said, coldly. 'We have very carefully saved all your faces. Your Royal Scepter was 'ported to its proper place. As for your being gone a week, you did that on purpose. After that civilization-wide, almost-successful coup, you retired to a private place with a lot of guards you knew you could trust – us. FirSec Daughtelna Starrlah has been so informed and has been caring for all routine matters. All you have to do is restore all psychics to full citizenship and let us give them new jobs and status ratings, entirely on abilities. After thorough study and so on – you know the exact squank to use – you've decided that psionics can be of great use to the Justiciate and is to be encouraged. You'll *have* to do something like that, anyway, to keep on living. Until we get the Edifice completely screened we'll have to do a lot more . . .'

'Oh? You can *screen* against the stuff?'

'Don't act so happy. Limited volumes against certain things, yes, but you'll need a lot of protection. Certainly as long as Laynch and his top people are alive; quite possibly until every Garshan psiontist is dead.'

At the cold certainty of Rodnar's tone Ranjak shrank visibly. 'But you and your psychics are just as much opposed to the Justiciate as the Garshans are.'

'You're so right. As it has been, that is, and as you present Justices want it to keep on being; a harsh, brutal, degrading, unjust and merciless despotism. It has denied all human rights to all except a minute fraction of the citizenry, and it . . .'

'You needn't elaborate,' Ranjak broke in. 'You have made your point. Why keep it, then? Even if I wished to change it – and there's no use in my pretending that I do – I couldn't. Believe it or not, I couldn't change it if my life depended on doing it.'

'I know you can't,' Rodnar agreed, and Ranjak breathed an audible sigh of relief. 'Three hundred billion stupid and ignorant people can't be changed in a month; nor, very much, in a decade. But over the decades, a government having some thought for the good of its people could do wonders. But with Laynch in the saddle and a self-perpetuating Council of Justices of Garshans set up, things would be worse than ever and they'd stay that way.'

Ranjak nodded. 'Probably so. I see what you mean. As a long-term project, it could possibly be made to work. I wouldn't like it . . . but of course I won't be here long enough to see much difference. If any.'

'Probably none at all. That's the idea, exactly. Slight changes over long periods – education, standard of living, and so on. Men of your stripe will change with the times; the Garshans won't. I'm stating that as a fact because, over the last thousand years, they haven't changed at all.'

Ranjak shook his head. 'There's too much sophistry in that argument. We haven't changed, either.'

'If you will pardon me, Your Magnificence, for . . .'

'My *what*?' the old man demanded. He was visibly shaken.

Rodnar grinned. 'Since I'm going to be one of your most loyal and devoted subjects I'd better be getting used to it.'

'We'll dispense with it for now. You were saying?'

141

'No sophistry. You *have* changed, and you're going to change the government. Not much, but a little here and a little there. Aren't you?'

'Admitted; but you are overlooking a point.' As a matter of fact, Ranjak had already changed more than he could have been compelled to admit. 'It is not of my own free will. You have used and will continue to use force; force with which I cannot possibly cope. Your argument is entirely fallacious.'

'Think a minute. Here's the clincher. Suppose Laynch were Supreme Justice and here arguing instead of you. I state as a fact that the only possible change any conceivable force could make in Sonednil Laynch of Garsh would be to change him from a live Garshan into a dead one.'

' Ranjak nodded. 'As you found necessary in the cases of the thirty two Grand Justices . . . I could name most of them, I think . . . but I would rather live. In fact, I can see some merit in your long-term program. Now, as for the short term?'

'It'll be to muster Grand Fleet. I don't know whether we can beat Laynch to the punch or not, but I'd rather have the fighting around Garsh than Slaar.'

'Naturally. Now as to details . . .'

'Details can wait, Your Magnificence,' Rodnar said, and he 'ported himself and Ranjak into the despot's sumptuous living quarters where he waited while the Tyrant changed apparel; then to the inner-sanctum private office in the Edifice of Justice.

In that familiar office the old man reverted instantly to his former self; stern, unbending, and dictatorial. For a minute or so Rodnar thought that he might have to do something about it, but he didn't. Ranjak, a firm pragmatist, had made a bargain and he was sticking to it. And why not? He was submitting to a little control, true, but no outsider knew it – and in exchange for that slight

142

concession he had not only his former full power, but also a surety of control that he had never thought possible. For getting so much the better of the bargain, who wouldn't make a few concessions? Particularly, when there was no alternative.

His return was without incident. He was the boss, accountable to no one for his comings and goings. His organization was very good. His people would carry on whenever or however long he chose to be away – or become eaglemeat. It was as simple as that.

While Rodnar stood inconspicuously in the background Ranjak punched a few buttons, issued a stream of curt orders, then called his First Secretary, telling her to bring in the tapes of whatever few matters might require his personal attention. Starrlah arrived in moments, all business, to be told to work out the earliest possible time for a meeting of the Council of Grand Justices, and to notify all surviving Grand Justices to attend.

While this was going on Rodnar kept up a steady stream of mental communication. 'Sweetheart – you look lovely this morning. So good to see you. It's been so long! Why, we haven't been together, for a day or two.' He noticed her heightening color, though her manner remained briskly professional, her expression unchanged. 'Careful, Starr – '

'Of course I'm careful, you darling idiot! But tell me – have you decided to let him know about us? We can't be tied down here with so much happening.'

Rod's thought was immediately serious. 'I'll tell him later today. You know he's making me Supreme Commander of the Guard of the Person – Status Five goes with the job – but a lot of flexibility will have to go with it too.'

Meanwhile – and this interchange took only seconds – Ranjak called for an eleven-way hookup and told his Cabinet of Advisors to be in his office in thirty minutes.

143

He snapped another order, then dismissed his FirSec with a wave of his hand.

In moments a crew of tailors came in pushing a machine and a rack of garments. Rodnar peeled off his clothes – and in fifteen minutes he was fitted with a royal-purple shirt, royal-golden shorts, and royal-silver sandals. Thus, when the ten advisors came in and bowed deeply – high-status people did not have to prostrate themselves – before standing stiffly at attention, Rodnar was rigidly erect to the right and behind Ranjak's throne-like chair.

'At ease,' the Supreme Justice said, and everyone relaxed a little. His gaze moved deliberately from person to person. Finally he spoke, his tones cold, his words carefully chosen.

'Anyone who refuses to admit the truth, knowing what the truth is, is a fool. The present truth is that psionics is a potent force. Properly directed, it can be of very great use to the State. Hence I did what I have done. This use of a hitherto wasted force has already produced important results in revealing a traitor in my cabinet. Sonluzor Lizor of Skane, from whom and for what treachery did you get that half-million junex that is now in Box NN728R in the Fifth Fiduciary?'

A man wearing the exact duplicate of Rodnar's uniform, screaming his innocence, threw himself on his face before the desk, but Ranjak's coldly stern expression did not change. 'Eaglemeat,' he said, jerking a thumb; and two burly guards entered to drag the screaming man out of the room. Ranjak went on, 'He, the Supreme Commander of the Guard of the Person, was to knife my complement and our children and our grandchildren, after I was assassinated. He was paid the mentioned sum in advance and was promised – falsely, of course – the Grand Justiceship of Skane.'

The nine facing him, beginning to turn pale, glanced at

each other apprehensively. Rodnar tossed a thought to Ranjak, who continued, 'I care nothing about ordinary nest-feathering, such as the two thousand junex Daughtnola Kada of Kange accepted for giving a certain man and his complement a certain pair of jobs . . .' A tall, good-looking woman turned white; then, as the Tyrant's face relaxed the merest trifle, flushed red, '. . . That is one of the perquisites of status. You all do it, and thousands of others. And the pair appointed are quite capable. Be very careful from now on, however, that greed does not result in the appointment of anyone unfit.' A pause, then he continued,

'I present to you Sonrodnar Rodnar of Slaar. He is replacing the traitor Lizor as Supreme Commander of the Guard of the Person. Rodnar, your place.'

Rodnar bowed deeply. 'Your Magnificence, I thank you,' he said, and took stance where the other man had stood.

'Having cleaned house,' the dictator went on, 'I will brief you on the situation regarding Garsh as it now is.' He did so. 'You will all begin immediately to put your departments on a full war footing. First strike is vital. Supreme Admiral Sonaxten Axolgan of Spath, I do not direct experts in the minutiae of their highly specialized crafts. You will, however, report to me from time to time, in broad, as to what is being done. But prepare without delay. Dismissed.'

They all backed out of the Presence except Rodnar who with a 'Your permission, Your Magnificence,' halted at the doorway. Ranjak smiled faintly. 'Of course, Rodnar. And what is on your mind?'

'Your Magnificence,' Rodnar began, keeping close watch on the Tyrant's mental reaction, 'I have news that may distress you. Your First Secretary Daughtelna Starrlah and I joined lives some time ago. We felt it was not –

expedient – then to register the transaction. We will now do so.' He paused.

There was surprise and regret in Ranjak's response. 'Does this mean that I will lose the best FirSec I ever had?'

Rodnar bowed. 'At least temporarily. It will be absolutely necessary that Starrlah and I take part in the attack on Garsh –'

'You mean she too – is a psiontist?' This was a shocker for the Tyrant. 'That during these years – ?'

Rodnar interrupted. 'Yes, she is a psiontist, but it has not been of long duration. She was a powerful latent with no recognizable psionic abilities until the Great X-storm. For her this produced a psychic trauma that suddenly released these powers, and now she is one of the most capable among us. And the two of us together are far greater than either of us alone. We will be far more useful in the coming battle than here in your service.'

Ranjak forced a smile but made no comment. Rodnar noted no reaction save surprise and regret.

'You will find, Your Magnificence, that Starrlah's First Assistant is quite capable, should you wish to promote her; and before I leave with the fleet I will have given you an incorruptible Guard of the Person with all key positions filled by psiontists. You will never have had such complete protection.'

And Ranjak thought, 'Nor as complete surveillance.' He added aloud, 'Is that all?' He sounded tired; it had been a trying day. 'You are dismissed.'

Rod backed out in approved fashion, then 'ported himself to Starrlah's office. Nothing needed to be said about what had happened; she had been an anxious observer. A fervent, exultant kiss – then she went on with her calling the farflung members of the Council of Justices.

CHAPTER 12

The Guard of the Person

At day's end Rodnar and Starrlah 'ported themselves up into their new apartment. Dwelling Unit Four Point Five Zero, Zero Zero of Quarters Five. Five because in the Justiciate the status of the higher-status one of any pair of complements was the status of the pair, and the Supreme Commander of the Guard of the Person was at the very top of Status Five.

There was, of course, no trace left of the previous occupant of the apartment. Even Starrlah was impressed by the magnificence of the furnishings and decorations of the place and both were awed by the beauty and perfection of art so lavishly displayed; but Rodnar, taking the girl by the shoulder, turned her gently around to face him. 'It's beautiful, Starr, I know – I certainly never expected to live to see Naizlon's original *Queen of the Ocean* in my own living room – but we've got work to do. Let's get at it.'

'Not just yet, Rod; I've got something important to do first.' She led him up to a full-length mirror and pointed. 'Just *look* at us side by side! I've simply *got* to do something about my hair before anything else . . . I wonder what color would look best with your new outfit . . . ?'

'Purple,' he said facetiously with a sly grin. 'Or purple and gold. Better yet, purple and gold and silver.'

'That's it!' she cried. '*Perfect*! Parted a little to the left of center, with one side purple, the other side gold, and a sharp streak of silver right down the middle. Thanks, you wonderful guy!'

He sobered. 'You wouldn't have the nerve.'

'I wouldn't? Watch my contrails! First thing in the morning. Now we can get to work.'

Their first care was to scan to its depths each mind of the Cabinet – Starr with her inside knowledge and Rod with his impartial analysis – and when *those* two probers got done with any mind, that mind had been through the wringer. Then, working separately, they went through the Guards of the Person, starting at the top and working down. The upper echelons were pretty solid stuff; career men and women mostly, who had grown up with the service and were doing their job. In the middle and lower brackets, however, they found quite a lot of eaglemeat – and, both now being of Status Five, either of them declared eaglemeat immediately upon discovering it, and it became so forthwith.

Neither was at all perturbed or felt any compunction about condemning fellow human beings to death. That was their job and that was their way of life; the fashion of their civilization and their culture.

Throughout the Justiciate there were no reformatories or jails or penitentiaries; no prisons of any kind. There were no juries; in fact no word meaning jury or any equivalent thereof. A civilian suspect was brought before an Arbiter; who, after hearing the evidence, announced his decision, from which there was no appeal. There were three possible decisions. Go free – pay a fine – become eaglemeat.

Government and military personnel were tried, usually very informally, by any convenient superior of Status Fifteen or better. The possible verdicts were the same as in civil life.

There was some corruption, malfeasance, and dirty work, of course; but not as much as might be supposed. Every person wearing a number had taken an oath that meant exactly what it said; plain-clothed spies abounded; and anyone caught violating their oath became eaglemeat in very short order.

However, the two psiontists were much more lenient than were most of the overlings of their time. They overlooked many punishable offenses, but they would not condone corruption or treason.

When Rodnar began to reorganize the Guard he was of course subjected to all the pressures that the about-to-be-displaced persons and their more-or-less powerful friends could bring to bear; but nothing worked. He was moderately wealthy through his bladesman's winnings, and he was aware that there were more important things in life than money.

Among these was the matter of status. Rodnar's status had been that of his father, forty seven; and through his victories in the arena he had gained status – but not in his wildest dreams had he thought of becoming a Five. Now both he and Starrlah were Fives. FIVES! Was he going to do anything that would jeopardize *that* status? Not by nine thousand clusters of suns!

And finally, and of over-riding importance, the Guard had to be the very best he could make it for the safety of the Justiciate and the defeat of Garsh.

While he was cleaning up the Guard, and seeing to it that every eligible Guardsman down to and including Status Fifteen was a capable psiontist, other things were happening.

The Justiciate was enlarged to one hundred eighty members; one from each loyal planet. This was a change from the arbitrary selection by His Magnificence of Chief Justices from those planets he deemed worthy. Those which had not been represented officially in the Justiciate had had planetary Chief Justices, of course; but they had had no direct voice in the affairs of the Justiciate as a whole. This was a source of dissatisfaction on many worlds; but none ever openly questioned the edicts of His Magnificence. Now this was changed.

The pioneer planet project Hope was abandoned before it really got started. The three Garshan planets – Garsh, Psi, and Quonike – had seceded from the Justiciate. The non-Garshan inhabitants of Garsh and Quonike had either emigrated or died. The Garshan population of one hundred eighty worlds had likewise either emigrated or died. In time, the strongest psychics of those hundred eighty worlds wore the purple, gold, and silver of the Guard of the Person.

By no means all of the psychics of the non-Garshan worlds, however, would join any such organization as the Guard of the Person – the hated 'Purps' – the Justiciate's powerful, dreaded enforcement arm.

The mystics, for instance, stayed away unanimously. They believed that the entire material universe was merely illusion; that the only Reality was in the mind and the things of the mind. That the only Reality rests in and is part of the completely immaterial entity that is the One. That each living creature possesses – on loan, so to speak, and enchained by the illusion that is the flesh – some portion of the One. By denial of the flesh, and by intense concentration upon Reality, he can eventually cast aside all illusion, fuse his ever-increasing portion of the One with the One and know the full, perfect, and eternal Truth.

Since neither Rodnar nor Starrlah could stomach any part of such squank, they did not try to recruit any mystics. Nor any pacifists. Nor any man or woman who could not pass fairly severe physical and mental tests. Thus it took a long time to fill all the places; but when it was done the quality of the corps was very high indeed. Every color of skin known to the one hundred and eighty

150

loyal planets – except of course for the red-brown of Garsh – was represented. There was not, nor could be, any racial discrimination where ability alone was the determining factor.

With everything organized and running smoothly, Rodnar called the one hundred seventy nine Grand Commanders of the Guard of the Person to a conference in the Edifice. He opened the meeting with, 'The Purps are now in position to –'

'Are *you* calling us "Purps"?' a surprised thought broke in.

Rodnar grinned. 'Why not? Everybody else does, always has, and probably always will. We're stuck with it. As I started to say, we are now in a position to operate as no police force in history has ever operated; and if we do a good job over the years that nickname will become a title of honor and respect, not a jeer. Any argument on that?'

There was a short and thoughtful silence, but no argument.

'To that end every planetary commander *must* act, always and in every decision for the good of the human race as a whole. In case of doubt a conference will thrash the matter out to substantial agreement or no action will be taken at that time.

'Next. In the matter of status we have all advanced tremendously, to the class of Fives. Also, we have all advanced tremendously in authority and responsibility. I am therefore adopting the system of equating psionic ability to status throughout the upper echelons of our organization. You Grand Commanders are now all Fives. Each of you has the exact decimal status rating of his or her psionic ability as determined by computation of all available data. Are there any beefs about this pecking order?'

There were no beefs. In fact, everyone was highly pleased.

'We thank you all. Now. Over the centuries, as the Tyranny has become more and more powerful and absolute, more and more people have been reduced to an animal existence. Thinkers have deplored this condition, but no one has been able to do anything about it. Every revolution or reform movement has been either crushed by the Justiciate or absorbed into it and become part of it. Knuaire of Spath reduced his thinking on this matter to four words, "Power, of itself, corrupts".

'I *think* that we Grand Commanders, by using all the psionic powers we have, can do something about this condition. To implement the method, however, we must give up one of our most cherished tenets. We must permit – in fact, we must *encourage* – in everything pertaining to our work . . .' He paused for a long five seconds, '. . . full and willing invasion of privacy.'

There was a concerted gasp at that, and a confused roar of thought. 'But why?' a woman demanded. 'I don't see any possible . . .' The thought died.

'I think you all see, but I'll draw you a diagram. There will be pressures and temptations that no world ever saw before. Things that I would not trust any living person, including my complement, Starrlah and myself, to resist. But with a hundred seventy nine other minds looking on, none of us would turn crooked. We couldn't. Non-psis would think that the other fellow was taking it too, so he'd fall. But we'd all know the other fellow was *not* taking it, and even without the tremendous mutual support we'd have, none of us would ever admit to being the weakest link in our chain of command. Would it work?'

The consensus was that it would work, and Sleht, now Grand Commander of the Guard of Skane, added, 'To say nothing of the fact you so delicately omitted, Rod, that anyone deciding to sell us out wouldn't live to collect his bribe.'

Rodnar grinned. 'It'll never come to that, I'm sure. It is agreed, then, that the corruptive agent, in order to be effective, would have to corrupt all of us at once. Considering the fact that we collectively have all the power there is – we actually *are* the Tyranny – can any of you think of anything that could make all of us turn traitor to the entire human race?'

There was a long and profoundly relieved silence. It *would* work!

'Very well,' Rodnar said. 'Think about it – see if there's anything all of us can't lick. Now let's try that mind-linkage thing. It'll be tough, compartmentalizing that way . . . it may take a lot of practice . . . but nobody'd peek, anyway.'

'*That's* for sure,' someone agreed, then added, doubtfully, 'I hope.'

There was a general laugh, and Rodnar said, 'No peeking, everybody, on honor. Say it.'

Still laughing, everybody said in unison, 'No peeking, on honor,' and then they tried the compartment-fusion.

It wasn't easy. In fact, it was the hardest mental work any of them had ever done. It wasn't at all like an open meeting of minds. It was still less like thinking into a group, in which process only surface thoughts were involved. It was analogous to dividing an open warehouse up into rooms, one of which could be thrown wide open while all the others remained tightly closed.

Everyone was skittish, jittery, and on a hair trigger. No one peeked, of course. What happened was just the opposite. At one time or another everyone leaked, generally a half dozen at once; spilling into the pool of police business such extraneous matters as fun-last-night, sex-affairs, hair-bleach, more-tonight, and so on. Whenever that happened solid blocks would snap up all over the place and they would have to start all over again. It was embarrassing to everyone; at times, extremely so.

However, those first ineffectual attempts showed so plainly what *could* be done that they all kept doggedly at it. Not one of them suggested abandoning the project. They worked at it all the rest of that day, slept in the Edifice that night, and tore into it again right after breakfast next morning. They worked until almost evening. Then, all of a sudden, one of them got the solution. She uttered a piercing mental shriek, showed everyone else the exact technique of doing it, and there ensued a meeting of minds of a kind, scope, size, and quality undreamed-of before in all space.

It was one tremendous mind, knowing everything of official business that any one of them had ever known, yet not befogged or cluttered up with anything except official business. Also, each individual mind now had the total police knowledge of the whole group. It was wonderful – aweful – utterly perfect – and for two long minutes they held that fusion; savoring it, appreciating it, marveling at it, reveling in it.

Then they broke it up and celebrated – a celebration that was not limited to the mental. Men yelled triumphantly; women shrieked ecstatically; men and women hugged and kissed each other and danced joyously throughout the big room. After the turmoil had subsided a little, Rodnar ordered up a banquet that was really a Royal Gorge.

At the end of that hectic feast Rodnar said, 'Thanks, all of you, for coming. More than thanks for what you have just done. We *thought* we were doing a job before, but now we *know* what we can do. We'll all drink a salute.' All stood up and raised their glasses as high as they could reach. 'To the Purps!' Rodnar shouted aloud.

'To the Purps!' came the response in unison, and they all downed their drinks. Then in perfect synchronization one hundred eighty one empty glasses clinked sharply against the bare tops of four long tables and one hundred eighty one persons disappeared. To where they disappeared and with whom, it was agreed, was private business.

Rodnar 'ported to his quarters where Starrlah waited. She knew, of course, of the successful completion of the meeting of the Grand Commanders of the Guard. After several minutes which had nothing to do with State business, Rodnar called for audience with His Magnificence Supreme Grand Justice Sonrathendak Ranjak, speaking to Starrlah's replacement, the new FirSec. Without delay he was admitted to the Presence, where, concisely but completely, he reported what had been accomplished; and that now, with the permission of His Magnificence, he and Starrlah would join the Grand Fleet.

Together, then, they 'ported out to a space-yard. They had figured out a thing. They didn't know whether or not it would work and they didn't have much time to check, since Grand Fleet was just about to blast off. If it *did* work, though, it would really be a something.

CHAPTER 13

The Attack on Garsh

Psychokinetics – sometimes called psychodynamics or telekinetics – is a subject to which very few non-psis have given serious consideration. Nothing worth while concerning it is in general circulation, since it can be handled only in the esoteric symbology of paraphysics and paramechanics; both of which disciplines are closed books to non-psionic minds.

Thus the belief is widespread that any psychic who can 'port a pencil one inch above a table's top can 'port anything anywhere he pleases. This belief is false. The laws of psionics are as immutable as those of mechanics. While it is true that the map is the territory, the map must be very finely detailed indeed – the psiontist must know the object's fine structure very well indeed – if great masses are to be handled psionically. Rodnar and Starrlah, however, did not know that – then.

Starr, before her explosive psionic development, was a strong, dynamic, brilliant woman. Rodnar found her an amazingly apt pupil. She quickly gained an impervious shield and achieved excellence in every common area of psionics including short- and long-range scanning, psychocontrol and teleportation.

Both could 'port themselves anywhere they wanted to go. Almost literally anywhere at all. Either of them could 'port a subspeedster from one solar system to another. So they decided to see what they could do with a superdreadnought.

They found out. Nothing. Neither of them could move it. Both of them together could not move it.

'Slankerosity!' Rodnar snorted in disgust. 'Just like trying to blow it away with our breaths!'

'Well, we'll have to do something else, then,' Starrlah said, practically.

Rodnar scowled. 'Such as?'

'Nothing definite – but maybe this,' and the two went into a lightning-fast exchange of ideas and plans. Finally Rodnar commented, 'I think we're ready to talk business with the admiral.'

Supreme Admiral Axolgan was amenable to reason, of course. If he had not been, someone else would have been Supreme Admiral. Wherefore, when the Grand Fleet of the Justiciate blasted off for Garsh, the Guard of the Person was left in charge of medium-grade personnel; every upper-bracket psiontist Purp, man or woman, was with the fleet.

Rodnar and Starrlah, while with the fleet, were not of it. They were together aboard a small scout-class cruiser; which, it had turned out, was the biggest vessel their combined powers could handle. They were hanging back, waiting for time zero minus sixty seconds – zero being the exact instant at which the Justiciate's immense fleet would emerge and begin to tear the ether apart with its beams.

Precisely on the count of sixty their cruiser emerged; within a thousand miles of Garsh's surface, well inside the Garshan defense in depth. Both scanned at top speed.

They knew they wouldn't have much time; much less than a minute. It wouldn't take nearly that long for the nearest Garshan battleship to detect their cruiser and bring a projector to bear on it, and if they were still there when that beam arrived – !!! – so they wouldn't be there then.

'You clicked, Rod,' the girl said.

'So far,' he agreed. 'But the crux is still ahead – but I don't *think* he's expecting us – if he is you'll have to dig him out – get with it!' and he launched his first bomb.

The capital city of Garsh was built on the precipitous face of a mountain; a mountain that plunged so deeply and so steeply into the ocean that the water a few hundred yards off shore was two hundred fathoms deep.

Rodnar's first bomb exploded against that city a scant quarter mile above sea level, with a power so appallingly vast as to jar the planet to its core; so incomprehensibly vast as to open half the faults of the planet's crust.

A huge part-sphere of emptiness appeared where buildings and rock and water had been; what had formerly been there had been transformed into sub-atomic debris. Then, as soon as matter could move and could become affected as such by the multi-million degree heat, the explosively-boiling water formed a wall and began to move violently and turbulently away. City and mountain, in the form of an incandescent liquid almost as fluid as water, rushed in torrents into the sea. Cubic miles of steam roared upward to join the hellish pillar of horribly transformed matter that was boiling straight up into the stratosphere. Higher and higher, more and ever more viciously raging, that pillar hurled itself upward, to spread finally into a mushroom cap many miles in diameter.

Neither Rodnar nor Starrlah observed anything of this, of course. They were too busy. She was scanning; he was launching bombs as fast as he could think. He annihilated the sixteen largest cities of Garsh before she told him to quit.

'Get ready!' she snapped. 'He *was* expecting us, the kfard, but I'm holding him . . . 'Port!'

They 'ported, a couple of milliseconds ahead of a beam that would have whiffed them out of existence, and braced themselves to meet the ultimately savage mental attack of Laynch and his complement. They took it on their shields and countered just as viciously – and just as effectively. Then two pairs of psionic battlers, probably the two strongest pairs of their whole space, stood still and fought.

While even the sense of perception was not at all clear in that rapidly-thickening murk of psionic force, they could 'see' well enough to fight. Laynch was standing stiffly still, with his right arm in a sling. His left hand gripped the back of a chair. His complement, a tall, splendidly proportioned woman, stood beside him, gripping the same chair. They were in a scout-destroyer, a vessel a little smaller than the Slaaran vessel, but big enough to carry plenty of bombs; each one of which was to have exploded in the vitals of a warship of the Justiciate. Each bomb, however, was still in its cell. Rodnar and Starrlah had known the earliest instant in which the Garshans could act and they had acted first. First by not very much, but by enough.

Both hawk-nosed faces looked more demonic than human. Both were twisted into grimaces of sheerest, starkest ferocity; the ultimately desperate ferocity of such conquest-lusting minds as theirs at seeing triumph, practically in grasp, turn so suddenly into frustration.

Rodnar, by contrast, *looked* relaxed. His physical self was standing apparently at ease; his face wore a grimly saturnine half-smile-half-sneer. But never were appearances more deceitful: he was putting out force enough to make the very subether boil.

Starrlah's whole body was tense. Her fists were clenched. Her face was set and pale. Her eyes were diamond-hard, steady, and utterly, bitterly cold.

In the flagship, at time zero minus twenty seconds, Supreme Admiral Sonaxten Axolgan of Spath whirled around to face Knuaire and Marrjyl, who were standing beside him. 'Well?' he demanded, savagely.

Knuaire's set face did not change; nor did the far-away

159

look in Marrjyl's eyes. 'No hold. Minus eighteen and counting.'

Knuaire's count-down was for their own information; it had nothing to do with either the absolute time of or the simultaneity of Grand Fleet's emergence. No. Zero time had been computed in nanoseconds and would take place by the nanosecond. Each ship had a timer operating on one single wavelength of monochromatic ultra-violet light. All timers were synchronized to within a very small fraction of the frequency. The operating leads from timer to operator, while only three inches long, were all made of the same composition of isotopically-analyzed silver; were all of the same length to within a thousandth of an inch; and were all kept at the same temperature – 4.28°K. Even so there was some error, but it didn't amount to more than a couple of miles.

'But what do you *see*?' Axolgan demanded.

'Nothing. It's so thick we can't drive a probe into it. They've got each other immobilized for the duration, is my best guess. I didn't expect anything like this, but Rodnar more than half did. So no hold. Minus eleven and counting.'

'Damned foolishness,' the admiral grumbled, half to himself. 'Only one planet. They *can't* have enough stuff to need half of this – nor a quarter.'

'You hope,' Knuaire said, quietly. 'Five – four – three – two – one – GO!'

The vast fleet emerged with battle screens full out and all its projectors began as one to blaze; and Axolgan got the shock of his not-too-war-filled life. All space around the planet was full of warships; the Garshan fleet was larger than his own! He said something to Knuaire, but got no answer. The psiontist-fusion was busy. *Very* busy. They were doing the work that Rodnar and Starrlah would have been doing if they had not been so hard at work elsewhere.

It is impossible to teleport anything into any volume protected by a capable psiontist; and Rodnar had insisted that every warship of Grand Fleet, of whatever tonnage, should have a psiontist aboard. Thus Grand Fleet could have been larger than it was, but Axolgan did not object to that. He thought it already four or five times too big for the job.

While the Garshan fleet was, at the moment of engagement, larger than the Justiciate fleet by two hundred twenty one units, the Guards outnumbered the Garshan psiontists by three hundred sixteen. Wherefore, in the first thirty seconds of plus time, five hundred thirty seven Garshan ships were blown out of space. Ragingly incandescent, furiously expanding fire-balls appeared where each unprotected warship had been.

Knuaire and Marrjyl came out of their trance and Knu spoke. 'Yours now, Admiral; you can fight the rest of this battle on conventional lines – I think. Plus thirty two and counting.'

'Thank the Power for that!' The old spacehound was very glad indeed to take over and to conduct the rest of the battle as a space-battle should be conducted.

Immediately upon emergence Grand Fleet had of course launched thousands of missiles. Immediately after detecting the invaders the Garshans had of course launched thousands of the same. Equally of course none of these missiles hit anything; automatic, instantly-reactive spotters and blasters and anti-missile missiles saw to that.

The dreadnoughts and supers drove up and slugged. The lighter, more maneuverable ships darted hither and thither; searching out heavies who were taking too much punishment, trying to slip a big one where it would do some good.

As soon as the battle situation began to stabilize, Axolgan began to use his numerical superiority. Percentage-wise it was small; but actually it was decisive. Through the linked minds of the psiontists he had full knowledge and, for the first time in his life, perfect control. Ten or fifteen of his 'loose' ships, all that were within striking distance of a target, would half-englobe one Garshan and pour in everything they could put out of vibratories, plasma beams, and atomic missiles. Objective – to blow the Garshan out of space before he could duck into subspace – was not attained very often, since it took almost perfect point-blank range placing of the attacking ships and almost perfect synchronization of their fire-power to do any really crippling damage before the automatic overload kickouts of the enemy could act.

Technically, however, a force-out was good business. Any ship forced to retreat that way weakened the enemy's formation and was out of action for some time – the exact length of time depending upon the quality and speed of its computers and the speed and ability of its astrogators – and every force-out increased Grand Fleet's numerical superiority. Thus the rate of force-out of Garshan vessels increased geometrically until, in just under two hours of ether-racking combat, all that was left of the Garshan fleet vanished at once. The Garshan admiral had decided to call it a day.

Although Grand Fleet hadn't made very many kills – only one hundred sixty six as compared with the psiontist's bag of five hundred thirty seven in the first thirty seconds of the battle – Axolgan was immensely pleased. One sixty six was excellent and he hadn't lost a ship. His astrogators and his powermen had been right up to the tips of their toes. Grand Fleet had done a Class A Triple-Prime job.

He was still smiling happily to himself when Rodnar and Starrlah appeared in his control room. (Laynch and his complement had disappeared with their fleet.) They both looked tired.

Rodnar glanced once at the admiral's smiling face and said aloud, 'Shall we break the bad news to him gently, Starr, about how many people we killed on Garsh, or let him stay happy until he finds it out for himself?'

Starr smiled a tired smile; her baptism of fire had been exhausting. 'Well, that's *one* way of breaking it gently, I suppose.'

The admiral's expression changed instantly. 'Don't tell me Garsh was *abandoned*!' he roared.

'Just that,' Rodnar informed him. 'Maybe a few technicians and supervisors on the automation, but I didn't perceive any. The net result of this whole operation is: scrub one abandoned planet.'

'Bub-bub-but . . . *how*?' Axolgan stuttered. 'How *could* they – and *why*?'

'That'd be guessing,' Rodnar said quietly. 'Knu, I told you Laynch has been plotting this thing for years . . . how wrong can a man get? Centuries – Laynch and his forefathers . . . finding Garsh empty rocked us back on our heels. What I'm wondering now is how many Garshan planets there are that nobody ever heard of.'

The admiral's jaw dropped in amazement and Knuaire stared, but Marrjyl had been thinking right along with Rodnar, perhaps a trifle ahead of him. 'So you think, just by pure dumb luck, we forced his hand? So they had to act before they were ready? Say another twenty-five years, or however long it would take for them to have more psiontists than we have?'

'I'm not thinking any more, Marr.' He grinned at her. 'I'm all thunk out, or else too damned tired to, I don't know which.' His gaze turned toward Starrlah. 'All I want to do right now is to go to bed and sleep for four solid days. How about it, sweetheart?'

'*Now* you're clicking, man of mine; you're really clicking.' She took his hand; and Rodnar addressed a final word to the admiral. 'The skeleton crew is bringing in the cruiser – and you will, of course, report to His Magnificence. We'll go planet-hunting later. After all, those Garshan worlds weren't developed in a day, and we won't find 'em in a day. The search will be our next order of business – but sleep comes first.' And Rodnar and Starrlah disappeared.

Marrjyl hooked arms with Knuaire and exclaimed, 'A right noble idea. Agreed, Knu? Sleep sounds very inviting.'

And a somewhat disconcerted Supreme Admiral Axolgan was alone.

In a conference room at the MetEnge headquarters on Newmars eight psiontists gathered at the suggestion of Carlyle Deston. In his call to each couple he had given the reason for his request – another venture into Second Space.

Because they had not seen each other for several weeks, time was spent in small talk, audible and enthusiastic.

Bernice Jones spoke above the hubbub, 'Not strictly necessary, of course,' swinging out the well-stocked portable bar by hand, 'but it's fun, especially since we're practically strangers. Drinks – smokes – name your poisons, ladies and gentlemen, and I'll play Hebe. I'll serve you with my own lily-white hands.'

'Bun the Barmaid, and a truly *rara avis* of the ilk.' Deston laughed and led a round of applause. Then, when all were settled, he went on, 'Okay, Herc, you aren't sold. Shoot.'

'I certainly am not. You know what happened to the *Explorer*. She lasted quick, and I do mean *quick*. Considering the stuff she had and how long it lasted, I'm dubious as all hell about going in with a thing that hasn't got screen enough to stop a flashlight nor a beam hot enough to light a cigarette. My personal opinion is that both you Destons are more than somewhat daft.'

'Hear, hear!' Train applauded, raising his glass. 'Or to put it somewhat less poetically – nuts. Squirrel food. The thing to do is wait for *Explorer Two*, so as to go in loaded for . . .'

'I object!' Barbara snapped. 'I object most strenuously to that system of nomenclature – it's strictly for cretins. *Explorer Two*! No imagination. Anyone with one-tenth of a brain ought to be ashamed of it.'

Train frowned. 'Can you think of a better one?'

'Of course I can. Almost *anything* would be better than *that*. Something original – distinctive. I was reading an old book a while ago . . .'

'A-ha!' Deston stage-whispered to Mrs Adams. 'The wench claims she can read printed words.'

Barbara faked a glare. 'That's all we'll have out of you, Babe. This old book was about ancient Africa – on Tellus, you know – when it was practically all unexplored jungles and swamps all full of poisonous snakes and monkeys and crocodiles. So I'm going to name our ship the *Safari* and if you don't know what that word means you can go and look it up.'

'Okay, but let's get back to business,' Deston said. 'That flat bust was my fault. I was over-confident. Cocky. It never even occurred to me that we might hit something it'd be smart to run away from. I wasn't even set to run, but this time I will be. *Believe me*, I will be! I'll do everything the sneaky way, and I mean *sneaky*. Carefully, furtively, on soft little feet. Timid like a mouse, and just as ready to scamper.'

The girls started to laugh and the men joined in. It was hard to visualize Carlyle Deston in the role of the Timid Soul; but they all knew that he could do it if he would, and he convinced him that this time he would.

Dr Andrew Adams made the deciding contribution to the discussion. 'My friends, I don't want to exert undue influence on your decision – but I can't stress too strongly our need for more data.' He hesitated, then continued with some uncertainty, 'For reasons which I can't pin-point, and which I suppose could be called instinctive, I believe more knowledge of Second Space is vital – and delay in acquiring that data could be very costly.'

Wherefore, a few days later, a light cruiser immerged and felt its way at low power through the indescribable something – or nothing? – that is subspace. Indescribable? Utterly. No ordinary passenger or spaceman ever looks into it. The ordinary mind cannot stand it. Psiontists can look at it – even though their physical senses reel at being extruded by force into that three-dimensionally-impossible region – but looking doesn't do even them any good. No two observers ever see the same things and not one of them likes what he sees. Thus the eight aboard the cruiser did not look with their eyes. They scanned with their three-dimensionally-impossible super-senses, which did not require transparent ports.

Ready for inter-space transit, Train said, 'We're taking it by steps this time. First step, rotation into alignment with Second Space, but we won't emerge. Ready? Hold onto your breakfasts.'

There came the well-remembered racking, battering, sense-shattering – but only momentary – shock of re-orientation. They scanned. They checked their instruments. Senses and meters and 'scopes alike told them that they were still in the same subspace they had known so long.

Jones' right hand reached for the EMERGE button, but stopped half way. 'You still think, Babe, they'll necessarily be friendly?'

'Maybe not exactly friendly,' Deston said, and paused.

'I can't say I'm exactly friendly myself. But they'll certainly be receptive, the same as we are. Damn it, Herc, they're *psiontists*. They *have* to be. Of approximately our own grade. Everything points that way. Those things we hit were automatics – they *must* have been. Minds of that caliber *can't* be barbarous enough to attack on sight without warning.'

'Automatic or not, *something* attacked us last time,' Train said dryly. 'Remember that, my friend.'

'I'm remembering it and I'll be ready to run, but I'm sure as sure that they've figured out things the same way we have. So I'm pretty sure that they're expecting us to visit them again.'

Barbara shuddered. 'What can they be like, do you suppose? Some kind of unspeakable monstrosities? Perhaps even indestructible entities of pure force?'

'That would be guessing and I'm a little afraid to guess. Okay, Herc, flip it – I'm set to flip her back in a musecond.'

Jones flipped it. Nothing happened except the peculiar 'feel' of Second Space; which, to the relief of all, subsided rapidly into normality.

Deston lifted his mental grip from the IMMERGE breaker and glanced at his board. 'Hey!' he yelped the thought. 'These instruments have gone hay-wire for fair! How about yours, Herc?'

'Here too.' Jones' eyes expressed his consternation. 'The kickouts ought to be yanking us out of here.'

'They can't. We're *in* space – a kind of space, anyway – remember?'

'Okay. So let's get the hell out of it, then.'

'Not for a sec. Didn't they act that way before?'

'I don't know.' Jones glanced at Bernice. '*We* don't know. We weren't here long enough and we were too busy to look. *Let's jet!*'

'Jetting!' Deston snapped the thought and snapped his finger down at the manual switch – and in that instant a far-questing synchronizing feeler of thought impinged upon their telepathic linkage and tuned itself precisely to it; and a razor-sharp, crystal-clear communication came in:

'Intelligences from another space, we greet. But *please* – either stop that frightful emanation or get out of our space . . .'

'Excuse it, please, we were already leaving.' Deston's finger had kept on moving, and fast; but so incomprehensible is the speed of thought that the message was finished in full before the cruiser's machinery could act:

'. . . but stay in subspace, please, and do not block this communication channel. We wish to confer with you as much as you must wish to confer with us. We follow you.'

CHAPTER 14

First Encounter

The Galaxian cruiser hung poised in subspace, with just enough power on to keep her from emerging into Second Space. Her crew of eight psiontists stood or sat frozen for perhaps fifteen seconds. Their expressions varied from astonishment to stupefaction. Even Adams the Imperturbable was no long writing down pot-hooks and symbols. He sat motionless, with notebook in left hand and ballpoint in right.

Deston, the first to recover, drew a tremendously deep breath. '*That* scared me a dime's worth. I claimed I expected it, but I see now that I didn't . . . I said they'd be intelligent, but I'm not a damn sure they don't suit me quite a much too well.'

White-faced, Barbara licked her lips and began to breathe again. 'Brother, I hear you testify. I'm scared witless. *Intelligent!* Listen – I quote – "Intelligences" – plural, you'll note – "from another space" – and if you don't think *that* made cold chills run up and down my back you're out of your mind – "we greet" – *that* bit helped a little – I've never in my life seen so much meaning packed into six words. I wonder how many of them there were?'

'Two,' Cecily said. Her hands were still fists, her freckles stood out boldly against the whiteness of her skin. 'Male and female – they'd have to be, of course, to work the Fourth Nume – in perfect sync. As perfect as Perce and I can do it.'

Bernice relaxed. 'That makes me feel better. If they're sexual they can't be *too* monstrous or incomprehensible.'

'That doesn't necessarily follow,' Stella Adams put in.

'Any two non-conjugate incommensurate three-dimensional spaces could very well be so variant that our numes would not . . .'

'Ps-s-s-st!' Jones cut in. 'They're here!'

The visitors came in sharp and clear, on the same extremely narrow, non-revealing band they had used before. 'We thank you, visiting intelligences, for waiting; and for the privilege of this contact. It is well that your customary mode of thought is diffuse, and not, like ours, on a sharply limited . . .'

'*Tighten it up!*' Cecily snapped.

'Ah? You can?' The Second Spacers' thought went clearly on. 'It is vastly more difficult to synchronize eight minds than two. Fortunately, however, the sidebands and leakages were enough to embolden us sufficiently to seek a meeting of minds; to assure us that our two races have some things in common. This is your first trans-spatial encounter, as it is ours. You are as apprehensive – to be truthful, as frightened – as we are. We have physical bodies based on the liquid state of the water that is two atoms of hydrogen mass one and one atom of oxygen mass sixteen . . .'

Thoughts – chemical, physical, and mathematical – flew lightning fast. Then came the coordination and comparison of basic standards. Temperature, of course, was easy. Water, nearly enough for a first approximation, froze at zero degrees and boiled at one hundred. Time and length, from unique spectral lines, were fairly simple. Pressure, by barometry, was very easy. Mass was a bit more difficult, but that of one cubic centimeter of ordinary water was close enough.

From that point on, progress was very rapid. Both races were warm-blooded oxygen breathers. Both were bisexual and were made of flesh. Of, as nearly as they could tell – neither Rodnar nor Starrlah knew too much biological chemistry – the same kind of flesh. The two atmospheres were very much alike in composition, temperature, and pressure. Body temperatures were, within human variation, the same. And, to the utter amazement of each side, the other was not only people-sized, but also near-people-shaped; erect, bifurcate, bilaterally symmetrical, one head on a neck, two eyes, two ears, one nose, one mouth . . .

Both sides lowered their screens enough to permit pseudo vision. The first reaction, of course, was one of almost stunned amazement. Then came a flashing exchange of thought, both between the groups and intra-group.

The three First Space girls looked first at Rodnar, but abandoned him quickly. They had much better men, they thought as one, of their own. Then:

'My God!' Cecily exclaimed. 'Just *look* at that emerald!' indicating the jewel hanging on a chain around Starrlah's neck. 'It's as big as an egg and it's genuine! And those gratings – '

'Those clothes – if you can call them that,' Barbara cut in. 'They're positively *shrunk* on; they're – '

'That *hair*!' Bernice said. 'Doesn't that three-tone job give you twinges of envy, Bobby?'

'A few, at that,' Barbara admitted. 'Maybe I'll try something like that some day. And aren't those bracelets and anklets simply *fabulous*? She's really a something. But who ever heard of an *ear*chain? Lobes never pierced or clamped – doesn't she want to, I wonder, or didn't it ever occur to them over here?'

And so on; and Starrlah, after scarcely a glance at the women, scanned the other-space men. 'Death of Eagles!' she tight-beamed to Rodnar. 'Just *look* at the size of those two men – and the *quality* of the bigger one – the craggy-faced one. Why, he could tear Laynch apart with those hands and eat half of him for lunch!'

171

Rodnar, however, was not communicating. He was observing with every sense he had; reading every sideband available; and filing every datum for future reference. He and Starrlah had just begun their search for the Garshan planets – a quest that inevitably had to be long and frustrating – and this had happened. This incredible contact with Other-Space beings was of tremendous importance; and he was taking advantage of every moment.

After a second or two Stella Adams assumed the position of hostess. 'It was a very pleasant surprise, friends of another space, to find people so much like ourselves. Will you please 'port yourselves aboard our ship so we can get acquainted? Strict protocol may perhaps call for the reverse, but you haven't room for all of us and we have plenty of room for you.'

'A second, please,' Deston said. 'I will, I think, second the invitation to you of the Justiciate; but first there is the matter of arms. The worn grips of your blasters and knives show that they are not merely ornamental. Will you join me in lowering shields sufficiently to reveal intentions?'

'Very gladly indeed.' Ten shields were lowered a little, revealing a tremendous amount of additional information, and the two Justicians smiled truly human smiles. Rodnar went on, 'I thought of suggesting a better contact myself, since there are eight of you and only two of us. You're not trying to make me think, are you, that physical weapons would be of any use against such minds as yours?'

'Frankly, I was wondering. I couldn't be sure, from such a superficial contact, whether they would be or not. Anyway, it'd be extremely embarrassing to invite supposed friends aboard and then have to throw them out.'

'It would be, at that,' and the two Slaarans came aboard. There was a moment of cautious sniffing . . .

'Okay?' Deston asked.

'Except for some strange – very peculiar – odors, which

of course were to be expected, it seems perfectly satisfactory. Have a whiff?' and Rodnar held out his rose-quartz flask – at the sight of which Cecily whistled expressively.

'Hold everything, man of other sp . . .' Starrlah broke off, flicked a feeler of thought at Deston, and went on, 'Deston? Carlyle? Carl? Babe? Squirt? Runt – surely not *Runt*?'

Deston laughed. 'Keep on digging, Starrlah, and you'll find I've been called lots of names worse than that. Since this, I hope, is only the beginning of a long acquaintance-ship, either Carl or Babe will do very nicely.'

'No.' Starrlah shook her head – even *that* gesture belonged also to Second Space! 'I don't know why, but your complement Daughtbar . . . no, Barbara of New-mars – wouldn't like it, so we'll call you Mister Des . . . *Now* what have I done? I see – I read a sideband of thought, "The Slaaran mode of thought seems to be one of truth rather than diplomacy" . . . your diplomacy, then, is in one-to-one correlation with lying.'

Adams laughed deeply. 'That, young lady, is putting it right into the well-known nut-shell.'

'I'm sorry, Starrlah,' Barbara rushed over and took both of the strange girl's hands in hers. 'Really I am. I was a little shocked, I admit, but I didn't understand you then. You'll both call him Babe, like the rest of us do. I'm Bobby Deston, the platinum blonde over there is Bun Jones, and the red-head is Curly Train. That big bruiser is Perce Train; the still bigger one is Herc Jones. This is Stella Adams . . .'

'But that's her real name . . . Oh, I see. We, too respect old people if they deserve it . . . Oh! I've made another – what do you call it? A break. A social error.'

'Think nothing of it, my dear.' Stella Adams laughed, and meant it. 'Variations in the proprieties are of course inevitable between two such widely variant cultures as our two. I can only hope that when we come to visit you I won't commit much more serious social errors than those.'

'That's true.' Starrlah nodded and went on, 'I like that idea of nicknames. We don't have anything like that, except just to shorten our own names – Rod for him and Starr for me. But I'm going to. I'm going to think up a good one for him. But Babe, about that noisome squampf Rod's offering you. If you're not lined with chemically-pure lead, sniff it easy – it tears at the lungs like the beak and claws of a wild mountain-king eagle.'

Deston sniffed cautiously, then inhaled deeply. The stuff was good! It was entirely different from anything he had ever had in his lungs before, but it was *very* good. Barbara tried it too, but she didn't like it at all. 'I don't like your poisonous Mexican cigarettes, either,' she said, 'and *that* stuff – "squampf" is exactly the right word – is even worse.'

'He *is* lined with lead,' Starrlah said, and went on explaining her emeralds – particularly her emerald flask – to the fascinated Cecily. 'Dress is a weakness with me,' she admitted. 'And emeralds are expensive, yes. Worked and carved like this, extremely so. But none of this cost me anything; it's been handed down from mother to daughter for over six hundred years . . .' and very shortly several brands of cigarettes and two flasks of inhalant were circulating freely.

This participation in social amenities did more to cement a friendly relationship between the mankinds of two spaces than any amount of purely cerebral exchange could have done.

Then they got down to business. First the Justicians went into the matter of the Galaxian interference – the X-storms with their incredible disruptive power; how they had studied them, finally building the mighty counter-generators which they had placed in the areas of space

174

indicating greatest activity. They told of the Great X-storm and the destruction of fifty nine of the sixty defensive structures; of the finding of the mass of rhenium alloy; of their tentative deductions.

Earlier storms, it now appeared, had been caused by leakage of the inimical energy generated by Galaxian liners from subspace into their space. When the Galaxian super-vessel was actually in their space the damage was of course much greater and vastly more widely spread.

In turn the Galaxians told of their problems – the occasional vanishing without trace of a subspacer; of Adams' deductions concerning the zeta field, created, it would appear, by the near-passage of vessels from first and Second Space, unlikely as this approach seemed in the vast emptiness.

At this point Adams spoke aloud, wonderingly, 'But why, really, the accompanying zeta field? In some way the Grahams must be involved, since those same Grahams create X-storms in the world of the Justiciate.' Adams halted, startled. 'Why did I say that? I don't *know* that the Grahams cause the X-storms! Or do I?' He fell silent, scowling blackly. One thought persisted, hidden, revealed to no one. The Operator!

Starrlah entered the discussion. 'May I ask – how long has subspace travel existed among the Galaxians?'

Deston answered. 'Approximately one hundred and seventy five years – but really extensive commerce has had a far shorter span. It was accelerated by the growth of colonization throughout the Galaxy. I suppose really heavy travel is no more than fifty or sixty years old.'

'Ours has a longer history – but it is significant that the scourge of X-storms seems to have intensified with the greater activity in your space.'

'An important datum,' Adams commented. 'It makes

more logical the elementary assumption that our subspace losses sprang from our own increase in flights.'

Referring to their current experimental venture into Second Space, Deston asked, 'How did you detect us – become aware of our entry? There obviously was something . . .'

Rodnar nodded emphatically. 'There certainly was! We detected the very beginnings of an X-storm. Our instruments went wild. Impossible readings. Your interference, however, was of such short duration – and at the first sign we began scanning, and fortunately were able to detect your thought pattern almost instantly – and your departure followed so promptly that no real damage was done to our cruiser.'

'It's quite understandable, I think,' Adams said. 'Your sixty generators were designed specifically to block some one component of our drive. Our own energies accumulated and back-fired. The *Explorer* encountered such intense fields and put out so much energy that she was crippled; the energies involved here were not of a magnitude to do your cruiser any real harm.'

'That's probably it,' Deston agreed. 'But they've got a drive that doesn't interfere with . . .'

'Naturally,' Adams said, dryly. 'Considering that the number of possibilities is very large it would be strange indeed, even if the two spaces were exactly alike – which is highly improbable – if their system would be the same as ours. Indeed, the fact of the interference would preclude the possibility of their being alike.'

Minds united then and flashed over the two systems. At the Chaytors, both Justicians were profoundly shocked. 'Eagledeath!' Rodnar snapped. The thought was perfectly clear, but all that the Galaxians got out of it was that it was an oath. '*What power*! But of course you wouldn't . . . ?'

Deston grinned. 'But of course I would. Except for the

176

few items we've been hiding from each other so carefully and so politely – planets, co-ords, and so on, you know – I'll tell you anything you want to know. In exchange, that is – you've got a lot of stuff we want to know about, too.'

'Such as?' Starrlah asked.

'You don't use Grahams or any facsimile thereof, and that's . . .'

Jones whistled. 'They don't, at that. InStell'd give a megabuck to get rid of 'em – cut maintenance ninety percent, as well as saving carrying spare units and five hundred miles of Graham wire on every liner . . . And maybe, as Doc suggested, the Grahams are the cause of the trouble in Second Space!'

'Almost certainly we'll find the Grahams at fault!' Adams displayed rare excitement. 'The Grahams interacting with something, some phase of Other Space. As you know, I try to avoid coming to conclusions without adequate data – but in this instance I believe we'll find that the Grahams are behind both the X-storms in Second Space and the zeta fields in subspace. And if this is so, the elimination of Grahams in our drive should solve both problems.' Adams hesitated. 'Call it a hunch if you like – but I shall be greatly disappointed if I'm mistaken.'

'I'd bet on a hunch of yours any day,' Deston exclaimed. 'And given a little time I think you'll come up with math to prove it.'

'Before continuing with mechanics,' Rodnar said then, 'I am emboldened to ask you a question of psionics. Your Chaytors, in some way or other, give you all the power you want. But how can you possibly control – direct and handle – enough power to whiff out fifty nine of our sixty generators in almost no time at all? I am a Subspace Technician First, and Starr and I are Psiontist Firsts; yet we can't understand it.'

Deston, Jones, and the Trains linked up and showed

177

them; and since the explanation was purely psionic, both Rodnar and Starrlah understood it instantly.

Discussion went on. Neither side could understand the subspace drive of the other. Nor did that fact surprise any of them, since all knew that each drive was the product of many decades of work by thousands of specialists. Hence, after only a few seconds of struggle, Deston said, 'No use. None of us knows enough detail. All of us together don't. I'll give you the manual.'

He 'ported the 'manual' – a tri-di projector and miles of tape – out of its cabinet and said, 'Better not try to study it here or to get it all at once. Take it home with you. We'll pick up another one back at Base. You carry something similar, I suppose?'

'Yes.' A metal-bound carrying case, about the size and shape of a steamer-trunk, appeared. 'That will give you everything you need, I think. May I suggest that we set up a communications relay in subspace, so that either side can get in touch with the other in case of difficulty?'

'That'd be smart – and easy.' It was easy and they set it up. Then Deston said, 'One more thing. Those blasters of yours. Plasma jets. We have plasma-jet projectors, but they weigh a hundred metric tons per each and take myriakilowatts of power. We have miniaturization, too, but it hasn't got *that* far. I don't suppose you have a manual on the blaster.'

'No. Something better.' Rodnar grinned and one of the utterly vicious hand-guns appeared on the low table at Deston's elbow. 'Here you are. Now we'll say goodbye and thanks.'

'Not quite yet, please,' Adams said. 'An operating manual, however complete, will not be enough. We will need much basic material, such as . . .' He told them at length what he wanted, and they got it for him.

Then the Justicians left; and, back in their little subspacer, gave way to emotions that were mixed indeed. During a long technical discussion they steadied down, and after they were back to normal Rodnar said, 'They impressed you, too, tremendously – especially their Captain Jones.'

'Yes. Very much so . . . in strange and contradictory ways . . . and yes, Herc Jones especially. If you weren't my complement, and if I were an experimenter, I would have suggested an experiment.' Starrlah was remorselessly, uncompromisingly honest with herself and with her mate. She did not like 'diplomacy'. 'But I couldn't really like him . . . or respect him. I can't understand how such really able psiontists can possibly be so weak-kneed. So wishy-washy. So . . . so senselessly squeamish. Can you?'

'No, I can't. From sidebands, however, I read enough to know that their civilization is vastly different from ours. It's much weaker . . . softer . . . gentler.'

'But how can you get anything *done* that way?'

'I don't know. We'll have to visit them some day – maybe – and find out.'

A pause, then Rodnar added, 'In the meantime, you realize of course that this must interrupt our search for the Garshan planets. If we can get the Other Space power source, their Chaytors, and some other improvements they may perhaps provide, it will make our job much easier . . .'

'Right now we need Knu and Marr . . .'

Aboard the Galaxian cruiser, after the Justicians had left, a tensely thoughtful silence endured for minutes.

'My . . . God . . .' Cecily breathed, finally. 'I expected to be surprised; but not that way or that much. That Starrlah *looks* like a highschool girl, but . . .' She paused, helplessly.

179

After another silence Barbara nodded. 'But she very definitely isn't. She's a hundred and forty pounds or so of unadulterated Bengal tigress. Babe, with their actual brains – and being top-bracket psiontists, too – how can they *possibly* be such utter, *utter* savages?' The Galaxians had done much sideband reading, too.

Deston shook his head and Bernice said, 'I can understand how a man could be, perhaps, but she's just as bad as he is. Why, they're actually killers!'

'They're weirdies, no fooling,' Train agreed. 'I wonder – just what kind of a culture could produce people like that?'

'For me,' Deston said, 'I'm not a damn bit sure I even want to find out – ever. Either one of them would just as soon cut your throat as give you the time of day.'

Dr Andrew Adams remained aloof from the discussion; but on a tight band he and Stella exchanged a thought. That startling vision they had caught of a race of utter savagery – it was not these beings – but there was a kinship. That glimpse had come out of Second Space! Had it been prudent to exchange information with their visitors? In retrospect it hardly seemed wise . . . yet at the moment it had seemed the logical thing to do. The Operator . . . ?

In GalMet's vast Research and Development Center on Galmetia, in a private laboratory, Deston, Jones and Adams worked on that enigmatic blaster from Second Space.

For a side-arm it was brutally heavy, weighing just under six pounds. Its barrel, made of a metalloid-ceramic unknown even to Adams, was eleven inches long and an inch and a half in outside diameter. There was no breech-block; no breech mechanism of any kind. The upper part of the thing was all barrel. The bore, only a quarter of an inch in diameter, centered the barrel and was wide open – full length and at both ends. It was aimed by sighting through the unobstructed bore.

Coils and complexes of insulated silver wire were imbedded in the barrel's substance, but there were no visible nodes. Both front and rear orifices were clean, smooth and bright, showing no burning, pitting, or erosion. In spite of this fact, however, the grips of the butt – which was located a couple of inches ahead of the rear orifice – showed so much wear that the checkerwork and knurling had all but disappeared.

Inside the butt, instead of a magazine or a power-pack, there were mazes within mazes of wire; solidly, immovably imbedded and connected to nothing at all – not even any one to any one of the others. There were only three moving parts: a trigger, a front-plate and a back-plate. All of these would move under the stress of operation, but not one of them could move more than an eighth of an inch and not one of them could touch anything except a stop molded into the ceramic.

The only replaceable item was an encapsulated pellet of U-235 the size and shape of a .45-caliber bullet; which, also, was not connected to anything. Deston knew it was Uranium Two Thirty Five, even though a scintillometer could not detect any radiation from it.

After studying the thing for four solid days without learning anything at all, they took it to the Laboratory of Standards, where a weighmaster spent two hours in weighing it to the limit of attainable accuracy. They then took it up into the hills, where they took turns firing it against a cliff; each in turn holding it until his hand was numb. After eight hours of this, after making a lake of incandescent obsidian, the weapon was just comfortably warm; and the front orifice – there had been no backward emission of any detectable kind – was as bright, as clean, as virgin as before.

Next morning they took it back to Standards, where the same expert weighed it again . . . and who, after lunch, reported that it apparently had lost approximately three one-hundredths of one milligram. 'But this loss,' the weighmaster concluded brightly, 'is no doubt due to wear – you handled it so much yesterday.'

Deston seethed quietly to himself all the way back to the laboratory, where he again drove into the thing and through it with every possible application of every sense he had and of all the lore at his command. Then he grabbed it, hurled it to the floor – where it made quite a dent in the polyplastic tile – and kicked it across the room; the while cursing it vividly.

'Tut-tut, my boy,' Adams soothed him. 'Mustn't let your anger get the better of you. That's a juvenile outlet.'

'Juvenile, hell!' Deston flared. 'I'm not even that. I'm a babe in arms . . . a fetus . . . a Mongoloid-idiot fetus, at that . . . you know what this whole damn business reminds me of? A gang of Australian bushmen trying to figure out a ram-jet engine. What I think we'd better do is admit we're licked and go call Rodnar and get some dope on it.'

Adams smiled. 'I came to that conclusion some time ago, and I hazard a guess that he needs more information very badly, too.'

'Huh?'

'As I told him at the time, any operating manual is insufficient. It takes too much for granted. For instance, what does your manual say to do when . . . say when, for instance, the square wave of 'scope twenty six begins to show round corners?'

'Why, you change your 4T6PD, of course . . .' Deston broke off and whistled.

'Precisely,' Adams said. 'Since everyone know exactly what a 4T6PD is, no additional information is necessary –

but how will your young friend find out that it itself is an extremely complicated plug-in unit?'

Deston nodded. 'That makes me feel better. They could be in the same jam we are, at that.'

'I'm sure of it. The basic material I brought back, while sufficient for the one purpose, does not cover the underlying theory of this weapon. The sciences of the two spaces developed along somewhat different lines. Thus I am sure Rodnar is having trouble, and I have it in mind to suggest a school in subspace, where scientists of each space may study the sciences of the other.'

'Could be . . .' Deston said. 'Sounds good, the way you say it. I'll call Rodnar and find out if he's as stupid as I am.'

He did so. Rodnar was. Knuaire, theoretician, and Marrjyl, designer, had been called in to work with him – and together they had gotten nowhere. Starrlah had been wanting for days to call Babe, but Rodnar had been dragging his feet – wanting 'just a little more time' to see if they couldn't get it without Galaxian help. The rest were sure he couldn't, and he himself was just about ready to give up.

Adams went briskly to work. Theoreticians of both sides were called in. They met in intense mental conference and agreed that it would take a long time for each group to absorb fully the basic knowledges of the other. All agreed that such an exchange would be of inestimable benefit to both. A starship was sent out from First Space and a few dozen psiontist-theoreticians went busily to work; with Adams, of course, as co-ordinator.

For the long pull, then, everything was on the beam; but Deston and his crew did not want to sit on their hands and wait. Neither did Rodnar and Starrlah – especially not Rodnar and Starrlah. They had some really important business to do that *had* to be done. Hence, even before the College was much more than started, a great deal of bartering went on; the largest item of which was swapping Chaytors for blasters.

Rodnar and Starrlah wanted also a light cruiser of the Galaxian fleet, in operating condition; for practical study, they said, and actual tests under various Second Space conditions. They would pay for it in blasters, manufactured goods, diamonds, emeralds, gold, or platinum, or they would swap a Justiciate vessel of the same class and tonnage for it.

Since the First Space engineers wanted a full Grahamless drive to study, the swap was made. The two Slaarans accepted delivery of the Galaxian cruiser in subspace and 'ported it to the Guard's shipyard on Slaar. There they made sketches of, and issued orders concerning, certain structural changes to be made in it; the principal one of which was the installation of an auxiliary Justiciate drive, so that it could operate in their space without blowing out every instrument within range. Then they 'ported themselves home to wait impatiently until the work was done.

CHAPTER 15

Garshan Espionage

Immediately after the defeat of the Garshan fleet and the discovery that the planet Garsh had been abandoned, Supreme Admiral Axolgan gave Psi and Quonike, the two inhabited planets of the Garshans, the logical treatment. Every military or semi-military installation, works, plant, base, fortress, or facility was bombed out of existence without warning or opportunity to evacuate personnel.

Regiment after regiment of space-marines landed. Martial law was declared and rigidly enforced. All weapons, down to knives having blades over two and one-quarter inches long, were confiscated and destroyed. The penalty for possessing a weapon one day after the issuance of the edict was death on the spot. Assembly was forbidden, but any group that formed in spite of that order was not dispersed. One horizontal, waist-high slash of a blaster ended it – as well as any bystanders near by – and neighborhood Garshans either cleaned up the mess or became part of it.

One hundred eighty thousand leading citizens, men and women, were seized. Their minds were read. Then they were shipped away unharmed (any more than had been necessary, that is) to feed the eagles of one hundred eighty planets at special celebrations. All those minds told the same story; a story that they all believed implicitly.

'Where are those warships?' the questioners had demanded of every person arrested. 'Where are the psiontists? Where are the ground officers and the staff?'

And every person gave the same answers. The Garshans were a proud race; holding honor vastly above life.

If they had not been ordered to submit they would all have killed themselves, too; but no high-status Garshan would ever be found alive. Rather than surrender and feed the eagles of the hated Justiciate, every Garshan captain had blown his vessel, with its full crew and their complements and their families, into impalpable vapor with an atomic bomb. Every psiontist and every officer aground had loaded a speedster with high explosive, taken his family aboard, gone out into deep space, and blown themselves to bits.

The prisoners all knew, beyond any shadow of doubt, that all this was true. That was the Garshan way. Any Garshan in any position of authority would have to do just that; he could not possibly do anything else.

The Justices were skeptical. Knuaire and Marrjyl were skeptical. Rodnar and Starrlah were extremely skeptical. They and thousands of other psiontists scanned all three planets, cubic yard by plotted cubic yard. Then ten thousand psiontists took to their subbers and scoured all explored space and beyond; and found nothing of what they sought.

Then Supreme Justice Ranjak called a special meeting of the Assembly of Justices, to which he invited the Grand Commanders of the Guard of the Person.

At that meeting Rodnar advocated, and then demanded, that the planets Garsh, Psi, and Quonike be bombed with cobalt and strontium and left barren for millennia to come. There were lots of inhabitable planets available and those three would make good examples.

Many others agreed with him, but the Assembly voted against the action by a substantial majority. Nor was this vote due entirely, or even largely, to the genocide involved. It took time, money, labor, material, and people to develop a new planet. One new planet was a tremendous burden for many years; three such, all at once, was unthinkable. Furthermore, those three planets were already highly developed, highly productive, and all contributing, each in a unique way, to the economy of the Justiciate. They would keep on doing so. As for being made examples, the way all Garshans would be treated would be a better example to all would-be rebels than would three barren planets. As for the high-status rebels still being alive somewhere . . . well, that was of course possible. With that possibility in mind the Guard of the Person would be even more vigilant than before. After all, that was their business, wasn't it? The Assembly of Justices adjourned.

The Garshans had always been fighters; they had been at war somewhere most of the time for over a thousand years. They were the Master Race, destined to rule all space. The pure blood of Garsh was the highest possible form of life; all other races were fit only to serve those of the pure blood. Nor was that blood diluted. Alone of all the races of man, they kept their blood pure. There were no Garshan half-breeds. Miscegenation, or even casual inter-racial liaison, made eaglemeat of both parties to the crime.

All this, the Creed of Garsh, was known throughout all explored space. What was known only to high-status Garshans was what was being done to implement that Creed. Only they knew that GREAT DAY was coming; the day when any surviving inferior races would live only to serve the Master Race. The real ability and the real brain-power of the entire Garshan race had been aimed for centuries at one objective – GREAT DAY.

Having real brains, the Garshans had never quite overstepped the line of aggression at which the Justiciate would wipe them out. Instead, they nibbled; and during that nibbling they made such contributions, particularly in technology, to the culture and to the economy that the Justiciate could not afford to wipe them out. Thus they grew and grew, as fast and as widespread as they could without provoking punitive action.

First, they conquered and practically enslaved all other races which for one reason or another had taken up residence on Garsh. Second, they fortified that planet and built a fleet that was ostensibly one unit of the Justiciate's Grand Fleet. Third, they conquered gradually and developed fully the planet Quonike. Fourth, they colonized an uninhabited planet, named it Psi, and advertised it as a haven and an ideal dwelling-place for psychics of all kinds and abilities, regardless of grade, power, status, age, race, color, or religion. At that point, as far as anyone not of the elect knew, they stopped expanding and devoted all their energies to development and consolidation.

As a matter of fact, however, they had not stopped their expansion at all. They had merely shifted it to a much healthier location in space – one not in the galaxy at all, but in a star-cluster well outside it. First one planet, then two, then three, and so on. Population exploded. Technology soared. Billions of pure-blood Garshans – the Master Race; the Ordained to Rule – were being driven and were driving themselves in a fashion sheerly impossible to any race other than one of starkly dedicated fanatics: which is what the Garshans were. They believed implicitly in Garshanism. They refused to consider any belief or any philosophy of life other than Garshanism. Their minds were closed.

At this time, then, when Emperor Laynch of Garsh was in the full prime of youth and strength, he and the Garshan Council of Advisors decided that everything was ready for Great Day. The date was set and detailed orders were given out. The exposure of the Justiciate psiontists advanced the date by the merest trifle.

Laynch himself was confident; proudly, superbly confident. He, the strongest of all Garshan psiontists, was therefore the strongest psiontist alive. That fact was axiomatic. Nevertheless he had tested its validity, over and over, on the proving grounds of the planet Psi and had proved it valid. It was unthinkable that any member of any inferior race could give him any trouble.

He was literally and terribly appalled, then, when Rodnar of Slaar stopped his knife four inches short of taking the life of the Supreme Justice. The fact that he could not free knife and hand from the Slaaran's grip didn't help a bit. The fact that a *woman* slashed his wrist added insult to injury. The fact that Wayrec, one of his top psiontist spies, died; and that the Guards were killing his people in a ratio of fifty to one was a bitter fact indeed; but it was a fact. Thus Laynch was seething with a scarcely-imaginable mixture of fury, chagrin, consternation, and frustration when he flashed the order for the surviving psiontists of his breed to 'port themselves back home.

He was even more furious and even more appalled when Rodnar and Starrlah held him and his complement to a scoreless tie while the Justiciate's Grand Fleet destroyed or forced out of action the mighty Garshan fleet that, with his help, would certainly have been victorious. It was in no gentle frame of mind, then, that Laynch sat on his throne in the Room of the Throne in the Edifice of Garsh – very similar to the Edifice of Justice – on the planet Newgarsh.

He was still seething; pent up; hovering one degree below his extremely high flash-point. Although no sign of strain showed in any lineament of his hard face or in any muscle of his hard body, even his iron control could not keep that almost overmastering fury out of his eyes. It had been only by the grimmest of grim resolve that he had forced himself to accept postponement of GREAT DAY and had sworn to work toward a new DAY exactly as he had worked before. It was all he could do now to keep from slashing to bits the man standing rigidly at attention before him.

This man, apparently a Slaaran, in full Guard uniform and with a sub-captain's insignia on the shoulders of his collarless purple shirt, was in fact Laynch's top Intelligence ace.

'Report!' Laynch snapped the thought.

'Thank you, All-Powerful,' the spy said, and that title was strictly true, as far as the Empire of Garsh was concerned. The spy went on, 'There were no – I repeat, NO – supernumerary psionic minds of Status Six or higher detectable on or within my range of the planet Slaar at time zero minus one second. At time zero plus one second there were over two hundred of them in the Room of the Throne itself. Therefore they must be able either: One, to screen their minds without using a perceptible shield, or: Two, to operate from and through a distance greater than my limit. Either of these alternatives, All-Powerful, leads unavoidably to the conclusion that their powers are greater than we supposed. They have concealed much from us.'

'I deduced that much myself.' Laynch's thought was dry and cold. 'There was no leakage of their counter-plan? No hints, bits, or scaps that you could piece together, as you did on so many other matters of great importance?'

'None whatever, All-Powerful, and that fact made me think along a new line. I re-analyzed all my data and found that all significant information leaked from psiontists of Status Six or lower. All leakages and sidebands emanating from Status Five have been trivial or false. This shows that all Fifth-Status sidebands and leaks are deliberate.'

'But they can't . . .' Laynch choked himself off. They could and they had. This was another bolus he would have to swallow. He went on, 'What do you recommend?'

'I recommend, All-Powerful, that I be authorized to use enough psionic power to work my way up, gradually and normally, to Status Five and displace one of the lowest-ranking Grand Commanders of the Guard by having a quarrel with him and killing him in a duel. Only so, I believe, can I learn what Sonrodnar Rodnar of Slaar – DAY curse his shade and shadow! – really has in mind.'

'There are two objections to that.' Laynch shook his head. He was cooling down and beginning to think with his usual clarity. 'It was decided that a sub-captain of Status Eleven was as high as you could safely go. Even if you could live to reach Five – which you will admit is doubtful – how long do you think you would last there?'

'Quite possibly long enough to learn something of value. I am expendable, All-Powerful.'

'Not *that* expendable, Yanark.' For the first time during the interview Laynch spoke aloud; his voice even carried a trace of something barely resembling warmth. 'I will bear the matter in mind, but nothing will be done at present. You are too valuable a man to risk on any small possibility of gain. Keep on as you have been doing. That is all.'

'I thank you, All-Powerful,' and Master Spy Sonraken Yanark of Slaar vanished.

His place was taken by an elderly, scholarly-looking man, apparently a yellow-skin; a brilliant mathematical theoretician who was attending the Interspatial Conference. He began to explain the actuality of different spaces, but very little information came through to Laynch.

'Call them co-ordinates,' Laynch ordered, finally. 'Not exact, you say, but the meaning is clear. You can't learn the co-ordinates of this other space or how to get there?'

'It is as yet impossible, All-Powerful. We have not as yet been able to establish stable reference planes in subspace, although we hope to be able to do so very shortly. In the meantime it requires a highly special and extremely rare type of psionic mind either to perceive the existent degree of incongruence or to exert the unique force required for interspatial rotation. Also, most unfortunately, these abilities, unlike other psionic powers, seem to be unteachable and non-transferable. Even the Doctor Adams, a very intelligent man, a highly capable Psiontist First, and the Supreme Director of the Other-Space force, does not possess that ability. There is in all his space only one matched pair who can do that type of work. Their names, completely unlike ours, seem to be Percival and Cecily . . .'

'Never mind names!' Laynch snapped. 'Where are they?'

'I thought of that, All-Powerful. They should be taken, studied, and used. Unfortunately, however, no one seems to know where they are. They seem to be Overstats, so that no one can give them orders. Fortunately, however . . .'

'Get to it, wind-bag! Isn't there *some* way of finding them?'

'I was coming to that, All-Powerful. The Other Space vessel in which our Conference is being held is now aligned with our space, not with theirs. Hence, before that vessel can return to its own space, of which event I will have ample notice, this uniquely-powered pair will of necessity come aboard. That will be the only possible time and place of taking them, All-Powerful.'

Laynch drew a deep breath of relief. 'You do use your brain occasionally, at that,' he said. There was no trace of the exultantly savage picture that appeared in his mind – a galaxy of pacifists whose knowledge and resources were his for the taking. The interview went on.

That interview was followed by another . . . and another . . . and still others . . .

At home, in Apartment Four Point Five Zero Zero Zero, Rodnar and Starrlah stared at each other wordlessly for seconds. Finally:

'Well?' she asked.

'W-e-l-l,' he replied, slowly. 'Yes. It stinks; the whole deal stinks. As the big Jones man said, "it stinks in spades".'

'You're clicking, man of mine. Those noisome Garshans aren't a bit deader than we are. Especially Laynch, the slankerous kfard.'

'And more especially the fleet,' he agreed. 'And *that* fleet wasn't built on any one planet. Nor on any eight or ten planets that we know anything about. I can answer that question now, Starr, about how stupid can a man get. I know all about . . .'

'Oh, I wouldn't say that, Rod.' She laughed, even while shaking her head. 'After all, you know, we didn't have much of anything to go on. But now we have and we'd better jet – and as that same Jones said, "You can play that in spades, Mister" . . . that meaning of the thought "spades" isn't clear . . . it's another one of their idioms that escapes me . . .'

'Don't get side-tracked, girl. You agree that there was no tip-off about our blocking their attack on the Justices.'

'None whatever. Laynch was the most surprised man in the universe. So Status Five is tight, but we knew that already. But I also agree that there must be a leak in the outfit somewhere. The big question is where. Right here on Slaar, don't you think?'

'That's my thought. There's a distance effect, especially on faint sidebands and leakages. He'll have to be up pretty close.'

'But there's very little leakage on the Sixth, Rod.'

'I know, but experts don't need much. They mosaic it, you know.'

'That's true . . . there's more, of course, as you go down . . . but they don't know anything really important down there . . . and on the Sixth, Rod, there simply *can't* be anything deliberate. No treason. We examined every one of them ourselves.'

'Likewise the Sevens, Eights, and Nines. So that tells us the "how". There's a hell of a good reader around here somewhere who knew altogether too much about that fleet action . . . a mind of at least Grade Six in a job no better than Ten . . . he could be a loner, but I don't think so. Do you?'

'I certainly do not . . . we're riding the same beam, Rod. Being a Purp would be his best chance, so he probably is one . . . and since that much down-status at that level simply isn't possible, he's a Garshan. He has to be.'

'I'm not so sure, Starr.' Rodnar frowned in thought. 'That doesn't necessarily follow. Spies of all races and colors work at the trade. Freelance. For hire to the highest bidder.'

Starrlah shook her head. 'I know, but this would almost have to be a special case. This is – *must* be – a high-up; someone real close to Laynch; and anyone who is for sale will sell out. Do you think that Laynch would trust anyone except a Garshan in this particular spot?'

'Probably not. You're right, I guess . . . So it's a Garshan we have to look for. One certainly with a bleached skin and probably but not quite as certainly with a plastic-surgery nose . . . We can check the numbers . . .' He broke off and grinned as she looked at him quizzically, then went on, 'I told you I was stupid. He'll prove to be Slaar-born, of course, with a pedigree as long as mine. His parents will be dead. So we'll look for skin-pigment and a nose-job. I don't imagine he could get every pigmented cell bleached alike, do you?'

'I certainly do not. It'd be impossible, is my guess. Especially since he's getting away with it for years and must get a little bit careless now and then. Or maybe they can't bleach clear through, or maybe several other things. So we go rig our minds up for spectroscopy and go through the Tens and Elevens like a couple of destroying angels.'

They consulted expert after expert in many different fields. First they studied the scars and marks and structures necessarily left by plastic surgery of the nose, which did not take long. Then they studied skin structure, skin pigmentation, and skin bleaching. They learned what the skin pigmentation was, in every race of man; how it developed and where and in what molecular form it occurred; the effect upon each such molecule of the various bleaches that could be employed. Then, applying these knowledges to the Garshan skin, they tuned their minds to the most probable molecular configuration and went out looking for it.

There were many thousands of men and women to be examined, but those two examiners could work very fast. Finding each individual was the bottle-neck; but even that did not take too long. Each Captain-of-Hundred knew exactly where each of his people was at all times – that was part of his job – so each Captain acted as guide, unknowingly, of course. Hundreds by hundreds, the search went on relentlessly.

CHAPTER 16

Quest – and Quarry

Jones had said that the building of the *Safari* would be a very long job. Ordinarily it would have been, requiring many months. However, when all the resources of such a tremendous organization as METALS AND ENERGY are put behind a crash-priority project, when expense is no object whatever, that project goes very fast. The work was divided into many sub-projects; to each of which was assigned all the people – picked people, too, experts all – who could work on it efficiently. And the work went on continuously; during twenty four hours per day every day.

There were new things in the internal structure of the giant craft, developments growing out of the several conferences; and design changes were needed to accommodate the Graham-less drive. Provision had to be made for avoidance of the kind of power over-load which had blown out the Chaytors; but these presented no insurmountable obstacles. After the fundamentals of the Second Space drive had been worked out and tested, they found the operation simpler and more efficient than the standard drive, hence there were no serious hold-ups at all. Instead of many months, the job was done in half that many weeks. Its cost was fantastic; but, as has been said, cost in this case was the least important of all the factors involved.

The immense warship-laboratory was finished and put through a series of grueling tests. A few bugs were found and were corrected. She was stocked with everything that anyone thought might prove useful on a voyage into the starkly unknown. Then came the selection of the personnel; or rather, of the population of the worldlet. All the couples who had made the previous crossing volunteered and were accepted; they and their children came aboard.

Stella Adams joined them, somewhat reluctantly leaving her Andy; but they felt it was important for her to provide the tight link between him and the *Safari* while he attended the Interspatial Conference. He could always 'port aboard the *Safari* if he were needed.

Recruiting went on. The tests were tough – that of interspatial rotation being very tough indeed – but there were thousands of applicants and in time all places were filled. Giant *Safari* immerged, rotated dimensionally, and emerged into Second Space. Deston called Rodnar, who interrupted his own work long enough to come, to check, and to report that the huge Galaxian sub-spacer was not putting out any X-interference at all. He was invited aboard, but had to decline. He was busier, he said, than any four men ought to be.

Then the galactic survey was begun. This was of course to be the merest, sketchiest preliminary; a hit-the-high-spots-only quickie of a few weeks instead of the years a real survey would require. With Adams at the Conference, he had sent Doctor Arthur Brashears, also a Fellow of the College, as a worthy substitute – and Theodore Jones was an astrogator second to none.

The most fiercely brilliant objects in that strange galaxy were nailed down first, into the primary grid. Then a couple of thousand somewhat feebler suns – sector-markers, these, each within psionic range of at least two others – would be tied together into a secondary grid, which would be tied solidly to the primary.

When this secondary grid was started, as soon as they knew that if they found anything of interest they could find it again, the Destons and the Trains and Bernice Jones began to tape down their quick-peek, hit-and-run

197

reconnaissances of a couple or three more-or-less-representative solar systems of each sector. Barbara, as before, worked on water and fuels; Deston on metals. Train handled the entire field of planetography. Bernice and Cecily, their minds so different yet so powerful, worked together on life. Bernice, exquisitely sensitive and of tremendous reach and scope, found it. Cecily, with her slashingly decisive analytical mind, aided by Stella Adams, classified it; or rather, and touching only the most obvious life-forms, they made a stab at phylum, class, and order. And Bernice, working with them mind to mind, put down their joint guesses as to the planet's ecology. It was not a scholarly effort, but even such rough notes as these might prove helpful, and doing it was fun.

It was their custom after supper to take a regular hour of loafing in the lounge. During one of these periods Deston said, 'Curly, for a while I've had a thought in mind. I know that Doc, besides being the boss, is probably the biggest wheel that ever lived. I'm sure, Stella, you'll agree. I also know that you Trains are very special stuff. Of course all of us to some degree can handle 'most every kind of psionic power, but in 'porting you two have abilities far beyond anything we can do. So – if the rest of us can take it – how about sharing the wealth?'

Cecily laughed. 'Of course. We should have done it before, I know; but honestly, I never thought of it except at exactly the wrong times. Link up, Perce . . . Ready, the rest of you?'

'Ready,' Barbara said. 'Pour it on, you two.'

The Trains 'poured it on', and it was stiff stuff. Brutally stiff. But those minds could take it, and they learned everything there was to know about interspatial relationships and interspatial rotation and orientation. But no amount of knowledge gave the others the sheer power of the Trains; the heavy 'porting remained their province.

Since subcaptains of the Guard were high-status persons – usually Elevens – each unmarried subcaptain on Slaar had a good two-room apartment all to himself. All these apartments were pretty much alike. The walls, ceilings, and floors were permanently decorated with a very good grade of art. The essential furniture, too, was assigned and was bolted immovably in place – in the exact places dictated by the artistic and esthetic unity of the room's total design. Thus the only latitude possible was in the tenant's personal belongings, each ordinarily-visible item of which had to be approved by the section's director of art.

In view of these restrictions, not much individuality was possible. The apartment of Subcaptain Sonraken Yanark of Slaar, however, was much more individual than most, since every movable thing in it was oriented to music. He had his own hi-fi set, which was just barely approvable for size. He had a bewildering array of recorders and other sound devices. He had all the music-oriented art he could get approved. Commodious closets were half filled with reels and spools of tape and wire, and a quarter of his pay went religiously to buy more.

His love of music amounted almost to fanaticism. He had two loves, his work and his music; and cared practically nothing for anything else. He had no hobbies other than music; no intimates, and no even-casual friends except a few other officers of the Guard and a few other music-lovers.

He had taken some pains, however, not to be too offensive or misanthropic about his isolationism. He went to occasional parties, although never twice with the same girl. Professionals, he said, were better than amateurs in any field; in the sexual as well as the musical. Occasionally he attended games and plays and meetings of various kinds, but he did not even pretend to enjoy them. He was merely and very obviously bored. Bored numb. Many times, in fact, he went to sleep quite openly. Wherefore, needless to say, his name did not appear on any list of eligible men.

Thus, without causing comment or arousing suspicion, he spent practically all of his free time alone in his own rooms. Supposedly and apparently he was listening to music and studying one or another branch of it. Actually he was scanning, reading, probing indetectably at governmental, regulatory, managerial, and executive minds up to and including those of Status Six. He very rarely got very much during any one 'period of relaxation', but he always got something. Bits and pieces. Scraps of this and that. Careless or deliberate bragging in bars. Unguarded minds in the heat of sexual passion. Angrily careless after-thoughts of differences of opinion concerning matters of high policy or decision or action – these were very informative indeed. Bills of lading – shipments – movements of money and men – these items and thousands of others went: first, into Yanark's coldly competent encyclopedic brain, and: second, onto a tape or wire. To all seeming, there was nothing but music on any of those records. It would have taken an expert of experts to find any trace of anything else; and, if found, it would have taken a platoon of experts months or years to break the code employed.

While each bit was of itself unimportant, the summation was informative indeed. Rodnar would have been appalled if he had even suspected how much Laynch's top Intelligence agent really knew. For, as a matter of fact, Yanark knew just about everything that was not kept tightly sealed behind the impenetrable and leak-proof shielding possible only to psiontists of Status Five.

Rodnar and Starrlah did not have to hunt up all of their subjects one by one, of course. Military-style inspections of hundreds were frequent, and by half-hundreds and quarter-hundreds even more so. With the men in formation, they could scan a hundred men in about half that many seconds. Target, feet. Not mainly to avoid the head, although that was a consideration: principally because the skin beneath and between the fourth and fifth toes was the best place to look. It was one of the hardest locations to get at, and the one that, in the opinion of both searchers, would be considered the least important.

It was at an inspection of hundreds that Starrlah found the spy. Action was thereupon so nearly instantaneous that it seemed automatic. Their two linked minds pounced as one, gripping the mind of the luckless wight so savagely that teleportation was impossible. So was the sending out of any signal. For the barest flick of time three figures stood where only one should have been; then there were none.

While no one had actually seen anything in detail, the captain and the three remaining subcaptains had a very good idea of what had happened, but not why. They knew it was Fifth-Status business, and as such was none of theirs. The less they knew about it the healthier they would be. Wherefore the inspection went on exactly as though the missing officer were still in his place.

None of the rank and file knew anything; nor was any one of them ever told.

And in the beautiful living room of their apartment the two Fives went savagely to work. Rodnar held the spy motionless; Starrlah hurled orders all over the city. Clerks by the dozen dropped whatever they were doing and scurried to filing cabinets and to machines. They found precisely what Rodnar and Starrlah had expected them to find – that the record of Sonraken Yanark of Slaar was flawless in every respect. So were his antecedents and his connections and everything pertaining thereto. He had been cleared as a Class A Double Prime security risk.

Neither of the Fives even thought of gentleness or of mercy in dealing with the spy. This was a Garshan. So the two minds drove in against their captive's hard-held block – and paused momentarily in surprise. This mind was a high Six or a low Five; much more powerful than either had expected. He must be near, or possibly at, the top of Laynch's whole Intelligence section!

'That is correct,' Yanark said aloud, through tight-locked teeth. 'Since you know that much there is no point in trying to deny it. But that is all you will learn from me. I am expendable. I can take anything you can give me; so do your damndest, you swinishly slankerous *white* kfards!'

Then Rodnar and Starrlah bore down and really put on the pressure; a pressure so unbearable that even a high Five would have been forced to leak; and after a quarter of a minute of that punishment some scraps of information did begin to come through. He reported directly to Laynch . . . they saw him standing before the Garshan throne – saw Laynch, his hand heavily bandaged and his right arm in a sling . . . but they already knew all that stuff . . .

'*Where* is Laynch?' The question was driven remorselessly in. '*Where* is the Garshan fleet? *Where* are the Garshan planets? How *many* Garshan planets are there in all?'

And sketchily, piece-wise, fuzzily, flickering in and out of existence, an almost unreadable picture began to form. A group of stars . . . yes, a star-cluster . . . in a line just to the right of the Eagle-Claw Nebula . . .

202

But the Garshan knew he was leaking, and he knew what to do about it. He was, even in his own mind, expendable. Wherefore, instantly and without hint of intent, he collapsed his shield; and when forces such as those tear into and through a completely unshielded mind there is nothing readable left in that mind. The man was probably already dead; but, just to make sure, Rodnar pulled his blade – only to be stopped cold in midstroke, knife, arm, and body alike, by the full power of Starrlah's mind.

'No, Rod, *no*! *Stop* it!'

'Huh? Wha'ja mean stop it?'

'I *won't* have blood all over this beautiful rug!'

'Oh. That makes sense, at that.' He sheathed his weapon, broke the spy's neck with his hands, and then, after assuring himself that the Garshan was unquestionably dead, he 'ported the corpse out into space and set it on a collision course with the sun.

A mental message to Rodnar's Second-in-Command, in which he was told only as much as he needed to know, resulted in the prompt 'porting of every movable item in the apartment of Sonraken Yanark into Guard's headquarters where experts promptly set to work on the long study of what the Garshan spy had accumulated. Obviously, of course, summaries and conclusions had long since made their way to Newgarsh.

CHAPTER 17

Revelations

Though they had eliminated Laynch's number one spy, Rodnar and Starrlah still had much to do. Each had devoted many hours to studying their problem, then they had compared results and had studied it together. They agreed that Laynch must have a Garshan psiontist attending the Interspatial Conference. Since Knuaire of Spath was a Fellow of that Conference, they asked him to find that Garshan and learn, if possible, what the spy was really doing. The Garshan was found without trouble and without any revelation of the search; and Knuaire 'ported into the RodStarr apartment that same evening.

'You were right,' he reported, after greetings had been exchanged and the three had settled down in the living-room. 'There is a Garshan Fellow – Marrjyl actually found him. Sonlanjann Skeejan of Skane. A yellow-skin with a reworked nose. I was never so shocked in my life. Damn it, I've known the man for years. He's one of the top theoreticians of all space. He has a string of degrees as long as your arm and publications to fill box after box. I checked his number. Everything is on the beam, clear back . . .'

'It would be; it'd have to be,' Rodnar said, and told Knuaire about Subcaptain Yanark of Slaar.

'I see. Bomb-proofing. Anyway, we went over him again, and found hundreds of cells showing unmistakable Garshan characteristics, even though he is doing – or getting – a very good bleach-and-dye job. So I'm sure he's a Garshan. As to what he's doing, he's studying. *How* he's studying! Except for me, I wouldn't wonder if he's getting more stuff than . . .'

'Hold it!' Rodnar broke in. 'I get a sideband there. You're taping their whole civilization?'

'I'm trying to,' Knuaire admitted, 'but it's a supreme mess. How it works at all is a mystery. I have ten reels of it so far and not a foot of it makes sense. It's such a weirdie, such an unbelievable mixture of . . .'

'We know that much about it ourselves,' Rodnar broke in. 'So when you get it published, we'll buy a set. But about that yellow-skinned scholar. He's studying. He's also, we know damn well, reporting to Laynch everything he learns. So, just to be on the safe side, I think we'd better . . .'

'Just a minute, Rod!' Starrlah snapped. 'I don't think so. Killing him would probably . . .'

'Huh? Are you getting squeamish?'

'No, I'm not. Listen. Killing that noisome Yanark was all right – and necessary. Spies always get killed if they get caught; that's an occupational hazard. Killing him didn't cause a ripple and won't. Laynch will know we did it, of course, but it won't pull any triggers – he must have been expecting it all along. But this Skeejan is an entirely different pan of sknarr. He's a *scholar*. Of course he's learning stuff for Laynch, but . . .'

'He's a Garshan,' Rodnar said, flatly. 'That makes eaglemeat of him. That alone.'

'Of course, but I said *listen*!' she snapped. 'If he gets it now – no matter how – Laynch will know we did it. So he'll know we aren't sticking to our regular business, but branching out all over the place. From there it won't be much of a jump – hardly a step, in fact – to the conclusion that we're coming out into his own star-cluster after him.'

'Um-m-m-m . . . Could be . . . and that *wouldn't* be good.'

'And besides, what could he possibly find out from those Big Domes that would do us any . . . Oh! Excuse that crack, Knu, please. I didn't mean . . .'

Knuaire laughed. 'Think nothing of it, Starr. I'll blame it on Thaskarr – that's one of his catch-words that really caught on. Starr's thought is sound, Rod, but both of you seem to be overlooking the point that any possible damage has already been done. Most of those Other-Space psiontists – and many of ours too, for that matter – are working screens-down most of the time. So Skeejan has had plenty of time to report anything Laynch is interested in.'

'Probably so, at that. For a check, what's your thought on what that would be?'

'As a long-term project, I'd say he wants all the data he can get on invading Other Space and conquering it. Short term, what he wants most is their rhenium technology – they do incredible things with it, especially in missiles – and of course their rhenium. None of their psiontists – with the possible exception of Adams, who can't read – know anything about it, from a practical standpoint. Not a kinto's worth.'

'That's about the way I see it . . . so we hadn't better kill Skeejan, at that. Maybe somebody else will expose him or we can take care of him later. Anything else, Knu?'

'Only one item of any importance. Interspatial transit. Did you know that it takes a perfectly-matched male-and-female pair to do it? That there's only one pair alive, as far as anyone knows, who *can* do it?'

'We certainly didn't . . . but wait – I remember – Cecily and Percival Train. What incredible power! They were tossing that ship around – dozens of times as big as anything Starr and I can move – like it was a bit of fluff. But I supposed the others could, too. There were no sidebands that those two were the only ones who could do the crossover from one space to the other.'

'There wouldn't be,' Starrlah said. 'They're above all that – they aren't the braggy type.'

'You can take it as a fact,' Knuaire said. 'Their psion-tists know it and make no secret of it. So the only way Laynch can get across to Other Space is for that pair to operate his ferry for him. You've met them, I haven't. Would they co-operate, do you think?'

'If I'm any judge, they wouldn't.'

'He'll take them and try to force them to do it, then.'

'*That* I'll make it a point to watch,' Starrlah said. 'They'll chew him to bits.'

'Are they *that* good?' Knuaire demanded.

'They're that good,' Rodnar said, slowly. 'Those eight, at least. Any of them could kill two of me . . .'

'But they wouldn't,' Starrlah put in practically. 'They're too . . . well, kind of squeamish. They wouldn't kill anybody unless they absolutely had to, not even that noisome Laynch.'

'That's my thought, too,' Rodnar agreed. 'But you can give a man plenty of punishment without killing him, and I think they'd do just that. However, except for those eight, there was nobody aboard that ship any better than we are – if as good.'

Knuaire thought for a second, then said, 'Adams is the only one in the Conference who would grade above medium Six; no one else there even compares with you two. So their space is probably safe from Laynch . . . unless he can take that couple by surprise. It might be a good idea to warn them . . . what do you think?'

'By all means,' Rodnar agreed.

'I'll take care of it, probably through Adams. Or – I'll be seeing Deston . . .'

'Tell him I'd like to talk with them before they leave.'

'I'll do that. They're weirdies, no question, but you have to admire 'em in some ways. One sure thing; their screens don't leak anything they want to keep inside.'

The conversation went on for another hour or so, then

Knuaire 'ported back to the Conference. Moments later Rodnar and Starrlah 'ported into his speedster and they took off. They knew where the star-cluster was – there was only one on any line just to the right of the Eagle-Claw Nebula – so they went there in one long subspace jump. Then they started to look.

Compared to a galaxy, or even to a spiral arm, a cluster is small. Nevertheless, it fills a lot of space and contains a lot of planets. Therefore it was a week before the psiontists' far-flung, ultra-sensitive detector web encountered a pattern of human thought. They located the planet and flashed up to it. It was Garshan.

Then the fine work began. In a way it was a repetition of their Orkstmen experience. Delicately, insidiously, they probed and studied, extremely careful not to touch, however fleetingly, any mind able to feel that touch. They examined minds and cards and filed documents. After hours, when offices were closed, they studied mile after mile of tape. They avoided observatories and other places where star-charts could have been found; they did not want to find any touchy Garshan psiontists – yet.

Such sketchy examinations as these, of only one part of one planet, would not except by pure luck reveal all the planets in the Garshan system. Each one, however, named and placed one or two or a few others; and these in turn supplied still others. They found the planet New-garsh, the Empire's capital world, but they did not stop there then. They kept on going until the circle was complete, until they knew surely that there were fifteen planets, and only fifteen planets, in the Garshan Empire. Then they went back to Newgarsh.

Now the really dangerous work started. Far above electronic detector range, they set their speedster in a carefully computed orbit around Newgarsh, fixed directly above the capital city, Garsh; and Rodnar and Starrlah lay

208

motionless on their beds, with every iota of their minds concentrated on their task.

They had to get the answers to three questions. Where was the Garshan fleet? What was its maximum strength? What was Laynch's plan?

They started at Status Fifteen and worked up, using the utmost care, with a delicacy of touch perfected during their session on old Garsh. They got – just as Yanark had done, but much faster – bits and pieces and fragments of information. They probed and probed and probed; and finally they got fairly complete answers to the first and second questions, and got a few hints as to the third. But no one knew Laynch's plan except himself. The only one else who knew much of anything about it was Supreme Admiral Songondo Grollo. Unlike Supreme Admiral Axolgan of the Justiciate, Grollo was a supersensitive psiontist, and as such he would react to the slightest touch of thought.

He did. With the first hint of reaction Rodnar and Starrlah appeared for an instant beside the admiral, but there was no eye present to see. Nor psionic alarm, for he had no time to send out a thought. They yanked him out into the little speedster. That speedster vanished; and, in subspace, went so fast and so far that there was no possibility of anyone tracing any element of its flight.

Well beyond the six-sigma limit of probability of detection or interference, Rodnar and Starrlah went to work on the mind of Admiral Grollo. They put on the pressure and held it; they bored and they probed and they dug and they stabbed. It is questionable whether any human mind could have withstood that brutally savage two-pronged attack; certainly Grollo's mind could not do so.

And, unfortunately for the Garshan cause, the admiral did not commit suicide at first contact. He was expendable – just as expendable as Yanark or as any other Garshan except Emperor Laynch – and he knew it. That is, he knew it in an empirical, didactic sort of way, but, deep down, he did not really believe it. He was too valuable a man to spare. Also, suicide was the coward's way; the easy way out. He was no coward, but a fighter; a strong and able fighter; the culmination of a thousand-years-long line of the strongest and ablest fighters of the Garshan race. Wherefore he set his blocks and fought back with all the fierce power and all the stubborn pride of his long heritage.

He leaked; and every scrap of information so released was seized and stored away. First, the inquisitors completed their knowledge of Grollo's own department, the Garshan Navy; its full roster of ships, where they had been built, where the bases were and how they were concealed, the present location of the fleet, what sealed orders were now in the admiral's hands, and so on – no details of which are of any importance here.

Then as to Laynch's plans; and here the first information obtained – it had to do with what the Emperor was going to do to Rodnar and Starrlah – was definite, detailed, and entirely new. Grollo was apparently the only real confidant Laynch had, except possibly for his complement, and the Emperor's thoughts about those two white psionists, even at second hand, frizzled to a crisp the very ether through which they passed.

Those thoughts, while interesting, were not really important, so the pair forced the admiral to think of something else; of what Laynch intended to do about the Justiciate and about Other Space. This field was not so productive, as even ultra-stubborn Grollo began to realize that he was giving away top-secret stuff; information that was never, under any conditions whatever, to be revealed. Wherefore Garsh's Supreme Admiral released his hard-held blocks and died instantly.

He had, however, resisted a little too long; had leaked a little too much. The two, after 'porting the corpse out into a sunward course in space, stared at each other for seconds before sending a thought or saying a word.

Before either spoke, Rodnar flashed a thought to Knuaire at the Interspatial Conference. 'Hope I'm not interrupting anything too important.' On Knu's instant reassurance he continued, 'Can you join us – now?' He gave a swift summary of what had happened and what they had learned, then followed with the co-ordinates.

That quickly they were a trio.

'Oh, I wish he'd fought a second longer!' Starrlah voiced her frustration. 'But he can't – he can't possibly do anything like . . . even if he could get across to Other Space . . . they *can't* have such missiles as that – a hundred and seventy five *thousand* gravities? Why, that's – it's preposterous!'

'Nevertheless it's true,' Knuaire said, quietly. 'It's common knowledge in the Conference. That rhenium alloy, you know.'

Rodnar did some fast mental arithmetic, then whistled though his teeth. 'I see. For a rough estimate – at a range of five hundred miles or so – one second's travel – they'd be logging about a thousand *miles* per second – and with Chaytor intake – they couldn't be stopped, Knu, by psionics or anything else.'

'I know that. So does Laynch. That's why he has got to have their rhenium. Or find a lot of it here, which he probably won't.'

'He'd rather have theirs, anyway,' Rodnar said.

'Oh, I wish we could have found out how he was going about it!' Starrlah exclaimed. 'He would have to force those Trains to do it for him and how could he? Can you extrapolate that far, Knu, with the data we got?'

'With a pretty high decrement of probability, yes.' The

master theoretician thought for minutes, then went on, 'There are several methods possible for him to use . . . the most probable of which, I believe, would be to concentrate everything they have of both physical and psionic power.'

'But that wouldn't get them anywhere,' Rodnar objected. 'The Trains would kill themselves first.'

'Would they? I considered that point in the light of everything I have learned about their culture and I am not at all sure that they would. We would, of course. So would any Garshan of status. However, the Galaxian system of thought – their entire culture – is vastly different from ours. They may not be weaker . . . that is, not exactly . . . softer? Gentler? There is no exact term of comparison. But you exchanged thoughts face to face with their strongest; what is your thought?'

'I see what you mean,' Rodnar said, slowly. 'The Trains could very well submit . . . temporarily, say, with the thought in mind to take corrective action, once back in their own space . . . knowing nothing of their space or their resources I have no idea of what such action would be . . . but yes, the Trains might do just that rather than leave all their fellows, men, women and children, stranded forever in a foreign space.'

'That's a thing, too,' Starrlah put in. 'Why under all the shining stars have they got their *children* along on such an exploration into the unknown as their expedition is?'

Both men shook their heads and the girl went on, 'That baffles me completely. It's the most cretinous idea I ever heard of – I'm going to ask that Bobby, next time I see her – but in the meantime we'd better get hold of Babe, don't you think, and warn him?'

Rodnar nodded. 'I think just that. If we're only partly right he hadn't better go anywhere near that Conference ship without having everything he's got loaded full up and on the trips.'

212

The subber immerged and hurtled toward the big subspace communications relay. Rodnar activated it and set out Deston's call. Minute after minute went by without reply.

'How far away can they get?' Starrlah demanded. 'This thing covers half the galaxy, doesn't it?'

'With the Chaytors and converters *they've* got they can go anywhere,' Rodnar said. 'So we'll get some more of these sets and pile 'em up in series until they'll cover the whole galaxy and half of intergalactic space. They must be reached.'

Suddenly Knuaire interposed, 'I'd like Marr in on this conference, if you don't mind, Rod – I think some heavy planning is in order.' Rod nodded; and with the thought Marrjyl appeared.

The Garshan Emperor's office, located between his private apartments and the Room of the Throne, was large and very ornate. Red and green, the colors of the Empire – a pure, intense, brilliant red and an equally pure and vivid green – were everywhere; in art, banners, streamers, and standards. Laynch's desk, a tremendous thing of fine hardwood, was so lavishly inlaid with flat-ground rubies and emeralds that it, too, was mostly red and green. The entire wall behind the desk was one huge mosaic picture, depicting in exquisite – if more than a little sickening – detail red-skinned warriors destroying all other races of man.

There were four secretaries, splendidly-proportioned young women wearing red shirts and green shorts. There were ministers of state – Supreme Lords of this and that – and guards by the score; all dressed in the royal colors. There were communicators and recorders of every kind known to the science of Second Space.

Laynch sat at his desk, both hands spread out flat on its

213

spectacularly-jeweled top. Both hands now looked alike; the surgeons had done such a perfect transplant job that no non-psi knew that they were not exactly alike. The psis knew, of course, but they were all very careful indeed not to think even fleetingly of that maimed right hand or how it had become that way. They did not want to feed the eagles.

As he sat there, Laynch's gorge began to rise. One of his Lords was late. 'You!' he snapped a mental order at his Supreme Commander of the Guard. 'Investigate!'

The officer vanished . . . and was gone a long half minute. He reappeared, saluted smartly, and reported. 'All-Powerful, no trace of Supreme Admiral Grollo is to be found. Not in his office, where all his staff supposed him to be. Nor at home, nor in any of his usual places, nor in any space I am able to scan for his pattern.'

Laynch's iron mask did not slip, but behind his shield his thoughts churned and seethed. He did not question the accuracy of the report, there was no need. If Sonrajan Rajan of Newgarsh could not find anyone whose pattern he knew, no other need look. Nor did the Emperor have to be told what had been done or who had done it.

For a moment his mind reveled in thoughts of what he would do to those two white psiontists when he caught them. Theirs would be deaths to be long remembered; under his personal supervision they would learn how long-drawn-out and how agonizing death could be; but he wasted very little time on that thought. He would have to catch them first.

The disappearance of his top spy had not been unexpected. Contingency plans had long since been made. Another psiontist, equally capable and equally well-hidden, had taken over. But this – the abduction of the Supreme Admiral out of his own office, tracelessly and without alarm – this was entirely unforeseen.

The great defect of Laynch's make-up was his stark inability to realize – to say nothing of being able to admit – that anyone else could be as good as he was. His one mind-to-mind engagement with the Slaarans had cracked that concept of innate superiority a little, but not too much; and this abduction . . . After all, Grollo was not Laynch, and they had undoubtedly ganged up on him . . . at least two to one, and quite possibly three or four. Very well, any knife could cut both ways. He skipped over the quality of the preliminary work that had been done. Any good psiontist, he assured himself, could do that.

Laynch's thinking had taken less than a second of time. 'Your report is received and approved!' he snapped; then sent a thought direct – an almost unheard-of procedure, this – to the Grand Admiral of the Fleet of Newgarsh. 'Cancel all previous orders. You are hereby promoted to be Supreme Admiral. Put entire Grand Fleet except the flagship *Garsh One* on maximum defensive alert. Have *Garsh One* ready to blast off on a special mission of indefinite duration in one hour. That is all.'

'Orders received, All-Powerful,' the answer snapped back. 'They are on record and are being executed.'

Then, in flashing thoughts, Laynch explained to the personages in his office what had happened and what he was going to do about it, concluding, 'You, Supreme Commander of the Guard; you, Lord of the Treasury; and you, Lord of Commerce; will make arrangements to be absent for a time. You and your complements will be aboard the *Garsh One* well before time zero. That is all.'

They were all aboard on time, and as the great warship bored through subspace toward Slaar Laynch explained as much of his plan as they should know. Those two obnoxious psiontists must be taken – alive if possible, dead if necessary. They were eight, the top eight psiontists of the Garshan race. They would operate as two quartets of two couples each. Each quartet would practise synchronization until its four minds acted and reacted as one. They would detect – flash up to objective – strike. One quartet would seize Rodnar of Slaar exactly as Rodnar and his complement had seized the Supreme Admiral; the other would seize Starrlah of Slaar. The new Supreme Admiral and the other powerful psiontists aboard would control any opposition that might arise.

With detector webs full out, then, the Garshan psiontists prowled and prowled. They did not find the two Slaarans – then. Instead, they found the mighty *Safari*.

'Eagles of Garsh!' a woman shrieked mental warning. 'What kind of a ship is that?'

But the seven other top Garshan minds, and half a dozen others of only slightly lesser ability, had also been holding the detector web. Thus, even before the woman's warning had begun, all those other minds were probing into the huge invader from Other Space. They had all heard of the *Safari*, of course; but, since none of the Big Brains at the Interspatial Conference knew much of anything factual about her, the information that the Garshan psiontists were now obtaining was all brand new.

Laynch knew that he would have only a very small fraction of a second of time in which to work; but such a mind as his, forewarned, can secure an incredibly large amount of information in an incredibly short time. The size of people gave him a rough unit of length, and he gasped mentally at the dimensions thus obtained. One lightning scan took him through the whole immense structure. He saw people – men, women, and *children* – going calmly about the everyday businesses and pleasures of life. He saw battery after battery of unfamiliar weapons of tremendous size and power. He saw engine-room after engine-room full of stand-by machines; any one of which monsters of power, he knew, could not only drive any warship of his fleet but would, at full power, tear itself loose from any possible anchorage in any warship of his fleet. He would *have* to have their rhenium!

He did not see, much to his surprised relief, any super-missiles; nor did he feel any thought of warfare or of conquest. His information had been correct; these people, in spite of their psionic powers and the powers of their weapons, were pacifists. They were soft, weak, flabby, non-aggressive. The mental atmosphere of the whole vast fabrication was one of *peace*! Those strange weapons, despite their terrific power, were intended primarily for *defense*!

After that first, ultra-fast sweep Laynch's mind snapped back to the room in which the Big Six were, but it was already too late to do anything about them, in spite of his fiercely-burning desire. The supersensitive Bernice Jones had already proofed the whole ship; that super-powered Cecily Train was already driving at Laynch's own mind a bolt of psychic force that made his senses reel. *That* white woman, at least, was no pacifist!

Laynch blocked, then, solidly, and pulled back, and *Garsh One* vanished. Vanished, and went fast and far. Then and only then did the Emperor take time to confer with his subordinates.

'We have seen and have studied the exploring vessel of the aliens of Other Space,' Laynch began. 'I am very glad indeed to have had this look at it. I had intended to seek it out later, but this encounter makes the taking of Rodnar and Starrlah of secondary importance. We must have that vessel and we *must* have access to the obviously large amount of rhenium available in Other Space.

'While the capture of such a large and powerful vessel would be impossible if manned by Garshans, in this case it will not prove so. That vessel is not – I repeat, NOT – a warship. It is a truism of warfare that any weapon, however potent, is only as good as the mind behind it; and the people of Other Space are, with a very few exceptions, weak, spineless, and squeamish pacifists.

'They have at least two minds of real power, but even those two are of such a nature that they will not prove to be any problem for the forces we will bring to bear.

'But before I go into any detailed planning, we must pool all the knowledge we obtained during the encounter. The total should be sufficient. Each of us will put into the pool every iota of information he perceived. I will construct the framework of that pool and make the first contribution of data. Here is the framework.

'I perceived . . .'

CHAPTER 18

The Garshan War

Aboard the *Safari* there was a short, stunned silence, followed by a quick but thorough check. Nothing of harm, physical or mental, had been suffered by any thing or any person aboard. The hit-and-run attacker had vanished to some place beyond even Bernice's prodigious range.

'He . . . they were trying to kill us,' Barbara said, flatly. 'They were trying to *kill* us.' Her eyes were still wide with surprise and shock.

'That's right,' Deston agreed, 'and for getting caught flatfooted and with our pants down, I'd say we did a pretty damned good job of keeping them from doing it.'

Cecily grinned. Rather feebly, but it was a grin. 'You know what that reminds me of? An old, old flat flickie I saw in a museum once. Redskins on the prairie, catching palefaces, burning 'em at the stake.'

Jones' face was deadly grim. 'Yeah . . . but funny? Indians are people . . .'

'D'you think I don't know that?' Cecily flared. 'Those damn *things* didn't even *look* like Indians, stupid! But if you'd rather I'd go into a fit of screaming hysterics and . . .'

'Steady, Sess.' Train put his arm around his quivering wife and glared at Jones.

'I'm sorry, Curly,' Jones said, quickly. 'Excuse it, please. I'm still in shock, I guess.'

'We're all still in shock,' Barbara put in, 'so let's take it easy, huh? But, Babe, just who was it who said that intelligent entities wouldn't try to kill on sight?'

'Guilty as charged, pet. All I can do is throw myself on

219

the mercy of the court. But listen. Did you, Bobby – or any of you – get any sidebands of thought from those Justicians – any indication at all – that there was anything like *that* in this whole damned space?'

The calm voice of Stella Adams surprised the six. She had been sitting quietly and unnoticed in the background.

'I can't answer your precise question, Babe – but I do have something to add to the total picture. Remember when Andy asked your permission to study your minds? After we had completed our project we received two unexplainable – communications, you might call them – and of course not from any of you.

'The first was a flash so brief, so fleeting that we couldn't be sure we actually received it. An intelligence of breadth and power and scope beyond our imagining. But not threatening or in any way negative. It was followed instantly by a totally different thought – and without question that second thought came from the same mind that just tried to kill us!'

In full detail, then, she described to her spellbound listeners the scene of the vision, and repeated verbatim the viciously savage words of the speaker behind the desk. 'Afterward,' she concluded, 'we scanned all areas of space we could reach seeking that specific thought pattern, but without success. It is now evident that for some reason beyond our knowledge we received a thought from Second Space.'

'But why didn't you tell us?' Cecily began, then added, 'But of course, you had your reasons.'

Stella's expression remained unruffled. 'Andy thought there was no point in talking about it until we secured more data. And now I think I'd better let him know about this.' She rose and went to their quarters to communicate with her husband in the privacy she preferred.

'Well I'll . . .' Deston didn't complete his exclamation

but concluded with a shrug, 'Andy's the boss. As for now, I'd say we'd better drill right out of here for that communicator and get hold of Rodnar – and we hadn't better let any space-barnacles grow on our plating while we're about it, either.'

'You can play *that* in spades, chum,' Jones said, and the huge subspacer took off at full blast.

Thus it was that Rodnar did not have to increase by very much the power of the highly special communicator; and in due course the four Justicians 'ported themselves into the lounge room of the *Safari*. Moments later Stella Adams reappeared. Introductions followed; and this time there was no stiffness about the meeting; each side was glad to see the other. Neither knew much about the other and both had plenty of reservations, but they shook hands all around and got down to business.

'I'd better begin,' Rodnar said, 'by giving you an idea about the political situation in our galaxy, since it now involves you.' In swift, graphic thoughts he sketched the structure of the Justiciate plus its history. He followed with a picture of Garsh and its position in the Justiciate; the centuries-long, grandiose planning of the red race to take over control of the one hundred eighty planets, eliminating all other races except for slaves necessary to serve what would then be the Garshan Empire. With occasional help from the other three Justicians he told of the recent abortive attempt of the then Grand Justice Laynch at a Garshan take-over; of the counter-measures that prevented his succeeding; and most recently Rodnar and Starr-lah's discovery of Laynch's plans for entry into and conquest of Other Space – immediate objective: rhenium – and specifically, the very real threat to the Trains.

The seven Galaxians had absorbed the flow of thoughts with intense interest, each keeping his own council. At Rodnar's conclusion Deston exclaimed:

'Ver-*ee* interesting! And a bright light begins to dawn. It makes what we just experienced all the more pertinent. I think we'd better take turns telling everybody what happened. I'll start; you, Curly, better be last. Here goes . . .'

When Cecily had finished, Rodnar stared at her in frowning, narrow-eyed concentration, then shook his head in baffled surprise. 'You weren't even *trying* to kill Laynch, then? Why – in all hells of your whole space – why not?'

'*Kill* him?' she asked, in equal surprise. 'Of course I wasn't – that was our first contact – how could I have been, possibly? Why, I'd never even *met* the guy! I didn't know anything about him. Even after I found out how rough he was playing it, all I was going to do to him was to bust him loose from his front teeth – and I'd've done it, too, in about another jillionth of a split mu-musecond.'

'Exactly . . . that's what I mean . . . and Laynch knows it.' Rodnar was still completely baffled. He thought for a few seconds then went on, 'But that could make it all the better, at that . . . he thinks you are all pacifists . . . but maybe you are. You all act like pacifists. Tell me. Could you – *would* you, I mean – kill? If all your lives depended on it? Our pacifists won't. They'd rather die themselves than take a human life.'

The six, dead serious now, looked at each other for a second, then Cecily said, 'There isn't a drop of martyr blood in me. I never have killed anyone, but I could if I had to, and I would. I don't know about you other girls, but – '

'Don't worry about Bun and me, Cecily,' Barbara said, quietly. 'We already have.' She silenced Deston's attempted protest and went on, 'Oh, I know, Babe – Uncle Andy gave you boys the credit in his autopsy reports, but – never mind the details. We have. As for Babe and Herc, Rodnar, while they were space-officers with InStell they were practically in the wholesale mayhem-and-killing business. And as for you, Perce – you're not exactly an innocent, either, are you? You didn't wear a gun all that time without using it at all, did you?'

'Not exactly, I'm afraid. No, I didn't.' Train shook his head as he answered the two questions specifically; but he did not elaborate.

And Rodnar, Starrlah, Marrjyl and Knuaire, seizing and reading hundreds of sidebands of thought, built themselves an entirely different picture of these supposedly peace-at-any-price denizens of Other Space than the one they had had before: a picture they liked much better and respected vastly more.

'I see . . . we're beginning to see, I mean,' Rodnar said, slowly. They were beginning – just beginning – to see what those strangers from Other Space really were. 'We *can* work together, after all; and if we do we should be able to win. Knu, as theoretician, taking these new data into account, what is your projection of the engagement?'

'In broad, and as respecting only those events whose probability approaches unity, it will almost certainly go like this . . .' and the Spathian thought into the pooled minds for several minutes.

'Nice – *very* nice!' Deston applauded. 'But how about in fine?'

'With the understanding that the probability will vary inversely as about the cube of the degree of fineness of detail . . .'

'At that price we don't want it,' Train cut in, decisively. 'Much better, Babe, don't you think, to play it by ear than to go in all set for the wrong things?'

'You couldn't be righter. So let's go over the things we are sure about again.'

They went over them again . . . and again . . . and again, six Galaxians and four Justicians, in an interspatial conference of another kind. Only Stella Adams remained in the background, storing every detail for later reporting to Andy.

After leaving the *Safari*, the four Justicians became very busy indeed. Rodnar and Starrlah had to work in utmost secrecy, since any leakage of their real plans to Laynch's spies would have been a double-prime disaster. Thus every Status-Five psiontist of the Justiciate – and this included the Grand Commanders of the Guard – knew what was going to happen and was drilled unrelentingly in the part each was to play. No one else knew that anything else was afoot.

No one, that is, except Supreme Admiral Axolgan; and he did not know anything until Knuaire of Spath and Marrjyl of Orm came aboard the flagship. They were armed with the full authority of His Supreme Justice Sonrathendak Ranjak of Slaar – and also with their own impermeable psionic shields.

After the Admiral was shown the ornately official document verifying their authority, he received his instructions. First and immediately every ship in the fleet must shield to the limit every sensitive instrument against any kind of interference including X-emanations. Second, as during the attack on Garsh, there must be a Psiontist Five aboard each ship, fully instructed, waiting and alert. These of course would be provided.

'But why – ' the Admiral began, then desisted.

Following, the Knuaire–Marrjyl fusion drew a detailed mental picture of Axolgan's part in the coming conflict.

'But that's the damndest way of fighting a battle anyone ever heard of,' the admiral grumbled.

'Enough!' Knuaire snapped aloud. 'This is going to be a kind of battle nobody ever heard of before. If we need you we'll really need you – and the psiontists will be in control.

You will do exactly as ordered. Make one slip – just one – and you feed the eagles. Is that clear? Hear and obey!'

'I hear and obey.' Axolgan saluted stiffly; and the Knuaire–Marrjyl pairing knew that the burly-hearted, tough-souled old spacehound, accustomed as he was to obeying orders exactly, would not make one slip . . . Then they began their waiting, in sync with Rodnar and Starrlah – even when the latter pair entered subspace. And waited – and waited . . . and waited.

As the day of adjournment of the First Session of the Interspatial Conference drew near, Emperor Laynch stepped up the tempo and intensity of his preparations. Planning had been done to the last detail. Calculating all the stress-factors, he piled the work on, at a rate precisely determined to bring every psiontist, every commander of men, and every firing officer to his peak of performance at time zero; yet without over-training any one of them.

And Laynch worked himself and his quartet of psionic operators at the same calculated rate. As a matter of fact, at zero time, the team-of-four of which he was the anchor man was probably the strongest team native to Second Space.

At noon of Adjournment Day, then, Laynch and his forces were ready. He watched the huge *Safari* approach the Conference ship; watched the Trains 'port themselves aboard; watched them chat unconcernedly and unsuspectingly with the departing psiontists of the Justiciate.

He was not surprised that the *Safari* wore impenetrable screen. That was now, of course, to be expected. That vessel could be and would be handled later; those two Trains were his present major concern. With cold intensity Laynch kept his mind fixed on his chronom. Split-second timing was essential because of the involvement, in subspace, of the immense Garshan fleet.

* * *

A couple of days before the Conference was to adjourn, the *Safari* made a quick flit to First Space, and when she got back there were only seven people aboard. There were to have been six, according to Deston's plan, but Stella Adams insisted on joining the group.

'I must be there,' she said flatly, with resolution that surprised the rest.

After telepathic communication with Andy Adams they realized that her presence, even if the part she played were passive, was highly important. As Adams expressed it, 'You youngsters have *so* much to learn! Would any of you – male or female – be complete without your complement? Of course you wouldn't! Though for the moment Stella and I are physically apart, I would be as a one-armed or one-eyed man without her. It was necessary that she be in Second Space when you had your full crew; it is just as vital now.'

Shortly after noon of Adjournment Day, then, the *Safari* and her crew were tensely alert. According to plan, Cecily and Perce Train 'ported themselves aboard the Conference ship to be ready, apparently, to take the First Space scientists back home. In the control room of the *Safari* the Destons and the Joneses were waiting. There were no longer any 'stand-by' machines as such aboard. Captain Theodore Jones, personally, had put every one of those monsters of power 'in sync and on the line.' Each was synchronized with every other to within the smallest measurable fraction of one wave-length of ultra-violet light; each was ready to pour out, with no time-lapse at all, its torrential myriakilowattage of unleashed power. Stella remained out of sight in the Adamses' quarters.

Of the four, Bernice was the only one who was tense. She was the detector, the giver-of-warning. She was touching – just barely touching, with the lightest possible contact even she could feel – the very outer fringes of Laynch's mind. Linked to her, lightly but definitely, were not only the other Galaxians but also Rodnar and Starrlah, who were still out in subspace but were ready instantly to emerge. This tension and this linkage were necessary because, although Laynch would have to initiate the action, several other actions would have to be practically simultaneous with his.

Quite a feat? Definitely; but Bernice was certain she could do it. Laynch could not act without an instant of self-preparation, she was sure. She was also sure that even if those Garshans' minds were linked as tightly as were those of the Galaxians that instant of preparation would give her time enough.

It did. The double quartet of Garshans struck at the Trains, and in the instant of that striking the Trains vanished from the Conference ship. In the same instant of time they materialized at their working stations aboard the *Safari* and hurled her right into the middle of the just-emerging Garshan fleet. And at the same moment, unnoticed, Andrew Adams appeared at his wife's side in their quarters; and instantly they went into full mental fusion, observing all that their minds could perceive.

Jones sat hunched at his board, eyes glaring at his master-meter, fingers curled around knobs, daring any one of those Gargantuan engines to wander off-sync by any fraction of a split red whisker. Bernice stood behind him; both hands fiercely gripping the back of his chair. Having done her first job, she was now holding psionic watch and ward, supremely alert for any unexpected thing that might happen.

Deston lay flat on his back on a davenport; eyes shut and jaw hard set. Barbara sat beside him, gripping both hands. Fused into one fourth-nume mind, they were placing their targets in a three-dimensional mental 'tank' and were plotting, for the Trains' benefit, the path of least travel.

As one the Justiciate fleet on the KnuMarr psionic signal emerged and instantly shut off all power. Rodnar and Starrlah had already emerged, in their First Space light cruiser.

With the Justiciate fleet in position, power off, they put every Graham their cruiser had on one-hundred-percent load and left it there; and as those terribly destructive Graham emanations filled space and subspace there came into being the second-worst X-storm ever observed.

Thus each Garshan war-ship, having emerged, was powerless either to maneuver or to immerge. All instruments and controls were dead. Officers and technicians went madly to work at rigging manual controls, but there was pitifully little that they could do.

Deston triggered his first Z-gun at his first target. There was no need to spare the horses, so he didn't. He worked his guns at maximum aperture and maximum blast; and when *that* beam struck it the Garshan warship literally exploded. That beam was over two hundred feet in diameter at the plane of impact; and, in spite of its dispersion, it was still so super-hellishly hot as to preclude all molecular and most atomic structures. Thus the effect was pretty much the same as though a few hundred tons of the vessel's own substance had been transformed instantly into low-grade fissionable material.

Simply, that warship disappeared. Where it had been there was a fireball so intensely, so frightfully hot that no fraction of its energy was in the visible spectrum. It would have to expand for seconds before any part of it would become visible.

Then the Trains flicked the *Safari* to Stop Two, where four Garshan ships were close enough to hit. At Stop

Three there were three . . . and so on . . . and on with devastating efficiency, taking appalling toll.

They had expected jury-rigged, hand-launched, and 'ported missiles, and they got them; but such things could not present any very serious threat. Bernice saw them all coming, and what few of them she could not handle, the Trains could.

Destruction proceeded apace. Then, as always, warfare was not sporting. In a perfectly-planned and perfectly-executed operation the victor emerged unscathed; the vanquished was totally destroyed.

This operation, however, was not perfectly planned and they all knew it. That was why Bernice, the most sensitive of them all, was on guard with every sense stretched full out; and suddenly she perceived something in the sub-ether; a disturbance; a peculiarly unfamiliar distortion. She didn't know what it was, but she didn't wait to learn anything about it.

'Flit!' she shrieked a mental warning.

The *Safari* 'flitted'.

The Trains were super-fast; but they were not quite fast enough to get their immense vessel away clean. In the instant of time while the *Safari* was immerging, while her rear gun was still in three-dimensional space, an atomic bomb exploded so close to her that it blew her whole tail-section squarely off.

Automatic bulkheads slammed shut, of course; and automatic decontaminators flashed on; but that had been a 'dirty' bomb and a lot of radiation came in.

'Wha'ja read, Babe?' Jones snapped. 'Thirty two here; high red.'

Deston glanced at his 'tell-tale' – the radiation meter – on his wrist. 'Thirty one – high red – I'll 'port the DCQ in here – strip, everybody, and make it *snappy*!'

Decontaminating the human body after an ordinarily

lethal dose of radiation was not a pleasant operation; but, if done soon enough, it was completely effective. There was, however, very little time to waste and no time at all for modesty. Thus, even though Bernice wailed 'Oh my God, Herc, not *again*?' she did not expect an answer to her question and she was the first undressed.

Clothing flew in all directions; the women grouped themselves around one of the DEKON* generators that Deston had 'ported into the room, the men around the other. Cupped hands grabbed up double handfuls of the thick, gooey, whipped-cream-like stuff frothing from the nozzles. Barbara and Bernice lathered and slathered the stuff all over themselves and each other and Cecily; the while showing the red-head just how to join the sport.

'What a shampoo!' Cecily exclaimed, rubbing the frothy cream vigorously into her scalp. 'I've read about this, of course, and seen it done on the tri-di, but you've both actually been through it. That'd make it easier, wouldn't it?'

'Just the opposite,' Bernice said, working busily on the red-head's back. 'They soft-pedal the part about inhaling both lungs full of the gunk. You cough so hard and so long you simply wish you could die.'

'*Inhale* it? *That* glop? Why, I thought it was a *gas* you inhaled!'

'That's what I said; they soft-pedal it. *Very* soft. It goes like this. I'm bigger than Bobby is, so I hold your head still in a head-lock. You exhale – clear empty. Then Bobby slaps a huge glob of the stuff over your nose and mouth and you inhale as fast and as hard as you can. If you don't get enough of it we both hold you down on the floor and give you some more while you're coughing and then you'll *really* wish you were dead. Okay?'

* DEKON. Decontaminant, Complete: Compound, Adsorbent, and Chelating: Type DCQ-429. E.E.S.

'Okay – I'll do my damndest, Bun. I'll inhale fast and hard.'

She did.

Ignoring the paroxysmally coughing, strangling, choking red-head writhing on the floor, Barbara said, 'Okay, Bun. Now I'll give it to you and have Babe give it to me. He can take it himself, but that's one thing I don't want ever even to try.'

While they were engaged in this most unpleasant but necessary task, Cecily, in the midst of coughing suddenly choked out:

'Stella!'

They had forgotten the seventh *Safari* passenger! Even as she coughed, Cecily sent her perception to the Adams suite. No one was there. Instantly she scanned the entire interior of the cruiser, reporting to the others; swiftly but thoroughly – and there were only six of them aboard.

Soberly Deston made the mental observation, 'Knowing Andy's powers, I'm not going to worry. You can bet your last buck – when trouble hit he whisked her away.'

The calm thought of Dr Adams came to the six simultaneously. 'You are correct, my friend. You didn't know it, but I was aboard, and when Cecily shrieked "Flit!" we did. We're on the RodStarr light cruiser. But you're busy with the DCQ – and in seconds we'll all be very busy.' He broke contact.

As smoothly as though it had been rehearsed, six minds became as one – two from First Space and four from Second Space – Andrew and Stella Adams, Rod and Starrlah, and Knuaire and Marrjyl. There followed the most wildly unorthodox tactic ever utilized in space warfare. It had been planned as a remote emergency measure – but it was ready. It required fantastic coordination, possible only to a linkage of top level psionic minds.

On signal Rodnar shut off the Grahams – power flicked

on in every Justiciate warship – missiles were launched at unprepared Garshan ships – an instantaneous flit – power off – and Grahams on. It happened with split second precision – and it worked. Because of the Justiciate fleet's shielding and because all power was off when the Grahams' disruptive emanations poured forth they escaped damage. Again and again at purely random intervals the procedure was repeated, inflicting devastating damage to the Garshan fleet with no retaliation.

In the *Safari* in subspace the endless half hour waiting period for complete decontamination finally ended; the six scraped most of the DCQ off their bodies, showered hastily, dressed, and prepared to go back into the fray. After the fact, they all knew how the successful attack had been accomplished. Suicide job. Some Garshan psiontist – and a good one – had 'ported that bomb inside a screened light cruiser, had 'ported that ship as close to the *Safari* as possible, and had died in the explosion. There would be more, they were certain.

They emerged – to find that the situation had changed greatly during their absence. The Garshan fleet had shrunk visibly. With their reappearance the Grahams remained on at full power and the remaining enemy ships centered their suicide attacks on the *Safari*. For the Galaxians it was a case of speed – flash in – blast – flash out. Fast as the Trains and Destons were, all too often they were just barely fast enough. The Garshan psiontists, aware of the only tactic that had worked, tried again and again. They were highly capable, completely expendable, and very, *very* fast. Although the Galaxians' hearts were in their throats half the time, the *Safari* was not actually struck again; and so the battle was finally won. Not a single Garshan ship remained in the entire region of Second Space.

Rodnar and Starrlah shut off their Grahams, and they,

Knuaire and Marrjyl, and Stella and Andrew Adams 'ported aboard the *Safari*. At sight of the latter, Deston exclaimed, 'Welcome aboard! And Doc – fighting isn't exactly in your line – but somehow you got into this one. And did quite well, from all I can gather.'

Adams smiled and shrugged deprecatingly. 'It seemed to be the thing to do under the circumstances. I joined Stella when Cecily and Perce 'ported in; and when the bomb was on its way we joined Rodnar and Starrlah.' He looked narrowly at Stella, then said to the rest, 'If you don't mind, we'll get some rest. It's been a trying time for us oldsters, you know.' As an afterthought, 'Someone should tell the people on the Conference ship just what happened, and that the Trains will be getting them back to First Space a bit later. I'll attend to it.' He linked arms with Stella. 'We'll see you at breakfast.' At Deston's nod they vanished.

Rodnar spoke for the Justicians. 'I think we too had better be on our way. Starr won't be fit to live with if she doesn't get some rest.'

Starrlah frowned in mock disapproval. 'Speak for yourself, Rod.'

They were tired, and showed it. Mere weariness, however, could not account for the expressions on the four Justician faces. They had seen what the Galaxians had done; and that had increased greatly their knowledge of the strangers. All were shivering inwardly at that knowledge: that the deadliest possible performer is not one whose ordinary life is one of violence, but a highly intelligent entity who, having coldly and accurately evaluated a situation and having come to a decision, proceeds coldly and ruthlessly to take whatever action is necessary to implement that decision.

'That was a mighty good job – a splendid job,' Rodnar said to Deston. 'With so many of their best psiontists

233

dead, mopping up Laynch and his empire will be much easier than we expected. A wonderful job, truly, for which we give you our deepest thanks. We owe you a lot. It is unfortunate that your ship was hit, but . . .' Rodnar paused. Unfamiliar with any expression of condolence, he simply did not know what to say.

'Think nothing of it, Rod.' Deston shrugged his shoulders. 'They didn't like us any better than they liked you; and, after all, it was us they were after, not you.'

'How many of 'em got away?' Jones asked. 'We lost a lot of time deconning ourselves. It seems our emergency plan worked very well.'

'It certainly did,' Knuaire answered. 'And very few if any at all escaped. Some of them rigged manual controls, but between you and the Navy I think we got them all. It's certain that the Garshan Navy is destroyed.'

'Good; that's one Navy we can spare,' Train said, and an awkward silence fell. There were a great many things each side wanted to talk about, but neither quite dared. They didn't know each other well enough yet; did not have enough in common. They liked each other well enough . . . in most ways . . . in *some* ways, at least, but . . .

For instance, Deston would not give Rodnar the formulae of interspatial transit. Not yet. He knew he wouldn't; he had no intention whatever of doing so. Perhaps they had no pair with the power of the Trains – but they *might*. Nevertheless, he felt guilty about not saying *anything* about it.

But Knuaire, who had as always been reading all available sidebands, held up his hand and smiled. 'Not yet, Babe. There's much too much for both of us to learn. There's lots of time. But why so funereal, everybody? It isn't as though we were parting forever, you know. The Conference meets again in forty days, and surely we'll all be here then?'

'Why, *of course* we will!' Barbara exclaimed, and everyone cheered up immensely. It has always been much easier to say 'See-you-later' than 'Good-bye.'

Starrlah, who had been looking closely at Deston, said, 'Babe, you look like a kinto's worth of eaglefood – you'd better get yourself some sleep.' Then, to them all, 'Forty days, then, you nice, nice people, you!' She waved her hand and the Justicians disappeared.

Deston smiled a bone-tired smile and said, 'You know, gang, that's the best advice I've had in a long time. I'm going to go to bed and sleep for one solid Galactic-Standard twenty-four-hour day.'

As though on signal the three couples 'ported to their rooms, and silence fell upon the great transpatial *Safari*.

Only in the Adams suite was there activity of a sort. Andrew and Stella faced each other across a little table, eyes meeting, hands gripping, minds fused. Their objective a galaxy, a planet, a room incalculably far removed from Second Space – a children's room on the night side of Newmars where two lovely youngsters, a boy and a girl, slept peacefully under the watch-care of two psiontist nurses.

The fusion touched those minds ever so lightly – and again they were conscious of an intellect of vast serenity and incredible scope. Awed but in full control the fusion asked, 'Isn't it logical to think we deserve some explanation? Or *are* we merely puppets?'

Their vision of Theodore Deston and Barbara Jones remained unchanged – two soundly sleeping children. But an answer came clearly in a thought with a strength and incisiveness they had never before encountered.

'The time for haste has passed and a great danger has been averted. The beginning of subspace interstellar travel set in motion events which, had they followed their course uninfluenced would inevitably have ended in the destruction of Galaxian civilization.

235

'Subspace transit with its inadvertent creation of X-storms in Second Space and with the infrequent destruction of our starships by our close approach to Second Space vehicles would have led to the eventual discovery of First Space by the science of the Garshans after their conquering of the Justiciate. So Laynch of Garsh had to be stopped.

'Many intellects had to be influenced – yours among them – to bring this about. Abilities had to be developed and intensified in a single generation. The need for such influence has ended and growth will now proceed at a normal pace. We can detect no adverse results in the future progress of humanity in First Space or in Second.' After the slightest pause, the thought concluded,

'Your minds are capable of accepting this truth in its totality. Others might not have that strength.'

Andrew and Stella Adams were aware of complete and final dismissal. Simultaneously they drew a deep breath, arose, and wordlessly prepared for bed. Sleep eluded them for a long time, and when it came it was troubled by a vision of a lovely little boy and girl peacefully asleep.

Epilogue

Many works are available on the subject of Theodore Warner Deston and Barbara Bernice Jones, his wife. These works range in tone from the scholarly through the flippant to the completely skeptical. After years of study, however, the chronicler has been forced to conclude that they were in fact the only pair of fully psionic human beings ever to live.

Only five facts about them are definitely known. One – they both were conceived in the theretofore starkly unknown environment of a zeta field. Two – their periods of gestation, which were extraordinarily long, were spent in that environment. Three – their parents were four of the strongest and ablest psiontists then alive. Four – there is no record that they themselves had issue. Five – after age sixty, no reference whatever to either of them is to be found.

Over the vista of the years it is impossible to understand the mental attitude of the psiontists of that age. Each insisted upon 'privacy'; a long-forgotten word that meant being *alone*. While it seems incredible, it is true; and this fact accounts for much of the difficulty in determining at this late date what that pair of supermen (they almost certainly *were* supermen) actually did. *How* they did it would of course, by definition, be incomprehensible to the strictly human mind.

It is not that no full-mind recordings of the Early Psionic Age have been found: the appalling truth seems to be that *no full-mind recordings were made*!

After years of study, the chronicler has concluded that events transpired substantially as follows:

Those two embryos began to think and to learn as soon as their brains began to form. Their minds were endowed from the first with superhuman powers, including those of trans-spatial and trans-temporal perception. Each learning event required the barest instant of objective time: long before their fingernails formed they had read and had understood every word and every symbol in the *Procyon*'s very comprehensive library.

Since subjective time is measured by the number of learning events experienced, they were mentally much more than adult at birth. They scanned times, spaces, and cultures. They studied, analyzed, computed, and decided what to do. For sixty years they did it. Then, having done what was best for all humanity, they . . .

The chronicler hesitates to record his considered opinion on imperishable tape, but to his mind only one conclusion is possible. There is no record that either of them ever died. At age sixty, probably simultaneously, they vanished. They did their work here and went somewhere else.

The probability is vanishingly small that a similar pair has appeared since or will appear in the foreseeable future. While many scientists have advocated the repetition of such pregnancies as controlled experiments, it never has been done and probably never will be done. Psionists of the requisite ability will not do it, and no others can.

As has been admitted, some material has been included here that is not incontrovertibly factual. There is only enough such material, however, to round out the treatment and make it complete.

It will be observed that this solution of the problem does not conflict with any fact; and that it explains all pertinent facts hitherto inexplicable, such as:

That the first psionists developed their tremendous powers so quickly, so easily, and at that particular time.

That interspatial transit was discovered and the course of

238

Second-Space civilization was changed at that particular time.

That the widely variant abilities of two different civilizations, in union both necessary and sufficient to crush the Garshan Empire, were brought together at that particular time.

That the Garshan GREAT DAY was just premature enough to insure its failure.

And many other facts hitherto ascribed to coincidence: these are only a few examples.

Respectfully submitted,
Edward E. Smith